Edgar Rice Burroughs was gifted with a limitless imagination. With it he created an entire culture for a vast planet—many races, many peoples, strange creatures, and stranger plants, an entire history stretching back through eons of time and extending itself into the future with scientific inventions only dreamed of even in our own time.

His imagination was coupled with an ability to write startlingly graphic prose, vivid with color and excitement, seething with action, and rich with the barbaric splendor of bygone ages.

LLANA OF GATHOL is the tenth book in a classic series of eleven volumes.

Edgar Rice Burroughs

MARS NOVELS

A PRINCESS OF MARS
THE GODS OF MARS
THE WARLORD OF MARS
THUVIA, MAID OF MARS
THE CHESSMEN OF MARS
THE MASTER MIND OF MARS
A FIGHTING MAN OF MARS
SWORDS OF MARS
SYNTHETIC MEN OF MARS
LLANA OF GATHOL
JOHN CARTER OF MARS

Published by Ballantine Books

LLANA
OF GATHOL

Edgar Rice Burroughs

BALLANTINE BOOKS • NEW YORK

TO
JOHN PHILIP BIRD

All rights reserved. Published in the United States by Ballantine
Books, a division of Random House, Inc., New York, and simul-
taneously in Canada by Ballantine Books of Canada, Ltd.,
Toronto, Canada.

Llana of Gathol was first published as four novelettes in
Amazing Stories Magazine as follows:
  "The City of Mummies," March 1941
  "Black Pirates of Barsoom," June 1941
  "Yellow Men of Mars," August 1941
  "Invisible Men of Mars," October 1941

ISBN 0-345-25829-0

This authorized edition published by arrangement with Edgar
Rice Burroughs, Inc.

Manufactured in the United States of America

First Edition: August 1963
Tenth Printing: December 1977

First Canadian Printing: September 1963

Cover art by Gino D'Achille

FOREWORD

LANIKAI is a district, a beach, a Post Office, and a grocery store. It lies on the windward shore of the Island of Oahu. It is a long way from Mars. Its waters are blue and beautiful and calm inside its coral reef, and the trade wind sighing through the fronds of its coconut palms at night might be the murmuring voices of the ghosts of the kings and chieftains who fished in its still waters long before the sea captains brought strange diseases or the missionaries brought mother-hubbards.

Thoughts of the past, mere vague imaginings, were passing idly through my mind one night that I could not sleep and was sitting on the lanai watching the white maned chargers of the sea racing shoreward beneath the floodlight of the Moon. I saw the giant kings of old Hawaii and their mighty chiefs clothed in feather cape and helmet. Kamehameha came, the great conqueror, towering above them all. Down from the Nuuanu Pali he came in great strides, stepping over cane fields and houses. The hem of his feather cape caught on the spire of a church, toppling it to the ground. He stepped on low, soft ground; and when he lifted his foot, the water of a slough rushed into his footprint, and there was a lake.

I was much interested in the coming of Kamehameha the King, for I had always admired him; though I had never expected to see him, he having been dead a matter of a hundred years or so and his bones buried in a holy, secret place that no man knows. However, I was not at all surprised to see him. What surprised me was that I was not surprised. I distinctly recall this reaction. I also recall that I hoped he would see me and not step on me.

While I was thinking these thoughts, Kamehameha stopped in front of me and looked down at me. "Well, well!" he said; "asleep on a beautiful night like this! I *am* surprised."

I blinked my eyes hard and looked again. There before me stood indeed a warrior strangely garbed, but it was not King Kamehameha. Under the moonlight one's eyes sometimes play strange tricks on one. I blinked mine again, but the warrior did not vanish. Then I knew!

Leaping to my feet, I extended my hand. "John Carter!" I exclaimed.

"Let's see," he said; "where was it we met last—the headwaters of the Little Colorado or Tarzana?"

"The headwaters of the Little Colorado in Arizona, I think," I said. "That was a long time ago. I never expected to see you again."

"No, I never expected to return."

"Why have you? It must be something important."

"Nothing of Cosmic importance," he said, smiling; "but important to me, nevertheless. You see, I wanted to see you."

"I appreciate that," I said.

"You see, you are the last of my Earthly kin whom I know personally. Every once in a while I feel an urge to see you and visit with you, and at long intervals I am able to satisfy that urge—as now. After you are dead, and it will not be long now, I shall have no Earthly ties—no reason to return to the scenes of my former life."

"There are my children." I reminded him. "They are your blood kin."

"Yes," he said, "I know; but they might be afraid of me. After all, I might be considered something of a ghost by Earth men."

"Not by my children," I assured him. "They know you quite as well as I. After I am gone, see them occasionally."

He nodded. "Perhaps I shall," he half promised.

"And now," I said, "tell me something of yourself, of Mars, of Dejah Thoris, of Carthoris and Thuvia and of Tara of Helium. Let me see! It was Gahan of Gathol that Tara of Helium wed."

"Yes," replied the war lord, "it was Gahan, Jed of the free city of Gathol. They have a daughter, one whose character and whose beauty are worthy of her mother and her mother's mother—a beauty which, like that of those other two, hurled nations at each other's throats in war. Perhaps you would like to hear the story of Llana of Gathol."

I said that I would, and this is the story that he told me that night beneath the coconut palms of Oahu.

LLANA OF GATHOL

LLANA OF GATHOL

BOOK 1

THE ANCIENT DEAD

1

No MATTER how instinctively gregarious one may be there are times when one longs for solitude. I like people. I like to be with my family, my friends, my fighting men; and probably just because I am so keen for companionship, I am at times equally keen to be alone. It is at such times that I can best resolve the knotty problems of government in times of war or peace. It is then that I can meditate upon all the various aspects of a full life such as I lead; and, being human, I have plenty of mistakes upon which to meditate that I may fortify myself against their recommission.

When I feel that strange urge for solitude coming over me, it is my usual custom to take a one man flier and range the dead sea bottoms and the other uninhabited wildernesses of this dying planet; for there indeed is solitude. There are vast areas on Mars where no human foot has ever trod, and other vast areas that for thousands of years have known only the giant green men, the wandering nomads of the ocher deserts.

Sometimes I am away for weeks on these glorious adventures in solitude. Because of them, I probably know more of the geography and topography of Mars than any other living man; for they and my other adventurous excursions upon the planet have carried me from the Lost Sea of Korus, in the Valley Dor at the frozen South to Okar, land of the black bearded Yellow Men of the frozen North, and from Kaol to Bantoom; and yet there are many parts of Barsoom that I have not visited, which will not seem so strange when there is taken into consideration the fact that although the area of Mars is like more than one fourth that of Earth its land area is almost eight million square miles greater. That is because Barsoom has no large bodies of surface water, its largest known ocean being entirely subterranean. Also, I think you will admit, fifty-six million square miles is a lot of territory to know thoroughly.

Upon the occasion of which I am about to tell you I flew northwest from Helium, which lies 30° south of the Equator which I crossed about sixteen hundred miles east of Exum, the Barsoomian Greenwich. North and west of me lay a vast, almost unexplored region; and there I thought to find the absolute solitude for which I craved.

I had set my directional compass upon Horz, the long deserted city of ancient Barsoomian culture, and loafed along at seventy-five miles an hour at an altitude of five hundred to a thousand feet. I had seen some green men northeast of Torquas and had been forced up to escape their fire, which I did not return as I was not seeking adventure; and I had crossed two thin ribbons of red Martian farm land bordering canals that bring the precious waters from the annually melting ice caps at the poles. Beyond these I saw no signs of human life in all the five thousand miles that lie between Lesser Helium and Horz.

It is always a little saddening to me to look down thus upon a dying world, to scan the endless miles of ocher, mosslike vegetation which carpets the vast areas where once rolled the mighty oceans of a young and virile Mars, to ponder that just beneath me once ranged the proud navies and the merchant ships of a dozen rich and powerful nations where today the fierce banth roams a solitude whose silence is unbroken except for the roars of the killer and the screams of the dying.

At night I slept, secure in the knowledge that my directional compass would hold a true course for Horz and always at the altitude for which I had set it—a thousand feet, not above sea level but above the terrain over which the ship was passing. These amazing little instruments may be set for any point upon Barsoom and at any altitude. If one is set for a thousand feet, as mine was upon this occasion, it will not permit the ship to come closer than a thousand feet to any object, thus eliminating even the danger of collision; and when the ship reaches its objective the compass will stop it a thousand feet above. The pilot whose ship is equipped with one of these directional compasses does not even have to remain awake; thus I could travel day and night without danger.

It was about noon of the third day that I sighted the towers of ancient Horz. The oldest part of the city lies upon the edge of a vast plateau; the newer portions, and they are countless thousands of years old, are terraced downward into a great gulf, marking the hopeless pursuit of the receding sea upon the shores of which this rich and powerful city once stood. The last poor, mean structures of a dying race have either disappeared or are only mouldering ruins now; but the splendid structures of her prime remain at the edge of the plateau, mute but eloquent reminders of her vanished grandeur—enduring monuments to the white-skinned, fair-haired race which has vanished forever.

I am always interested in these deserted cities of ancient Mars. Little is known of their inhabitants, other than what can be gathered from the stories told by the carvings which ornament the exteriors of many of their public buildings and the few remaining murals which have withstood the ravages of time and the vandalism of the green hordes which have overrun many of them. The extremely low humidity has helped to preserve them, but more than all else was the permanency of their construction. These magnificent edifices were built not for years but for eternities. The secrets of their mortars, their cements, and their pigments have been lost for ages; and for countless ages more, long after the last life has disappeared from the face of Barsoom, their works will remain, hurtling through space forever upon a dead, cold planet with no eye to see, with no mind to appreciate. It is a sad thing to contemplate.

At last I was over Horz. I had for long promised myself that some day I should come here, for Horz is, perhaps, the oldest and the greatest of the dead cities of Barsoom. Water built it, the lack of water spelled its doom. I often wonder if the people of Earth, who have water in such abundance, really appreciate it. I wonder if the inhabitants of New York City realize what it would mean to them if some enemy, establishing an air base within cruising radius of the first city of the New World, should successfully bomb and destroy Croton Dam and the Catskill water system. The railroads and the highways would be jammed with refugees, millions would die, and for years, perhaps forever, New York City would cease to be.

As I floated lazily above the deserted city I saw figures moving in a plaza below me. So Horz was not entirely deserted! My curiosity piqued, I dropped a little lower; and what I saw dashed thoughts of solitude from my mind—a lone red man beset by half a dozen fierce green warriors.

I had not sought adventure, but here it was; for no man worthy of his metal would abandon one of his own kind in such a dire extremity. I saw a spot where I might land in a nearby plaza; and, praying that the green men would be too engrossed with their engagement to note my approach, I dove quickly and silently toward a landing.

Fortunately I landed unobserved, screened by a mighty tower which rose beside the plaza I had selected. I had seen that they were fighting with long-swords, and so I drew mine as I ran in the direction of the unequal struggle. That the red man lived even a few moments against such odds bespoke the excellence of his swordsmanship, and I hoped that he would hold out until I reached him; for then he would have the best sword arm in all Barsoom to aid him and the sword that had tasted the blood of a thousand enemies the length and breadth of a world.

I found my way from the plaza in which I had landed, but only to be confronted by a twenty-foot wall in which I could perceive no opening. Doubtless there was one, I knew; but in the time that I might waste in finding it my man might easily be killed.

The clash of swords, the imprecations, and the grunts of fighting men came to me distinctly from the opposite side of the wall which barred my way. I could even hear the heavy breathing of the fighters. I heard the green men demand the surrender of their quarry and his taunting reply. I liked what he said and the way he said it in the face of death.

My knowledge of the ways of the green men assured me that they would try to capture him for purposes of torture rather than kill him outright, but if I were to save him from either fate I must act quickly.

There was only one way to reach him without loss of time, and that way was open to me because of the lesser gravitation of Mars and my great Earthly strength and agility. I would simply jump to the top of the wall, take a quick survey of the lay of the land beyond, and then drop down, long-sword in hand, and take my place at the side of the red man.

When I exert myself, I can jump to incredible heights. Twenty feet is nothing, but this time I miscalculated. I was several yards from the wall when I took a short run and leaped into the air. Instead of alighting on the top of the wall, as I had planned, I soared completely over it, clearing it by a good ten feet.

Below me were the fighters. Apparently I was going to land right in their midst. So engrossed were they in their sword play that they did not notice me; and that was well for me; as one of the green men could easily have impaled me on his sword as I dropped upon them.

My man was being hard pressed. It was evident that the

green men had given up the notion of capturing him, and were trying to finish him off. One of them had him at a disadvantage and was about to plunge a longsword through him when I alighted. By rare good luck I alighted squarely upon the back of the man who was about to kill the red man, and I alighted with the point of my sword protruding straight below me. It caught him in the left shoulder and passed downward through his heart, and even before he collapsed I had planted both feet upon his shoulders; and, straightening up, withdrawn my blade from his carcass.

For a moment my amazing advent threw them all off their guard, and in that moment I leaped to the side of the red man and faced his remaining foes, the red blood of a green warrior dripping from my point.

The red man threw a quick glance at me; and then the remaining green men were upon us, and there was no time for words. A fellow swung at me and missed. Gad! what a blow he swung! Had it connected I should have been as headless as a rykor. It was unfortunate for the green man that it did not, for mine did. I cut horizontally with all my Earthly strength, which is great on Earth and infinitely greater on Mars. My longsword, its edge as keen as a razor and its steel such as only Barsoom produces, passed entirely through the body of my antagonist, cutting him in two.

"Well done!" exclaimed the red man, and again he cast a quick glance at me.

From the corner of my eye I caught an occasional glimpse of my unknown comrade, and I saw some marvelous swordsmanship. I was proud to fight at the side of such a man. By now we had reduced the number of our antagonists to three. They fell back a few steps, dropping their points, just for a breathing spell. I neither needed nor desired a breathing spell; but, glancing at my companion, I saw that he was pretty well exhausted; so I dropped my point too and waited.

It was then that I got my first good look at the man whose cause I had espoused; and I got a shock, too. This was no red man, but a white man if I have ever seen one. His skin was bronzed by exposure to the sun, as is mine; and that had at first deceived me. But now I saw that there was nothing red-Martian about him. His harness, his weapons, everything about him differed from any that I had seen on Mars.

He wore a headdress, which is quite unusual upon Barsoom. It consisted of a leather band that ran around the head just above his brows, with another leather band crossing his head from right to left and a second from front to rear. These bands were highly ornamented with carving and set with jewels and precious metals. To the center of the band that crossed his forehead was affixed a flat piece of gold in the shape of a spearhead with the point up. This, also, was beautifully carved and bore a strange device inlaid in red and black.

Confined by this headdress was a shock of blond hair— a most amazing thing to see upon Mars. At first I jumped to the conclusion that he must be a thern from the far south-polar land; but that thought I discarded at once when I realized that the hair was his own. The therns are entirely bald and wear great yellow wigs.

I also saw that my companion was strangely handsome. I might say beautiful were it not for the effeminateness which the word connotes, and there was nothing effeminate about the way this man fought or the mighty oaths that he swore when he spoke at all to an adversary. We fighting men are not given to much talk, but when you feel your blade cleave a skull in twain or drive through the heart of a foe-man, then sometimes a great oath is wrenched from your lips.

But I had little time then to appraise my companion, for the remaining three were at us again in a moment. I fought that day, I suppose, as I have always fought; but each time it seems to me that I have never fought so well as upon that particular occasion. I do not take great credit for my fighting ability, for it seems to me that my sword is inspired. No man could think as quickly as my point moves, always to the right spot at the right time, as though anticipating the next move of an adversary. It weaves a net of steel about me that few blades have ever pierced. It fills the foeman's eyes with amazement and his mind with doubt and his heart with fear. I imagine that much of my success has been due to the psychological effect of my swordsmanship upon my adver-saries.

Simultaneously my companion and I each struck down an antagonist, and then the remaining warrior turned to flee. "Do not let him escape!" cried my comrade-in-arms, and leaped in pursuit, at the same time calling loudly for help, something he had not done when close to death before the points of six swords. But whom did he expect to answer his appeal in this dead and deserted city? Why did he call for help when the last of his antagonists was in full flight? I was puzzled; but having enlisted myself in this strange adventure, I felt that I should see it through; and so I set off in pursuit of the fleeing green man.

He crossed the courtyard where we had been engaged and made for a great archway that opened out into a broad avenue. I was close behind him, having outstripped both him and the strange warrior. When I came into the avenue I saw the green man leap to the back of one of six thoats waiting there, and at the same time I saw at least a hundred warriors pouring from a nearby building. They were yellow-haired white men, garbed like my erstwhile fighting companion, who now joined in the pursuit of the green man. They were armed with bows and arrows; and they sent a volley of missiles after the escaping quarry, whom they could never hope to overtake, and who was soon out of range of their weapons.

The spirit of adventure is so strong within me that I often yield to its demands in spite of the dictates of my better judgment. This matter was no affair of mine. I had already done all, and even more than could have been expected of me; yet I leaped to the back of one of the remaining thoats and took off in pursuit of the green warrior.

3

There are two species of thoat on Mars: the small, comparatively docile breed used by the red Martians as saddle animals and, to a lesser extent, as beasts of burden on the farms that border the great irrigation canals; and then there are the huge, vicious, unruly beasts that the green warriors use exclusively as steeds of war.

These creatures tower fully ten feet at the shoulder. They have four legs on either side and a broad, flat tail, larger at the tip than at the root, that they hold straight out behind while running. Their gaping mouths split their heads from their snouts to their long, massive necks. Their bodies, the upper portion of which is a dark slate color and exceedingly smooth and glossy, are entirely devoid of hair. Their bellies are white, and their legs shade gradually from the slate color of their bodies to a vivid yellow at the feet, which are heavily padded and nailless.

The thoat of the green man has the most abominable disposition of any creature I have ever seen, not even the green men themselves excepted. They are constantly fighting among themselves, and woe betide the rider who loses control of his terrible mount; yet, paradoxical as it may appear, they are ridden without bridle or bit; and are controlled solely by telepathic means, which, fortunately for me, I learned many years ago while I was prisoner of Lorquas Ptomel, jed of the Tharks, a green Martian horde.

The beast to whose back I had vaulted was a vicious devil,

and he took violent exception to me and probably to my
odor. He tried to buck me off; and, failing that, reached
back with his huge, gaping jaws in an effort to seize me.

There is, I might mention, an auxiliary method of control
when these ugly beasts become recalcitrant; and I adopted
it in this instance, notwithstanding the fact that I had won
grudging approval from the fierce green Tharks by control-
ling thoats through patience and kindness. I had time for
neither now, as my quarry was racing along the broad avenue
that led to the ancient quays of Horz and the vast dead sea
bottoms beyond; so I laid heavily upon the head and snout
of the beast with the flat of my broadsword until I had beat-
en it into subjection; then it obeyed my telepathic commands, and set out at great speed in pursuit.

It was a very swift thoat, one of the swiftest that I had
ever bestrode; and, in addition, it carried much less weight
than the beast we sought to overtake; so we closed up rapidly
on the escaping green man.

At the very edge of the plateau upon which the old city
was built we caught up with him, and there he stopped and
wheeled his mount and prepared to give battle. It was then
that I began to appreciate the marvelous intelligence of my
mount. Almost without direction from me he maneuvered into
the correct positions to give me an advantage in this savage
duel, and when at last I had achieved a sudden advantage
which had almost unseated my rival, my thoat rushed like a
mad devil upon the thoat of the green warrior tearing at its
throat with his mighty jaws while he tried to beat it to its
knees with the weight of his savage assault.

It was then that I gave the *coup de grace* to my beaten
and bloody adversary; and, leaving him where he had fallen,
rode back to receive the plaudits and the thanks of my new-
found friends.

They were waiting for me, a hundred of them, in what
had probably once been a public market place in the ancient city of Horz. They were not smiling. They looked sad.
As I dismounted, they crowded around me.

"Did the green man escape?" demanded one whose ornaments and metal proclaimed him a leader.

"No," I replied; "he is dead."

A great sigh of relief arose from a hundred throats. Just
why they should feel such relief that a single green man had
been killed I did not then understand.

They thanked me, crowding around me as they did so;
and still they were unsmiling and sad. I suddenly realized
that these people were not friendly—it came to me intuitively,
but too late. They were pushing against me from all sides, so

that I could not even raise an arm; and then, quite suddenly at a word from their leader, I was disarmed.

"What is the meaning of this?" I demanded. "Of my own volition I came to the aid of one of your people who would otherwise have been killed. Is this the thanks I am to receive? Give me back my weapons and let me go."

"I am sorry," said he who had first spoken, "but we cannot —do otherwise. Pan Dan Chee, to whose aid you came, has pleaded that we permit you to go your way; but such is not the law of Horz. I must take you to Ho Ran Kim, the great jeddak of Horz. There we will all plead for you, but our pleas will be unavailing. In the end you will be destroyed. The safety of Horz is more important than the life of any man."

"I am not threatening the safety of Horz," I replied. "Why should I have designs upon a dead city, which is of absolutely no importance to the Empire of Helium, in the service of whose Jeddak, Tardos Mors, I wear the harness of a war lord."

"I am sorry," exclaimed Pan Dan Chee, who had pushed his way to my side through the press of warriors. "I called to you when you mounted the thoat and pursued the green warrior and told you not to return, but evidently you did not hear me. For that I may die, but I shall die proudly. I sought to influence Lan Sohn Wen, who commands this utan, to permit you to escape, but in vain. I shall intercede for you with Ho Ran Kim, the jeddak; but I am afraid that there is no hope."

"Come!" said Lan Sohn Wen; "we have wasted enough time here. We will take the prisoner to the jeddak. By the way, what is your name?"

"I am John Carter, a Prince of Helium and Warlord of Barsoom," I replied.

"A proud title, that last," he said; "but of Helium I have never heard."

"If harm befalls me here," I said, "you'll hear of Helium if Helium ever learns."

I was escorted through still magnificent avenues flanked by beautiful buildings, still beautiful in decay. I think I have never seen such inspiring architecture, nor construction so enduring. I do not know how old these buildings are, but I have heard Martian savants argue that the original dominant race of white-skinned, yellow-haired people flourished fully a million years ago. It seems incredible that their works should still exist; but there are many things on Mars incredible to the narrow, earthbound men of our little speck of dust.

At last we halted before a tiny gate in a colossal, fortress-like edifice in which there was no other opening than this small gate for fifty feet above the ground. From a balcony fifty feet above the gate a sentry looked down upon us. "Who comes?" he demanded, although he could doubtless see who came, and must have recognized Lan Sohn Wen.

"It is Lan Sohn Wen, Dwar, commanding the 1st Utan of The Jeddak's Guard, with a prisoner," replied Lan Sohn Wen.

The sentry appeared bewildered. "My orders are to admit no strangers," he said, "but to kill them immediately."

"Summon the commander of the guard," snapped Lan Sohn Wen, and presently an officer came onto the balcony with the sentry.

"What is this?" he demanded. "No prisoner has ever been brought into the citadel of Horz. You know the law."

"This is an emergency," said Lan Sohn Wen. "I must bring this man before Ho Ran Kim. Open the gate!"

"Only on orders from Ho Ran Kim himself," replied the commander of the guard.

"Then go get the orders," said Lan Sohn Wen. "Tell the Jeddak that I strongly urge him to receive me with this prisoner. He is not as other prisoners who have fallen into our han's in times past."

The officer re-entered the citadel and was gone for perhaps fifteen minutes when the little gate before which we stood swung outward, and we were motioned in by the commander of the guard himself.

"The Jeddak will receive you," he said to the dwar, Lan Sohn Wen.

The citadel was an enormous walled city within the ancient city of Horz. It was quite evidently impregnable to any but attack by air. Within were pleasant avenues, homes, gardens, shops. Happy, carefree people stopped to look at me in astonishment as I was conducted down a broad boulevard toward a handsome building. It was the palace of the Jeddak, Ho Ran Kim. A sentry stood upon either side of the portal. There was no other guard; and these two were there more as a formality and as messengers than for protection, for within the walls of the citadel no man needed protection from another; as I was to learn.

We were detained in an ante room for a few minutes while we were being announced, and then we were ushered down a long corridor and into a medium size room where a man sat at a desk alone. This was Ho Ran Kim, Jeddak of Horz. His skin was not as tanned as that of his warriors, but his hair was just as yellow and his eyes as blue.

I felt those blue eyes appraising me as I approached his desk. They were kindly eyes, but with a glint of steel. From me they passed to Lan Sohn Wen, and to him Ho Ran Kim spoke.

"This is most unusual," he said in a quiet, well modulated voice. "You know, do you not, that Horzans have died for less than this?"

"I do, my Jeddak," replied the dwar; "but this is a most unusual emergency."

"Explain yourself," said the Jeddak.

"Let me explain," interrupted Pan Dan Chee, "for after all the responsibility is mine. I urged this action upon Lan Sohn Wen."

The Jeddak nodded. "Proceed," he said.

4

I couldn't comprehend why they were making such an issue of bringing in a prisoner, nor why men had died for less, as Ho Ran Kim had reminded Lan Sohn Wen. In Helium, a warrior would have received at least commendation for bringing in a prisoner. For bringing in John Carter, Warlord of Mars, a common warrior might easily have been ennobled by an enemy prince.

"My Jeddak," commenced Pan Dan Chee, "while I was beset by six green warriors, this man, who says he is known as John Carter, Warlord of Barsoom, came of his own volition to fight at my side. From whence he came I do not know. I only know that at one moment I was fighting alone, a hopeless fight, and that at the next there fought at my side the greatest swordsman Horz has ever seen. He did not have to come; he could have left at any time, but he remained; and because he remained I am alive and the last of the six green warriors lies dead by the ancient waterfront. He would have escaped had not John Carter leaped to the back of a great thoat and pursued him.

"Then this man could have escaped, but he came back. He fought for a soldier of Horz. He trusted the men of Horz. Are we to repay him with death?"

Pan Dan Chee ceased speaking, and Ho Ran Kim turned his blue eyes upon me. "John Carter," he said, "what you have done commands the respect and sympathy of every man of Horz. It wins the thanks of their Jeddak, but——" He hesitated. "Perhaps if I tell you something of our history, you will understand why I must condemn you to death." He paused for a moment, as though in thought.

At the same time I was doing a little thinking on my own account. The casual manner in which Ho Ran Kim had

sentenced me to death had rather taken my breath away.
He seemed so friendly that it didn't seem possible that he was
in earnest, but a glance at the glint in those blue eyes assured me that he was not being facetious.

"I am sure," I said, "that the history of Horz must be
most interesting; but right now I am most interested in learning why I should have to die for befriending a fighting man
of Horz."

"That I shall explain," he said.

"It is going to take a great deal of explaining, your majesty," I assured him.

He paid no attention to that, but continued. "The inhabitants of Horz are, as far as we know, the sole remaining
remnant of the once dominant race of Barsoom, the Orovars.
A million years ago our ships ranged the five great oceans,
which we ruled. The city of Horz was not only the capital of
a great empire, it was the seat of learning and culture of the
most glorious race of human beings a world has ever known.
Our empire spread from pole to pole. There were other races
on Barsoom, but they were few in numbers and negligible in
importance. We looked upon them as inferior creatures. The
Orovars owned Barsoom, which was divided among a score
of powerful jeddaks. They were a happy, prosperous, contented people, the various nations seldom warring upon one another. Horz had enjoyed a thousand years of peace.

"They had reached the ultimate pinnacle of civilization
and perfection when the first shadow of impending fate darkened their horizon—the seas began to recede, the atmosphere
to grow more tenuous. What science had long predicted was
coming to pass—a world was dying.

"For ages our cities followed the receding waters. Straits
and bays, canals and lakes dried up. Prosperous seaports
became deserted inland cities. Famine came. Hungry hordes
made war upon the more fortunate. The growing hordes of
wild green men overran what had once been fertile farm
land, preying upon all.

"The atmosphere became so tenuous that it was difficult to
breathe. Scientists were working upon an atmosphere plant,
but before it was completed and in successful operation all
but a few of the inhabitants of Barsoom had died. Only the
hardiest survived—the green men, the red men, and a few
Orovars; then life became merely a battle for the survival of
the fittest.

"The green men hunted us as we had hunted beasts of
prey. They gave us no rest, they showed us no mercy. We
were few; they were many. Horz became our last city of ref-
uge, and our only hope of survival lay in preventing the out-

side world from knowing that we existed; therefore, for ages we have slain every stranger who came to Horz and saw an Orovar, that no man might go away and betray our presence to our enemies.

"Now you will understand that no matter how deeply we must regret the necessity, it is obvious that we cannot let you live."

"I can understand," I said, "that you might feel it necessary to destroy an enemy; but I see no reason for destroying a friend. However, that is for you to decide."

"It is already decided, my friend," said the Jeddak. "You must die."

"Just a moment, O Jeddak!" exclaimed Pan Dan Chee. "Before you pass final judgment, consider this alternative. If he remains here in Horz, he cannot carry word to our enemies. We owe him a debt of gratitude. Permit him then to live, but always within the walls of the citadel."

There were nods of approval from the others present, and I saw by his quickly darting eyes that Ho Ran Kim had noticed them. He cleared his throat. "Perhaps that is something that should be given thought," he said. "I shall reserve judgment until the morrow. I do so largely because of my love for you, Pan Dan Chee; inasmuch as, because it was due to your importunities that this man is here, you must suffer whatever fate is ordained for him."

Pan Dan Chee was certainly surprised, nor could he hide the fact; but he took the blow like a man. "I shall consider it an honor," he said, "to share any fate that may be meted to John Carter, Warlord of Barsoom."

"Well said, Pan Dan Chee!" exclaimed the Jeddak. "My admiration for you increases as does the bitterness of my sorrow when I contemplate the almost inescapable conviction that on the morrow you die."

Pan Dan Chee bowed. "I thank your majesty for your deep concern," he said. "The remembrance of it will glorify my last hours."

The Jeddak turned his eyes upon Lan Sohn Wen, and held them there for what seemed a full minute. I would have laid ten to one that Ho Ran Kim was about to cause himself further untold grief by condemning Lan Sohn Wen to death. I think Lan Sohn Wen thought the same thing. He looked worried.

"Lan Sohn Wen," said Ho Ran Kim, "you will conduct these two to the pits and leave them there for the night. See that they have good food and every possible comfort, for they are my honored guests."

"But the pits, your majesty!" exclaimed Lan Sohn Wen.

"They have never been used within the memory of man. I do not even know that I can find the entrance to them."

"That is so," said Ho Ran Kim, thoughtfully. "Even if you found them they might prove very dirty and uncomfortable. Perhaps it would be kinder to destroy John Carter and Pan Dan Chee at once."

"Wait, majesty," said Pan Dan Chee. "I know where lies the entrance to the pits. I have been in them. They can easily be made most comfortable. I would not think of altering your plans or causing you immediately the deep grief of sorrowing over the untimely passing of John Carter and myself. Come, Lan Sohn Wen! I will lead the way to the pits of Horz!"

5

It was a good thing for me that Pan Dan Chee was a fast talker. Before Ho Ran Kim could formulate any objections we were out of the audience chamber and on our way to the pits of Horz, and I can tell you that I was glad to be out of sight of that kindly and considerate tyrant. There was no telling when some new humanitarian urge might influence him to order our heads lopped off instanter.

The entrance to the pits of Horz was in a small, windowless building near the rear wall of the citadel. It was closed by massive gates that creaked on corroded hinges as two of the warriors who had accompanied us pushed them open.

"It is dark in there," said Pan Dan Chee. "We'll break our necks without a light."

Lan Sohn Wen, being a good fellow, sent one of his men for some torches; and when he returned, Pan Dan Chee and I entered the gloomy cavern.

We had taken but a few steps toward the head of a rock hewn ramp that ran downward into Stygian darkness, when Lan Sohn Wen cried, "Wait! Where is the key to these gates?"

"The keeper of the keys of some great jeddak who lived thousands of years ago may have known," replied Pan Dan Chee, "but I don't."

"But how am I going to lock you in?" demanded Lan Sohn Wen.

"The Jeddak didn't tell you to lock us in," said Pan Dan Chee. "He said to take us to the pits and leave us there for the night. I distinctly recall his very words."

Lan Sohn Wen was in a quandary, but at last he hit upon an avenue of escape. "Come," he said, "I shall take you back to the Jeddak and explain that there are no keys; then it will be up to him."

"And you know what he will do!" said Pan Dan Chee.

"What?" asked Lan Sohn Wen.

"He will order us destroyed at once. Come, Lan Sohn Wen, do not condemn us to immediate death. Post a guard here at the gates, with orders to kill us if we try to escape."

Lan Sohn Wen considered this for a moment, and finally nodded his head in acquiescence. "That is an excellent plan," he said, and then he detailed two warriors to stand guard; and arranged for their relief, after which he wished us good night and departed with his warriors.

I have never seen such courteous and considerate people as the Orovars; it might almost be a pleasure to have one's throat slit by one of them, he would be so polite about it. They are the absolute opposites of their hereditary enemies, the green men; for these are endowed with neither courtesy, consideration, nor kindness. They are cold, cruel, abysmal brutes to whom love is unknown and whose creed is hate.

Nevertheless, the pits of Horz was not a pleasant place. The dust of ages lay upon the ramp down which we walked. From its end a corridor stretched away beyond the limits of our torchlight. It was a wide corridor, with doors opening from it on either side. These, I presumed, were the dungeons where ancient jeddaks had confined their enemies. I asked Pan Dan Chee.

"Probably," he said, "though our jeddaks have never used them."

"Have they never had enemies?" I asked.

"Certainly, but they have considered it cruel to imprison men in dark holes like this; so they have always destroyed them immediately they were suspected of being enemies."

"Then why are the pits here?" I demanded.

"Oh, they were built when the city was built, perhaps a million years ago, perhaps more. It just chanced that the citadel was built around the entrance."

I glanced into one of the dungeons. A mouldering skeleton lay upon the floor, the rusted irons that had secured it to the wall lying among its bones. In the next dungeon were three skeletons and two magnificently carved, metal bound chests. As Pan Dan Chee raised the lid of one of them I could scarce repress a gasp of astonishment and admiration. The chest was filled with magnificent gems in settings of elaborate beauty, specimens of forgotten arts, the handicraft of master craftsmen who had lived a million years ago. I think that nothing that I had ever seen before had so impressed me. And it was depressing, for these jewels had been worn by lovely women and brave men who had disappeared into an oblivion so complete that not even a memory of them remained.

My reverie was interrupted by the sound of shuffling feet behind me. I wheeled; and, instinctively, my hand flew to where the hilt of a sword should have been but was not. Facing me, and ready to spring upon me, was the largest ulsio I had ever seen.

These Martian rats are fierce and unlovely things. They are many legged and hairless, their hide resembling that of a new-born mouse in repulsiveness. Their eyes are small and close set and almost hidden in deep, fleshy apertures. Their most ferocious and repulsive features, however, are their jaws, the entire bony structure of which protrudes several inches beyond the flesh, revealing five sharp, spadelike teeth in each jaw, the whole suggesting the appearance of a rotting face from which much of the flesh has sloughed away. Ordinarily they are about the size of an Airedale terrier, but the thing that leaped for me in the pits of Horz that day was as large as a small puma and ten times as ferocious.

As the creature leaped for my throat, I struck it a heavy blow on the side of its head and knocked it to one side; but it was up at once and at me again; then Pan Dan Chee came into the scene. They had not disarmed him, and with short-sword he set upon the ulsio.

It was quite a battle. That ulsio was the most ferocious and most determined beast I had ever seen, and it gave Pan Dan Chee the fight of his life. He had knocked off two of its six legs, an ear, and most of its teeth before the ferocity of its repeated attacks abated at all. It was almost cut to ribbons, yet it always forced the fighting. I could only stand and look on, which is not such a part in a fight as I like to take. At last, however, it was over; the ulsio was dead, and Pan Dan Chee looked at me and smiled.

He was looking around for something upon which he might wipe the blood from his blade. "Perhaps there is something in this other chest," I suggested; and, walking to it, I lifted the lid.

The chest was about seven feet long, two and a half wide and two deep. In it lay the body of a man. His elaborate harness was encrusted with jewels. He wore a helmet entirely covered with diamonds, one of the few helmets I had ever seen upon Mars. The scabbards of his long-sword, his short-sword, and his dagger were similarly emblazoned.

He had been a very handsome man, and he was still a handsome corpse. So perfectly was he preserved that, in so far as appearances went, he might still have been alive but for the thin layer of dust overlying his features. When I blew this away he looked quite as alive as you or I.

"You bury your dead here?" I asked Pan Dan Chee, but he shook his head.

"No," he replied. "This chap may have been here a million years."

"Nonsense!" I exclaimed. "He would have dried up and blown away thousands of years ago."

"I don't know about that," said Pan Dan Chee. "There were lots of things that those old fellows knew that are lost arts today. Embalming, I know, was one of them. There is the legend of Lee Um Lo, the most famous embalmer of all time. It recounts that his work was so perfect that not even the corpse, himself, knew that he was dead; and upon several occasions they arose and walked out during the funeral services. The end of Lee Um Lo came when the wife of a great jeddak failed to realize that she was dead, and walked right in on the jeddak and his new wife. The next day Lee Um Lo lost his head."

"It is a good story," I said, laughing; "but I hope this chap realizes that he is dead; because I am about to disarm him. Little could he have dreamed a million years ago that one day he was going to rearm The Warlord of Barsoom."

Pan Dan Chee helped me raise the corpse and remove its harness; and we were both rather startled by the soft, pliable texture of the flesh and its normal warmth.

"Do you suppose we could be mistaken?" I asked. "Could it be that he is not dead?"

Pan Dan Chee shrugged. "The knowledge and the arts of the ancients are beyond the ken of modern man," he said.

"That doesn't help a bit," I said. "Do you think this chap can be alive?"

"His face was covered with dust," said Pan Dan Chee, "and no one has been in these pits for thousands and thousands of years. If he isn't dead, he should be."

I quite agreed, and buckled the gorgeous harness about me without more ado. I drew the swords and the dagger and examined them. They were as bright and fine as the day they had received their first polish, and their edges were keen. Once again, I felt like a whole man, so much is a sword a part of me.

As we stepped out into the corridor I saw a light far away. It was gone almost in the instant. "Did you see that?" I asked Pan Dan Chee.

"I saw it," he said, and his voice was troubled. "There should be no light here, for there are no people."

We stood straining our eyes along the corridor for a repe-

tition of the light. There was none, but from afar there
echoed down that black corridor a hollow laugh.

6

Pan Dan Chee looked at me. "What," he asked, "could
that have been?"

"It sounded very much like a laugh to me," I replied.

Pan Dan Chee nodded. "Yes," he agreed, "but how can
there be a laugh where there is no one to laugh?" Pan Dan
Chee was perplexed.

"Perhaps the ulsios of Horz have learned to laugh," I suggested with a smile.

Pan Dan Chee ignored my flippancy. "We saw a light and
we heard a laugh," he said thoughtfully. "What does that convey to you?"

"The same thing that it conveys to you," I said: "that
there is some one down here in the pits of Horz beside
us."

"I do not see how that can be possible," he said.

"Let's investigate," I suggested.

With drawn swords we advanced; for we did not know the
nature nor the temper of the owner of that laugh, and there
was always the chance that an ulsio might leap from one of
the dungeons and attack us.

The corridor ran straight for some distance, and then commenced to curve. There were many branches and intersections,
but we kept to what we believed to be the main corridor. We
saw no more lights, heard no more laughter. There was not a
sound in all that vast labyrinth of passageways other than the
subdued clanking of our metal, the occasional shuffling of our
sandalled feet, and the soft whisperings of our leather harnesses.

"It is useless to search farther," said Pan Dan Chee at
last. "We might as well start back."

Now I had no intention of going back to my death. I
reasoned that the light and the laugh indicated the presence
of man in these pits. If the inhabitants of Horz knew nothing
of them; then they must enter the pits from outside the citadel, indicating an avenue of escape open to me. Therefore, I
did not wish to retrace our steps; so I suggested that we rest
for a while and discuss our future plans.

"We can rest," said Pan Dan Chee, "but there is nothing
to discuss. Our plans have all been made for us by Ho Ran
Kim."

We entered a cell which contained no grim reminders of

past tragedy; and, after wedging one of our torches in a niche in the wall, we sat down on the hard stone floor.

"Perhaps your plans have been made for you by Ho Ran Kim," I said, "but I make my own plans."

"And they are—?" he asked.

"I am not going back to be murdered. I am going to find a way out of these pits."

Pan Dan Chee shook his head sorrowfully. "I am sorry," he said, "but you are going back to meet your fate with me."

"What makes you think that?" I asked.

"Because I shall have to take you back. You well know that I cannot let a stranger escape from Horz."

"That means that we shall have to fight to the death, Pan Dan Chee," I said; "and I do not wish to kill one at whose side I have fought and whom I have learned to admire."

"I feel the same way, John Carter," said Pan Dan Chee. "I do not wish to kill you; but you must see my position— if you do not come with me willingly, I shall have to kill you."

I tried to argue him out of his foolish stand, but he was adamant. I was positive that Pan Dan Chee liked me; and I shrank from the idea of killing him, as I knew that I should. He was an excellent swordsman, but what chance would he have against the master swordsman of two worlds? I am sorry if that should sound like boasting; for I abhor boasting—I only spoke what is a fact. I am, unquestionably, the best swordsman that has ever lived.

"Well," I said, "we don't have to kill each other at once. Let's enjoy each other's company for a while longer."

Pan Dan Chee smiled. "That will suit me perfectly," he said.

"How about a game of Jetan?" I asked. "It will help to pass the time pleasantly."

"How can we play Jetan without a board or the pieces?" he asked.

I opened the leather pocket pouch such as all Martians carry, and took out a tiny, folding Jetan board with all the pieces—a present from Dejah Thoris, my incomparable mate. Pan Dan Chee was intrigued by it, and it *is* a marvelously beautiful piece of work. The greatest artist of Helium had designed the pieces, which had been carved under his guidance by two of our greatest sculptors.

Each of the pieces, such as Warriors, Padwars, Dwars, Panthans, and Chiefs, were carved in the likeness of well-known Martian fighting men; and one of the Princesses was a beautifully executed miniature carving of Tara of Helium, and the other Princess, Llana of Gathol.

I am inordinately proud of this Jetan set; and because the figures are so tiny, I always carry a small but powerful reading glass, not alone that I may enjoy them but that others may. I offered it now to Pan Dan Chee, who examined the figures minutely.

"Extraordinary," he said. "I have never seen anything more beautiful." He had examined one figure much longer than he had the others, and he held it in his hand now as though loath to relinquish it. "What an exquisite imagination the artist must have had who created this figure, for he could have had no model for such gorgeous beauty; since nothing like it exists on Barsoom."

"Every one of those figures was carved from life," I told him.

"Perhaps the others," he said, "but not this one. No such beautiful woman ever lived."

"Which one is it?" I asked, and he handed it to me. "This," I said, "is Llana of Gathol, the daughter of Tara of Helium, who is my daughter. She really lives, and this is a most excellent likeness of her. Of course it cannot do her justice since it cannot reflect her animation nor the charm of her personality."

He took the little figurine back and held it for a long time under the glass; then he replaced it in the box. "Shall we play?" I asked.

He shook his head. "It would be sacrilege," he said, "to play at a game with the figure of a goddess."

I packed the pieces back in the tiny box, which was also the playing board, and returned it to my pouch. Pan Dan Chee sat silent. The light of the single torch cast our shadows deep and dark upon the floor.

These torches of Horz were a revelation to me. They are most ingenious. Cylindrical, they have a central core which glows brightly with a cold light when exposed to the air. By turning back a hinged cap and pushing the central core up with a thumb button, it becomes exposed to the air and glows brightly. The farther up it is pushed and the more of it that is exposed, the more intense the light. Pan Dan Chee told me that they were invented ages ago, and that the lighting results in so little loss of matter that they are practically eternal. The art of producing the central core was lost in far antiquity, and no scientist since has been able to analyze its composition.

It was a long time before Pan Dan Chee spoke again; then he arose. He looked tired and sad. "Come," he said, "let's have it over with," and he drew his sword.

"Why should we fight?" I asked. "We are friends. If I go

away, I pledge my honor that I will not lead others to Horz. Let me go, then, in peace. I do not wish to kill you. Or, better still, you come away with me. There is much to see in the world outside of Horz and much to adventure."

"Don't tempt me," he begged, "for I want to come. For the first time in my life I want to leave Horz, but I may not. Come! John Carter. On guard! One of us must die, unless you return willingly with me."

"In which case both of us will die," I reminded him. "It is very silly, Pan Dan Chee."

"On guard!" was his only reply.

There was nothing for me to do but draw and defend myself. Never have I drawn with less relish.

7

Pan Dan Chee would not take the offensive, and he offered very little in the way of defense. I could have run him through at any time that I chose from the very instant that I drew my sword. Almost immediately I realized that he was offering me my freedom at the expénse of his own life, but I would not take his life.

Finally I backed away and dropped my point. "I am no butcher, Pan Dan Chee," I said. "Come! put up a fight."

He shook his head. "I cannot kill you," he said, quite simply.

"Why?" I asked.

"Because I am a fool," he said. "The same blood flows in your veins and hers. I could not spill that blood. I could not bring unhappiness to her."

"What do you mean?" I demanded. "What are you talking about?"

"I am talking about Llana of Gathol," he said, "the most beautiful woman in the world, the woman I shall never see but for whom I gladly offer my life."

Now, Martian fighting men are proverbially chivalrous to a fault, but this was carrying it much further than I had ever seen it carried before.

"Very well," I said; "and as I don't intend killing you there is no use going on with this silly duel."

I returned my sword to its scabbard, and Pan Dan Chee did likewise.

"What shall we do?" he asked. "I cannot let you escape; but, on the other hand, I cannot prevent it. I am a traitor to my country. I shall, therefore, have to destroy myself."

I had a plan. I would accompany Pan Dan Chee back al-

most to the entrance to the pits, and there I would over-
power, bind, and gag him; then I would make my escape, or
at least I would try to find another exit from the pits. Pan
Dan Chee would be discovered, and could face his doom without the stigma of treason being attached to his name.

"You need not kill yourself," I told him. "I will accompany you to the entrance to the pits; but I warn you that
should I discover an opportunity to escape, I shall do so."

"That is fair enough," he said. "It is very generous of you.
You have made it possible for me to die honorably and
content."

"Do you wish to die?" I asked.

"Certainly not," he assured me. "I wish to live. If I live, I
may some day find my way to Gathol."

"Why not come with me, then?" I demanded. "Together
we may be able to find our way out of the pits. My flier
lies but a short distance from the citadel, and it is only about
four thousand haads from Horz to Gathol."

He shook his head. "The temptation is great," he said, "but
until I have exhausted every resource and failed to return
to Ho Ran Kim before noon tomorrow I may do nothing else
but try."

"Why by noon tomorrow?" I asked.

"It is a very ancient Orovaran law," he replied, "which
limits the duration of a death sentence to noon of the day one
is condemned to die. Ho Ran Kim decreed that we should die
tomorrow. If we do not, we are not in honor bound to return to him."

We set off a little dejectedly for the doorway through which
we were expected to pass to our doom. Of course, I had no
intention of doing so; but I was dejected because of Pan Dan
Chee. I had come to like him immensely. He was a man of
high honor and a courageous fighter.

We walked on and on, until I became convinced that if
we had followed the right corridor we should long since have
arrived at the entrance. I suggested as much to Pan Dan
Chee, and he agreed with me; then we retraced our steps
and tried another corridor. We kept this up until we were all
but exhausted, but we failed to find the right corridor.

"I am afraid we are lost," said Pan Dan Chee.

"I am quite sure of it," I agreed, with a smile. If we were
sufficiently well lost, we might not find the entrance before
the next noon; in which event Pan Dan Chee would be free
to go where he pleased, and I had a pretty good idea of where
he pleased to go.

Now, I am no matchmaker; nor neither do I believe in
standing in the way to prevent the meeting of a man and a

maid. I believe in letting nature take her course. If Pan Dan Chee thought he was in love with Llana of Gathol and wished to go to Gathol and try to win her, I would only have discouraged the idea had he been a man of low origin or of a dishonorable nature. He was neither. The race to which he belonged is the oldest of the cultured races of Barsoom, and Pan Dan Chee had proved himself a man of honor.

I had no reason to believe that his suit would meet with any success. Llana of Gathol was still very young, but even so the swords of some of the greatest houses of Barsoom had been lain at her feet. Like nearly all Martian women of high degree she knew her mind. Like so many of them, she might be abducted by some impetuous suitor; and she would either love him or slip a dagger between his ribs, but she would never mate with a man she did not love. I was more fearful for Pan Dan Chee than I was for Llana of Gathol.

We retraced our steps and tried another corridor, yet still no entrance. We lay down and rested; then we tried again. The result was the same.

"It must be nearly morning," said Pan Dan Chee.

"It is," I said, consulting my chronometer. "It is almost noon."

Of course I didn't use the term *noon;* but rather the Barsoomian equivalent, 25 xats past the 3rd zode, which is 12 noon Earth time.

"We must hurry!" exclaimed Pan Dan Chee.

A hollow laugh sounded behind us; and, turning quickly, we saw a light in the distance. It disappeared immediately.

"Why should we hurry?" I demanded. "We have done the best we could. That we did not find our way back to the citadel and death is no fault of ours."

Pan Dan Chee nodded. "And no matter how much we may hurry, there is little likelihood that we shall ever find the entrance."

Of course this was wishful thinking, but it was also quite accurate thinking. We never did find the entrance to the citadel.

"This is the second time we have heard that laugh and seen that light," said Pan Dan Chee. "I think we should investigate it. Perhaps he who makes the light and voices the laugh may be able to direct us to the entrance."

"I have no objection to investigating," I said, "but I doubt that we shall find a friend if we find the author."

"It is most mystifying," said Pan Dan Chee. "All my life I have believed, as all other inhabitants of Horz have believed, that the pits of Horz were deserted. A long time ago, perhaps ages, some venturesome men entered the pits to in-

vestigate them. These incursions occurred at intervals, and
none of those who entered the pits ever returned. It was
assumed that they became lost, and starved to death. Perhaps
they, too, heard the laughter and saw the lights!"

"Perhaps," I said.

8

Pan Dan Chee and I lost all sense of time, so long were we
in the pits of Horz without food or water. It could not have
been more than two days, as we still had strength; and more
than two days without water will sap the strength of the best
of men. Twice more we saw the light and heard the laughter. That laugh! I can hear it yet. I tried to think that it was
human. I didn't want to go mad.

Pan Dan Chee said, "Let's find it and drink its blood!"

"No, Pan Dan Chee," I counselled. "We are men, not
beasts."

"You are right," he said. "I was losing control."

"Let's use our heads," I said. "He knows always where we
are, because always he can see the light of our torch. Suppose
we extinguish it, and creep forward silently. If he has curiosity, he will investigate. We shall listen attentively, and we
shall hear his footfalls." I had it all worked out beautifully,
and Pan Dan Chee agreed that it was a perfect plan. I
think he still had in mind the drinking of the creature's blood,
when we should find it. I was approaching a point when I
might have taken a drink myself. God! If you have never
suffered from hunger and thirst, don't judge others too
harshly.

We extinguished the torch. We each had one, but there was
no use in keeping both lighted. The light of one could have
been raised to a brilliancy that would have blinded. We crept
silently forward in the direction that we had last seen the
light. Our swords were drawn. Three times already we had
been set upon by the huge ulsios of these ancient pits of
Horz, but at these times we had had the advantage of the
light of our torch. I could not but wonder how we would
come out if one of them attacked us now.

The darkness was total, and there was no sound. We clung
to our weapons so that they would not clank against our
metal. We lifted our sandalled feet high and placed them
gently on the stone flooring. There was no scuffing. There was
no sound. We scarcely breathed.

Presently a light appeared before us. We halted, waiting,
listening. I saw a figure. Perhaps it was human, perhaps not.

I touched Pan Dan Chee lightly on the arm, and moved forward. He came with me. We made no sound—absolutely no sound. I think that we each held his breath.

The light grew brighter. Now I could see a head and shoulder protruding from a doorway at the side of the corridor. The thing had the contour of humanity at least. I could imagine that it was concerned over our sudden disappearance. It was wondering what had become of us. It withdrew within the doorway where it had stood, but the light persisted. We could see it shining from the interior of the cell or room into which the THING had withdrawn.

We crept closer. Here might lie the answer to our quest for water and for food. If the THING were human, it would require both; and if it had them, we should have them.

Silently we approached the doorway from which the light streamed out into the corridor. Our swords were drawn. I was in the lead. I felt that if the THING had any warning of our approach, it would disappear. That must not happen. We must see IT. We must seize IT, and we must force IT to give us water—food and water!

I reached the doorway, and as I stepped into the opening I had a momentary glimpse of a strange figure; and then all was plunged into darkness and a hollow laugh reverberated through the Stygian blackness of the pits of Horz.

In my right hand I held the long-sword of that long dead Orovaran from whose body I had filched it. In my left hand I held the amazing torch of the Horzians. When the light in the chamber was extinguished, I pushed up the thumb button of my torch; and the apartment before me was flooded with light.

I saw a large chamber filled with many chests. There was a simple couch, a bench, a table, bookshelves filled with books, an ancient Martian stove, a reservoir of water, and the strangest figure of a man my eyes had ever rested upon.

I rushed at him and held my sword against his heart, for I did not wish him to escape. He cowered and screamed, beseeching his life.

"We want water," I said; "water and food. Give us these and offer us no harm, and you will be safe."

"Help yourselves," he said. "There is water and food here, but tell me who you are and how you got here to the pits of ancient Horz, dead Horz—dead for countless ages. I have been waiting for ages for some one to come, and now you have come. You are welcome. We shall be great friends. You shall stay here with me forever, as all the countless others have. I shall have company in the lonely pits of Horz." Then he laughed maniacally.

It was evident that the creature was quite mad. He not only looked it, he acted it. Sometimes his speech was inarticulate gibber; often it was broken by meaningless and inopportune laughter—the hollow laugh that we had heard before.

His appearance was most repulsive. He was naked except for the harness which supported a sword and a dagger, and the skin of his malformed body was a ghastly white—the color of a corpse. His flabby mouth hung open, revealing a few yellow, snaggled fangs. His eyes were wide and round, the whites showing entirely around the irises. He had no nose; it appeared to have been eaten away by disease.

I kept my eye on him constantly while Pan Dan Chee drank; then he watched him while I slaked my thirst, and all the while the creature kept up a running fire of senseless chatter. He would take a word like calot, for instance, and keep repeating it over and over just as though he were carrying on a conversation. You could detect an interrogatory sentence by his inflection, as also the declarative, imperative, and exclamatory. All the time, he kept gesturing like a Fourth of July orator.

At last he said, "You seem very stupid, but eventually you may understand. And now about food: You prefer your ulsio raw, I presume; or shall I cook it?"

"Ulsio!" exclaimed Pan Dan Chee. "You don't mean to say that you eat ulsio!"

"A great delicacy," said the creature.

"Have you nothing else?" demanded Pan Dan Chee.

"There is a little of Ro Tan Bim left," said the THING, "but he is getting a bit high even for an epicure like me."

Pan Dan Chee looked at me. "I am not hungry," I said. "Come! Let's try to get out of here." I turned to the old man. "Which corridor leads out into the city?" I asked.

"You must rest," he said; "then I will show you. Lie down upon that couch and rest."

I had always heard that it is best to humor the insane; and as I was asking a favor of this creature, it seemed the wise thing to do. Furthermore, both Pan Dan Chee and I were very tired; so we lay down on the couch and the old man drew up a bench and sat down beside us. He commenced to talk in a low, soothing voice.

"You are very tired," he said, over and over again monotonously, his great eyes fixed first upon one of us and then upon the other. I felt my muscles relaxing. I saw Pan Dan Chee's lids drooping. "Soon you will be asleep," whispered the old man of the pits. "You will sleep and sleep and sleep, perhaps for ages as have these others. You will only awaken when I tell you to or when I die—and I shall never die. You robbed

Hor Kai Lan of his harness and weapons." He looked at me as he spoke. "Hor Kai Lan would be very angry were he to awaken and find that you have stolen his weapons, but Hor Kai Lan will not awaken. He has been asleep for so many ages that even I have forgotten. It is in my book, but what difference does it make? What difference does it make who wears the harness of Hor Kai Lan? No one will ever use his swords again; and, anyway, when Ro Tan Bim is gone, maybe I shall use Hor Kai Lan. Maybe I shall use you. Who knows?"

His voice was like a dreamy lullaby. I felt myself sinking into pleasant slumber. I glanced at Pan Dan Chee. He was fast asleep. And then the import of the THING'S words reached my reasoning mind. By hypnosis we were being condemned to a living death! I sought to shake the lethargy from me. I brought to bear what remained to me of my will power. Always my mind has been stronger than that of any Martian against whose mind I have pitted it.

The horror of the situation lent me strength: the thought of lying here for countless ages collecting the dust of the pits of Horz, or of being eaten by this snaggled toothed maniac! I put every ounce of my will power into a final, terrific effort to break the bonds that held me. It was even more devastating than a physical effort. I broke out into violent perspiration. I felt myself trembling from head to feet. Would I succeed?

The old man evidently realized the battle I was making for freedom, as he redoubled his efforts to hold me. His voice and his eyes wrapped themselves about me with almost physical force. The THING was sweating now, so strenuous were its endeavors to enthrall my mind. Would it succeed?

9

I was winning! I knew that I was winning! And the THING must have known it, too; for I saw it slipping its dagger from the sheath at its side. If it couldn't hold me in the semblance of death, it would hold me in actual death. I sought to wrench myself free from the last weakening tentacles of the THING'S malign mental forces before it could strike the fatal blow that would spell death for me and the equivalent of death for Pan Dan Chee.

The dagger hand rose above me. Those hideous eyes glared down into mine, lighted by the Hellish fires of insanity; and then, in that last instant, I won! I was free. I struck the dag-

ger hand from me and leaped to my feet, the good longsword
of Hor Kai Lan already in my hand.

The THING cowered and screamed. It screamed for help
where there was no help, and then it drew its sword. I
would not defile the fine art of my swordsmanship by crossing
blades with such as this. I recalled its boast that Pan Dan
Chee and I would sleep until it awoke us or it died. That
alone was enough to determine me—I would be no duelist,
but an executioner and a liberator.

I cut once, and the foul head rolled to the stone floor of
the pits of Horz. I looked at Pan Dan Chee. He was awaken-
ing. He rolled over and stretched; then he sat up and looked
at me, questioningly. His eyes wandered to the torso and the
head lying on the floor.

"What happened?" he asked.

Before I could reply, I was interrupted by a volley of
sound coming from the chamber in which we were and from
other chambers in the pits of Horz.

We looked quickly around us. Lids were being raised on
innumerable chests, and cries were coming from others the
lids of which were held down by the chests on top of them.
Armed men were emerging—warriors in gorgeous harness.
Women, rubbing their eyes and looking about them in bewilderment.

From the corridor others began to converge upon the
chamber, guided by our light.

"What is the meaning of this?" demanded a large man,
magnificently trapped. "Who brought me here? Who are you?"
He looked around him, evidently bewildered, as though searching for some familiar face.

"Perhaps I can enlighten you?" I said. "We are in the pits
of Horz. I have been here only a few hours, but if this dead
thing on the floor spoke the truth some of you must have
been here for ages. You have been held by the hypnotic power of this mad creature. His death has freed you."

The man looked down at the staring head upon the floor.
"Lum Tar O!" he exclaimed. "He sent for me—asked me to
come and see him on an important matter. And you have
killed him. You must account to me—tomorrow. Now I must
return to my guests."

There was a layer of dust on the man's face and body. By
that I knew that he must have been here a long time, and
presently my surmise was substantiated in a most dramatic
manner.

The awakened men and women were forcing their way
from the chests in which they had been kept. Some of those
in the lower tiers were having difficulty in dislodging the

chests piled on top of them. There was a great clattering and tumult as empty chests toppled to the floor. There was a babel of conversation. There were bewilderment and confusion.

A dusty nobleman crawled from one of the chests. Instantly he and the large man who had just spoken recognized one another. "What is the matter with you?" demanded the latter. "You are all covered with dust. Why did you come down? Come! I must get back to my guests."

The other shook his head in evident bewilderment. "Your guests, Kam Han Tor!" he exclaimed. "Did you expect your guests to wait twenty years for you to return."

"Twenty years! What do you mean?"

"I was your guest twenty years ago. You left in the middle of the banquet and never returned."

"Twenty years? You are mad!" exclaimed Kam Han Tor. He looked at me and then at the grinning head upon the floor, and he commenced to weaken. I could see it.

The other man was feeling of his own face and looking at the dust he wiped from it. "You, too, are covered with dust," he said to Kam Han Tor.

Kam Han Tor looked down at his body and harness; then he wiped his face and looked at his fingers. "Twenty years!" he exclaimed, and then he looked down at the head of Lum Tar O. "You vile beast!" he exclaimed. "I was your friend, and you did this to me!" He turned then to me. "Forget what I said. I did not understand. Whoever you may be, permit me to assure you that my sword is always in your service."

I bowed in acknowledgment.

"Twenty years!" repeated Kam Han Tor, as though he still could not believe it. "My great ship! It was to have sailed from the harbor of Horz the day following my banquet—the greatest ship that ever had been built. Now it is old, perhaps obsolete; and I have never seen it. Tell me— did it sail well? Is it still a proud ship?"

"I saw it as it sailed out upon Throxeus," said the other. "It was a proud ship indeed, but it never returned from that first voyage; nor was any word ever heard of it. It must have been lost with all hands."

Kam Han Tor shook his head sadly, and then he straightened up and squared his shoulders. "I shall build another," he said, "an even greater ship, to sail the mightiest of Barsoom's five seas."

Now I commenced to understand what I had suspected but could not believe. It was absolutely astounding. I was looking at and conversing with men who had lived hundreds of thousands of years ago, when Throxeus and the other four

oceans of ancient Mars had covered what are now the vast
desert wastes of dead sea bottom; when a great merchant
marine carried on the commerce of the fair-skinned, blond
race that had supposedly been extinct for countless ages.

I stepped closer to Kam Han Tor and laid a hand upon
his shoulder. The men and women who had been released
from Lum Tar O's malicious spell had gathered around us,
listening. "I am sorry to disillusion you, Kam Han Tor," I
said; "but you will build no ship, nor will any ship ever
again sail Throxeus."

"What do you mean?" he demanded. "Who is to stop Kam
Han Tor, brother of the jeddak, from building ships and
sailing them upon Throxeus?"

"There is no Throxeus, my friend," I said.

"No Throxeus? You are mad!"

"You have been here in the pits of Horz for countless
ages," I explained, "and during that time the five great
oceans of Barsoom have dried up. There are no oceans.
There is no commerce. The race to which you belonged is
extinct."

"Man, you are mad!" he cried.

"Do you know how to get out of these pits?" I asked—
"out into the city proper—not up through the—" I was going
to say citadel but I recalled that there had been no citadel
when these people had been lured to the pits.

"You mean not up through my palace?" asked Kam Han
Tor.

"Yes," I said, "not up through your palace, but out toward
the quays; then I can show you that there is no longer a
Throxeus."

"Certainly I know the way," he said. "Were these pits not
built according to my plans!"

"Come, then," I said.

A man was standing looking down on the head of Lum
Tar O. "If what this man says is true," he said to Kam Han
Tor, "Lum Tar O must have lived many ages ago. How then
could he have survived all these ages? How have we survived?"

"You were existing in a state of suspended animation,"
I said; "but as for Lum Tar O—that is a mystery."

"Perhaps not such a mystery after all," replied the man.
"I knew Lum Tar O well. He was a weakling and a coward
with the psychological reactions of the weakling and the coward. He hated all who were brave and strong, and these he
wished to harm. His only friend was Lee Um Lo, the most
famous embalmer the world had ever known; and when Lum
Tar O died, Lee Um Lo embalmed his body. Evidently he

did such a magnificent job that Lum Tar O's corpse never realized that Lum Tar O was dead, and went right on functioning as in life. That would account for the great span of years that the thing has existed—not a human being; not a live creature, at all; just a corpse the malign brain of which still functioned."

As the man finished speaking there was a commotion at the entrance to the chamber. A large man, almost naked, rushed in. He was very angry. "What is the meaning of this?" he demanded. "What am I doing here? What are you all doing here? Who stole my harness and my weapons?"

It was then that I recognized him—Hor Kai Lan, whose metal I wore. He was very much excited, and I couldn't blame him much. He forced his way through the crowd, and the moment he laid eyes upon me he recognized his belongings.

"Thief!" he cried. "Give me back my harness and my weapons!"

"I'm sorry," I said; "but unless you will furnish me with others, I shall have to keep these."

"Calot!" he fairly screamed. "Do you realize to whom you are speaking? I am Hor Kai Lan, brother of the jeddak."

Kam Han Tor looked at him in amazement. "You have been dead over five hundred years, Hor Kai Lan," he exclaimed, "and so has your brother. My brother succeeded the last jeddak in the year 27M382J4."

"You have all been dead for ages," said Pan Dan Chee. "Even that calendar is a thing of the dead past."

I thought Hor Kai Lan was going to burst a blood vessel then. "Who are you?" he screamed. "I place you under arrest. I place you all under arrest. Ho! the guard!"

Kam Han Tor tried to pacify him, and at least succeeded in getting him to agree to accompany us to the quays to settle the question of the existence of Throxeus, which would definitely prove or disprove the unhappy truths I had been forced to explain to them.

As we started out, led by Kam Han Tor, I noticed the lid of a chest moving slightly. It was raised little by little, and I could see two eyes peering out through the crack made by the lifting of the lid; then suddenly a girl's voice cried, "John Carter, Prince of Helium! May my first ancestor be blessed!"

10

Had my first ancestor suddenly materialized before my eyes, I could not have been more surprised than I was to hear my name from the interior of one of those chests in the pits of Horz.

As I started to investigate, the lid of the chest was thrown aside; and a girl stepped out before me. This was more surprising than my first ancestor would have been, for the girl was Llana of Gathol!

"Llana!" I cried; "what are you doing here?"

"I might ask you the same question, my revered progenitor," she shot back, with that lack of respect for my great age which has always characterized those closest to me in bonds of blood and affection.

Pan Dan Chee came forward rather open-mouthed and goggle-eyed. "Llana of Gathol!" he whispered as one might voice the name of a goddess. The roomful of anachronisms looked on more or less apathetically.

"Who is this person?" demanded Llana of Gathol.

"My friend, Pan Dan Chee of Horz," I explained.

Pan Dan Chee unbuckled his sword and laid it at her feet, an act which is rather difficult to explain by Earthly standards of conduct. It is not exactly an avowal of love or a proposal of marriage. It is, in a way, something even more sacred. It means that as long as life lasts that sword is at the service of him at whose feet it has been laid. A warrior may lay his sword at the feet of a man or a woman. It means lifetime loyalty. Where the object of that loyalty is a woman, the man may have something else in mind. I am sure that Pan Dan Chee did.

"Your friend acts with amazing celerity," said Llana of Gathol; but she stooped and picked up the sword and handed it back to Pan Dan Chee *hilt first!* which meant that she was pleased and accepted his offer of fealty. Had she simply refused it, she would have left the sword lying where it had been placed. Had she wished to spurn his offer, she would have returned his sword to him *point* first. That would have been the final and deadly insult. I was glad that Llana of Gathol had returned Pan Dan Chee's sword hilt first, as I rather liked Pan Dan Chee. I was particularly glad that she had not returned it point first; as that would have meant that I, as the closest male relative of Llana of Gathol available, would have had to fight Pan Dan Chee; and I certainly didn't want to kill him.

"Well," interrupted Kam Han Tor, "this is all very interesting and touching; but can't we postpone it until we have gone down to the quays."

Pan Dan Chee bridled, and laid a hand on the hilt of his sword. I forestalled any unseemly action on his part by suggesting that Kam Han Tor was wholly right and that our private affairs could wait until the matter of the ocean, so vital to all these other people, had been settled. Pan Dan Chee agreed; so we started again for the quay of ancient Horz.

Llana of Gathol walked at my side. "Now you may tell me," I said, "how you came to be in the pits of Horz."

"It has been many years," she began, "since you were in the kingdom of Okar in the frozen north. Talu, the rebel prince, whom you placed upon the throne of Okar, visited Helium once immediately thereafter. Since then, as far as I have ever heard, there has been no intercourse between Okar and the rest of Barsoom."

"What has all that to do with your being in the pits of Horz?" I demanded.

"Wait!" she admonished. "I am leading up to that. The general belief has been that the region surrounding the North Pole is but sparsely inhabited and by a race of black-bearded yellow men only."

"Correct," I said.

"Not correct," she contradicted. "There is a nation of red men occupying a considerable area, but at some distance from Okar. I am under the impression that when you were there the Okarians themselves had never heard of these people.

"Recently there came to the court of my father, Gahan of Gathol, a strange red man. He was like us, yet unlike. He came in an ancient ship, one which my father said must have been several hundred years old—obsolete in every respect. It was manned by a hundred warriors, whose harness and metal were unknown to us. They appeared fierce and warlike, but they came in peace and were received in peace.

"Their leader, whose name was Hin Abtol, was a pompous braggart. He was an uncultured boor; but, as our guest, he was accorded every courtesy. He said that he was Jeddak of Jeddaks of the North. My father said that he had thought that Talu held that title.

"'He did,' replied Hin Abtol, 'until I conquered his country and made him my vassal. Now I am Jeddak of Jeddaks of the North. My country is cold and bleak outside our glazed cities. I would come south, looking for other lands in which my people may settle and increase.'

"My father told him that all the arable lands were settled and belonged to other nations which had held them for centuries.

"Hin Abtol merely shrugged superciliously. 'When I find what I wish,' he said, 'I shall conquer its people. I, Hin Abtol, take what I wish from the lesser peoples of Barsoom. From what I have heard, they are all weak and effete; not hardy and warlike as are we Panars. We breed fighting men, in addition to which we have countless mercenaries. I could conquer all of Barsoom if I chose.'

"Naturally, that sort of talk disgusted my father; but he kept his temper, for Hin Abtol was his guest. I suppose that Hin Abtol thought that my father feared him, his kind often believing that politeness is a sign of weakness. I know he once said to my father, 'You are fortunate that Hin Abtol is your friend. Other nations may fall before my armies, but you shall be allowed to keep your throne. Perhaps I shall demand a little tribute from you, but you will be safe. Hin Abtol will protect you.'

"I do not know how my father controlled his temper. I was furious. A dozen times I insulted the fellow, but he was too much of an egotistical boor to realize that he was being insulted; then came the last straw. He told Gahan of Gathol that he had decided to honor him by taking me, Llana of Gathol, as his wife. He had already bragged that he had seven!

"'That,' said my father, 'is a matter that I cannot discuss with you. The daughter of Gahan of Gathol will choose her own mate.'

"Hin Abtol laughed. 'Hin Abtol,' he said, 'chooses his wives—they have nothing to say about it.'

"Well, I had stood about all I could of the fellow; and so I decided to go to Helium and visit you and Dejah Thoris. My father decided that I should go in a small flier manned by twenty-five of his most trusted men, all members of my personal Guard.

"When Hin Abtol heard that I was leaving, he said that he would have to leave also—that he was returning to his own country but that he would come back for me. 'And I hope we have no trouble about it,' he said, 'for it would be too bad for Gathol if she made an enemy of Hin Abtol the Panar, Jeddak of Jeddaks of the North.'

"He left the day before I set out, and I did not change my plans because of his going. As a matter of fact, I had been planning on this visit for some time.

"My ship had covered scarce a hundred haads on the journey toward Helium, when we saw a ship rise from the edge of a sorapus forest ahead of us. It came slowly toward us, and presently I recognized its ancient lines. It was the ship of Hin Abtol the Panar, so-called Jeddak of Jeddaks of the North.

"When we were close enough it hailed us, and its captain told us that something had gone wrong with their compass and they were lost. He asked to come alongside that he might examine our charts and get his bearings. He hoped, he said, that we might repair his compass for him.

"Under the circumstances there was nothing to do but accede to his request, as one does not leave a disabled ship without offering aid. As I did not wish to see Hin Abtol, I went below to my cabin.

"I felt the two ships touch as that of the Panar came alongside, and an instant later I heard shouts and curses and the sounds of battle on the upper deck.

"I rushed up the ladder, and the sight that met my eyes filled me with rage. Nearly a hundred warriors swarmed over our deck from Hin Abtol's ancient tub. I have never seen greater brutality displayed by even the green men. The beasts ignored the commonest ethics of civilized warfare. Outnumbering us four to one, we had not a chance; but the men of Gathol put up a most noble fight, taking bloody toll of their attackers; so that Hin Abtol must have lost fully fifty men before the last of my brave Guard was slaughtered.

"The Panars threw my wounded overboard with the dead, not even vouchsafing them the *coup de grace*. Of all my crew, not one was left alive.

"Then Hin Abtol swaggered aboard. 'I told you,' he said, 'that Hin Abtol chooses his wives. It would have been better for you and for Gathol had you believed me.'

" 'It would have been better for you,' I replied, 'had you never heard of Llana of Gathol. You may rest assured that her death will be avenged.'

" 'I do not intend to kill you,' he said.

" 'I shall kill myself,' I told him, 'before I shall mate with such an ulsio as you.'

"That made him angry, and he struck me. 'A coward as well as an ulsio,' I said.

"He did not strike me again, but he ordered me below. In my cabin I realized that the ship was again under way, and looking from the port I saw that it was heading north—north toward the frozen land of the Panars.

11

"Early the following morning, a warrior came to my cabin. 'Hin Abtol commands that you come at once to the control room,' he said.

" 'What does he want of me?' I demanded.

" 'His navigator does not understand this ship or the instruments,' the fellow explained. 'He would ask you some questions.'

"I thought quickly. Perhaps I might frustrate Hin Abtol's plans if I could have a few minutes with the controls and the instruments, which I knew as well as we know the face of a loved one; so I followed the warrior above.

"Hin Abtol was in the control room with three of his officers. His face was a black scowl as I entered. 'We are off our course,' he snapped, 'and during the night we have lost touch with our own ship. You will instruct my officers as to these silly instruments that have confused them.' With that, he left the control room.

"I looked around the horizon in every direction. The other ship was nowhere in sight. My plan was instantly formed. Had the other ship been able to see us, it could not have succeeded. I knew that if this ship on which I was prisoner ever reached Panar I would have to take my own life to escape a fate worse than death. On the ground I might also meet death, but I would have a better chance to escape.

" 'What is wrong?' I asked one of the officers.

" 'Everything,' he replied. 'What is this?'

" 'A directional compass,' I explained; 'but what have you done to it? It is a wreck.'

" 'Hin Abtol could not understand what it was for, which made him very angry; so he started taking it apart to see what was inside.'

" 'He did a good job,' I said, '—of taking it apart. Now he, or another of you, should put it together again.'

" 'We don't know how,' said the fellow. 'Do you?'

" 'Of course not.'

" 'Then what are we to do?'

" 'Here is an ordinary compass,' I told him. 'Fly north by this, but first let me see what other harm has been done.'

"I pretended to examine all the other instruments and controls, and while I was doing so, I opened the buoyancy tank valves; and then jammed them so that they couldn't be closed.

" 'Everything is all right now,' I said. 'Just keep on north by this compass. You won't need the directional compass.' I might have added that in a very short time they wouldn't need any compass as far as navigating this ship was concerned. Then I went down to my cabin.

"I knew that something would happen pretty soon, and sure enough it did. I could see from my porthole that we were losing altitude—just dropping slowly lower and lower—and directly another warrior came to my cabin and said that I was wanted in the control room again.

"Once more Hin Abtol was there. 'We are sinking,' he told me—a fact that was too obvious to need mention.

" 'I have noticed that for some time,' I said.

" 'Well, do something about it!' he snapped. 'You know all about this ship.'

" 'I should think that a man who is thinking of conquering all of Barsoom ought to be able to fly a ship without the help of a woman,' I said.

"He flushed at that, and then he drew his sword. 'You will tell us what is wrong,' he growled, 'or I'll split you open from your crown to your belly.'

" 'Always the chivalrous gentleman,' I sneered; 'but, even without your threat, I'll tell you what is wrong.'

" 'Well, what is it?' he demanded.

" 'In fiddling around with these controls, either you or some equally stupid brute has opened the buoyancy tank valves. All you have to do is close them. We won't sink any lower then, but we'll never go any higher, either. I hope there are no mountains or very high hills between here and Panar.'

" 'Where are the valves?' he asked.

"I showed him.

"They tried to close them; but I had made such a good job of jamming them that they couldn't, and we kept right on dropping down toward the ocher vegetation of a dead sea bottom.

"Hin Abtol was frantic. So were his officers. Here they were, thousands of haads from home—twenty-five men who had spent the greater parts of their lives in the glazed, hot-house cities of the North Polar lands, with no knowledge, or very little, of the outside world or what nature of men, beasts, or other menaces might dispute their way toward home. I could scarcely refrain from laughing.

"As we lost altitude, I saw the towers of a city in the distance to the north of us; so did Hin Abtol. 'A city,' he said. 'We are fortunate. There we can find mechanics to repair our ship.'

" 'Yes,' I thought; 'if you had come a million years ago, you would have found mechanics. They would have known nothing about repairing a flier, for fliers had not been invented then; but they could have built you a stanch ship wherein you could have sailed the five seas of ancient Barsoom,' but I said nothing. I would let Hin Abtol find out for himself.

"I had never been to Horz; but I knew that those towers rising in the distance could mark only that long dead city, and I wished the pleasure of witnessing Hin Abtol's disappointment after he had made the long and useless trek."

"You are a vindictive little rascal," I said.

"I'm afraid I am," admitted Llana of Gathol; "but, in this instance, can you blame me?"

I had to admit that I could not. "Go on," I urged. "Tell me what happened next."

"Will we never reach the end of these abominable pits!" exclaimed Kam Han Tor.

"You should know," said Pan Dan Chee; "you have said that they were built according to your plans."

"You are insolent," snapped Kam Han Tor. "You shall be punished."

"You have been dead a million years," said Pan Dan Chee. "You should lie down."

Kam Han Tor laid a hand upon the hilt of his longsword. He was very angry; and I could not blame him, but this was no time to indulge in the pleasure of a duel.

"Hold!" I said. "We have more important things to think of now than personal quarrels. Pan Dan Chee is in the wrong. He will apologize."

Pan Dan Chee looked at me in surprise and disapproval, but he pushed his sword back into its scabbard. "What John Carter, Prince of Helium, Warlord of Barsoom, commands me to do, I do," he said. "To Kam Han Tor I offer my apology."

Well, Kam Han Tor graciously accepted it, and I urged Llana of Gathol to go on with her story.

"The ship dropped gently to the ground without incurring further damage," she continued. "Hin Abtol was undecided at first as whether to take all his men with him to the city or leave some to guard the ship. Finally he concluded that it might be better for them all to remain together in the event they should meet with a hostile reception at the gates of the city. You would have thought, from the way he spoke, that twenty-five Panars could take any city on Barsoom.

" 'I shall wait for you here,' I said. 'There is no reason why I should accompany you to the city.'

" 'And when I came back, you would be gone,' he said. 'You are a shrewd wench, but I am just a little bit shrewder. You will come with us.'

"So I had to tramp all the way to Horz with them, and it was a very long and tiresome tramp. As we approached the city, Hin Abtol remarked that it was surprising that we saw no signs of life—no smoke, no movement along the avenue which we could see paralleling the plain upon which the city faced, the plain that had once been a mighty ocean.

"It was not until we had entered the city that he realized that it was dead and deserted—but not entirely deserted, as we were soon to discover.

"We had advanced but a short distance up the main avenue when a dozen green warriors emerged from a building and fell upon the Panars. It might have been a good battle, John Carter, had you and two of the warriors of your guard been pitted against the green men; but these Panars are no warriors unless the odds are all on their side. Of course they outnumbered the green men, but the great size and strength and the savage ferocity of the latter gave them the advantage over such weak foemen.

"I saw but little of the fight. The contestants paid no attention to me. They were too engrossed with one another; and as I saw the head of a ramp close by, I dodged into it. The last I saw of the engagement revealed Hin Abtol running at the top of his speed back toward the plain with his men trailing behind him and the green men bringing up the rear. For the sublimation of speed, I accord all honors to the Panars. They may not be able to fight, but they can run."

12

"Knowing that the green men would return for their thoats and that I must, therefore, hide, I descended the ramp," Llana went on. "It led into the pits beneath the city. I intended going in only far enough to avoid discovery from above and to have a head start should the green men come down the ramp in search of me; as I knew they might—they would not quickly forego an opportunity to capture a red woman for torture or slavery.

"I had gone down to the end of the ramp and a short distance along a corridor, when I saw a dim light far ahead. I thought this worth investigating, as I did not wish to be taken unexpectedly from behind and, perhaps, caught between two enemies; so I followed the corridor in the direction of the light, which I presently discovered was retreating. However, I continued to follow it, until presently it stopped in a room filled with chests.

"Looking in, I saw a creature of most horrid mein—"

"Lum Tar O," I said. "The creature I killed."

"Yes," said Llana. "I watched him for a moment, not knowing what to do. A lighted torch illuminated the chamber. He carried another in his left hand. Presently he became alert. He seemed to be listening intently; then he crept from the room."

"That must have been when he first heard Pan Dan Chee and me," I suggested.

"I presume so," said Llana of Gathol. "Anyway, I was left

alone in the room. If I went back the way I had come, I might run into the arms of a green man. If I followed the horrid creature I had just seen, I would doubtless be in just as bad a fix. If I only had a place to hide until it would be safe to come out of the pits the way I had entered!

"The chests looked inviting. One of them would provide an excellent hiding place. It was just by the merest chance that the first one I opened was empty. I crept into it and lowered the lid above me. The rest you know."

"And now you are coming out of the pits," I said, as we started up a ramp at the top of which I could see daylight.

"In a few moments," said Kam Han Tor, "we shall be looking upon the broad waters of Throxeus."

I shook my head. "Do not be too disappointed," I said.

"Are you and your friend in league to perpetrate a hoax upon me?" demanded Kan Han Tor. "Only yesterday I saw the ships of the fleet lying at anchor off the quay. Do you think me a fool, that you tell me there is no longer any ocean where an ocean was yesterday, where it has been since the creation of Barsoom? Oceans do not disappear overnight, my friend."

There was a murmur of approval from those of the fine company of nobles and their women who were within earshot. They were loath to believe what they did not wish to believe and what, I realized, must have seemed an insult to their intelligence.

Put yourself in their place. Perhaps you live in San Francisco. You go to bed one night. When you awaken, a total stranger tells you that the Pacific Ocean has dried up and that you may walk to Honolulu or Guam or the Philippines. I'm quite sure that you wouldn't believe him.

As we came up into the broad avenue that led to the ancient sea front of Horz, that assembly of gorgeously trapped men and women looked about them in dumfounded astonishment upon the crumbling ruins of their once proud city.

"Where are the people?" demanded one. "Why is the Avenue of Jeddaks deserted?"

"And the palace of the jeddak!" exclaimed another. "There are no guards."

"There is no one!" gasped a woman.

No one commented, as they pushed on eagerly toward the quay. Before they got there they were already straining their eyes out across a barren desert of dead sea bottom where once the waters of Throxeus had rolled.

In silence they continued on to the Avenue of Quays. They simply could not believe the testimony of their own eyes. I

cannot recall ever having felt sorrier for any of my fellow
men than I did at that moment for these poor people.

"It is gone," said Kam Han Tor in a scarcely audible
whisper.

A woman sobbed. A warrior drew his dagger and plunged
it into his own heart.

"And all our people are gone," said Kam Han Tor. "Our
very world is gone."

They stood there looking out across that desert waste; behind them a dead city that, in their last yesterday, had teemed
with life and youth and energy.

And then a strange thing happened. Before my eyes, Kam
Han Tor commenced to shrink and crumble. He literally
disintegrated, he and the leather of his harness. His weapons
clattered to the pavement and lay there in a litle pile of dust
that had been Kam Han Tor, the brother of a jeddak.

Llana of Gathol pressed close to me and seized my arm.
"It is horrible!" she whispered. "Look! Look at the others!"

I looked about me. Singly, in groups of two or three, the
men and women of ancient Horz were returning to the dust
from which they had sprung—"Earth to earth, ashes to ashes,
dust to dust!"

"For all the ages that they have lain in the pits of Horz,"
said Pan Dan Chee, "this disintegration has been going slowly
on. Only Lum Tar O's obscene powers gave them a semblance
of life. With that removed final dissolution came quickly."

"That must be the explanation," I said. "It is well that it
is so, for these people never could have found happiness in
the Barsoom of today—a dying world, so unlike the glorious
world of Barsoom in the full flush of her prime, with her
five oceans, her great cities, her happy, prosperous peoples,
who, if history speaks the truth, had finally overthrown all
the war lords and war mongers and established peace from
pole to pole."

"No," said Llana of Gathol, "they could never have been
happy again. Did you notice what handsome people they
were? and the color of their skins was the same as yours,
John Carter. But for their blond hair they might have been
from your own Earth."

"There are many blond people on Earth," I told her. "Maybe, after all the races of Earth have intermarried for many
ages, we shall develop a race of red men, as has Barsoom.
Who knows?"

Pan Dan Chee was standing looking adoringly at Llana of
Gathol. He was so obvious that it was almost painful, and I
could see that it annoyed Llana even while it pleased her.

"Come," I said. "Nothing is to be gained by standing here.

My flier is in a courtyard nearby. It will carry three. You will come with me, Pan Dan Chee? I can assure you a welcome in Helium and a post of some nature in the army of the jeddak."

Pan Dan Chee shook his head. "I must go back to the Citadel," he said.

"To Ho Ran Kim and death," I reminded him.

"Yes, to Ho Ran Kim and death," he said.

"Don't be a fool, Pan Dan Chee," I said. "You have acquitted yourself honorably. You cannot kill me, and I know you would not kill Llana of Gathol. We shall go away, carrying the secret of the forgotten people of Horz with us, no matter what you do; but you must know that neither of us would use our knowledge to bring harm to your people. Why then go back to your death uselessly? Come with us."

He looked straight into the eyes of Llana of Gathol. "Is it your wish that I come with you?" he asked.

"If the alternative means your death," she replied; "then it is my wish that you come with us."

A wry smile twisted Pan Dan Chee's lip, but evidently he saw a ray of hope in her noncommital answer, for he said to me, "I thank you, John Carter. I will go with you. My sword is yours, always."

13

I had no difficulty in locating the courtyard where I had landed and left my flier. As we approached it, I saw a number of dead men lying in the avenue. They were sprawled in the grotesque postures of death. Some of them were split wide open from their crowns to their bellies. "The work of green men," I said.

"These were the men of Hin Abtol," said Llana of Gathol.

We counted seventeen corpses before we reached the entrance to the courtyard. When I looked in, I stopped, appalled—my flier was not there; but five more dead Panars lay near where it had stood.

"It is gone," I said.

"Hin Abtol," said Llana of Gathol. "The coward abandoned his men and fled in your flier. Only two of his warriors succeeded in accompanying him."

"Perhaps he would have been a fool to remain," I said. "He would only have met the same death that they met."

"In like circumstances, John Carter would have been a fool, then," she shot back.

Perhaps I would, for the truth of the matter is that I like to fight. I suppose it is all wrong, but I cannot help it. Fighting has been my profession during all the life that I can recall. I fought all during the Civil War in the Confederate Army. I fought in other wars before that. I will not bore you with my autobiography. Suffice it to say that I have always been fighting. I do not know how old I am. I recall no childhood. I have always appeared to be about thirty years old. I still do. I do not know from whence I came, nor if I were born of woman as are other men. I have, so far as I know, simply always been. Perhaps I am the materialization of some long dead warrior of another age. Who knows? That might explain my ability to cross the cold, dark void of space which separates Earth from Mars. I do not know.

Pan Dan Chee broke the spell of my reverie. "What now?" he asked.

"A long walk," I said. "It is fully four thousand haads from here to Gathol, the nearest friendly city." That would be the equivalent of fifteen hundred miles—a very long walk.

"And only this desert from which to look for subsistence?" asked Pan Dan Chee.

"There will be hills," I told him. "There will be deep little ravines where moisture lingers and things grow which we can eat; but there may be green men, and there will certainly be banths and other beasts of prey. Are you afraid, Pan Dan Chee?"

"Yes," he said, "but only for Llana of Gathol. She is a woman—it is no adventure for a woman. Perhaps she could not survive it."

Llana of Gathol laughed. "You do not know the women of Helium," she said, "and still less one in whose veins flows the blood of Dejah Thoris and John Carter. Perhaps you will learn before we have reached Gathol." She stooped and stripped the harness and weapons of a dead Panar from his corpse and buckled them upon herself, The act was more eloquent than words.

"Now we are three good sword arms," said Pan Dan Chee with a laugh, but we knew that he was not laughing at Llana of Gathol but from admiration of her.

And so we set out, the three of us, on that long trek toward far Gathol—Llana of Gathol and I, of one blood and two worlds, and Pan Dan Chee of still another blood and of an extinct world. We might have seemed ill assorted, but no three people could have been more in harmony with each other—at least at first.

For five days we saw no living thing. We subsisted en-

tirely upon the milk of the mantalia plant, which grows
apparently without water, distilling its plentiful supply of milk
from the products of the soil, the slight moisture in the air, and
the rays of the sun. A single plant of this species will give
eight or ten quarts of milk a day. They are scattered across
the dead sea bottoms as though by a beneficent Providence,
giving both food and drink to man and beast.

My companions might still have died of thirst or starvation had I not been with them, for neither knew that the
quite ordinary looking plants which we occasionally passed
carried in their stems and branches this life-giving fluid.

We rested in the middle of the day and slept during the
middle portion of the nights, taking turns standing guard—a
duty which Llana of Gathol insisted on sharing with us.

When we lay down to rest on the sixth night, Llana had
the first watch; and as I had the second, I prepared to sleep
at once. Pan Dan Chee sat up and talked with Llana.

As I dozed off, I heard him say, "May I call you my
princess?"

That, on Barsoom, is the equivalent of a proposal of marriage on Earth. I tried to shut my ears and go to sleep, but I
could not but hear her reply.

"You have not fought for me yet," she said, "and no
man may presume to claim a woman of Helium until he has
proved his metal."

"I have had no opportunity to fight for you," he said.

"Then wait until you have," she said, shortly; "and now
good-night."

I thought she was a little too short with him. Pan Dan
Chee is a nice fellow, and I was sure that he would give a
good account of himself when the opportunity arose. She
didn't have to treat him as though he were scum. But then,
women have their own ways. As a rule they are unpleasant
ways, but they seem the proper ways to win men; so I suppose they must be all right.

Pan Dan Chee walked off a few paces and lay down on
the other side of Llana of Gathol. We always managed to
keep her between us at all times for her greater protection.

I was awakened later on by a shout and a hideous roar.
I leaped to my feet to see Llana of Gathol down on the
ground with a huge banth on top of her, and at that instant Pan Dan Chee leaped full upon the back of the mighty
carnivore.

It all happened so quickly that I can scarcely visualize it
all. I saw Pan Dan Chee dragging at the great beast in an
effort to pull it from Llana's body, and at the same he was
plunging his dagger into its side. The banth was roaring

hideously as it tried to fight off Pan Dan Chee and at the same time retain its hold upon Llana.

I sprang close in with my short-sword, but it was difficult to find an opening which did not endanger either Llana or Pan Dan Chee. It must have been a very amusing sight; as the four of us were threshing around on the ground, all mixed up, and the banth was roaring and Pan Dan Chee was cursing like a trooper when he wasn't trying to tell Llana of Gathol how much he loved her.

But at last I got an opening, and drove my short-sword into the heart of the banth. With a final scream and a convulsive shudder, the beast rolled over and lay still.

When I tried to lift Llana from the ground, she leaped to her feet. "Pan Dan Chee!" she cried. "Is he all right? Was he hurt?"

"Of course I'm all right," said Pan Dan Chee; "but you? How badly are you hurt?"

"I am not hurt at all. You kept the brute so busy it didn't have a chance to maul me."

"Thanks be to my ancestors!" exclaimed Pan Dan Chee fervently. Suddenly he turned on her. "Now," he said, "I have fought for you. What is your answer?"

Llana of Gathol shrugged her pretty shoulders. "You have not fought a man," she said, "—just a little banth."

Well, I never did understand women.

BOOK 2

THE BLACK PIRATES OF BARSOOM

IN MY former life on earth I spent more time in the saddle than I did on foot, and since I have been here on the Planet of Barsoom I have spent much time in the saddle or on the swift fliers of the Navy of Helium; so naturally I did not look forward with any great amount of pleasure to walking fifteen hundred miles. However, it had to be done; and when a thing has to be done the best plan is to get at it, stick to it, and get it over with as quickly as possible.

Gathol is southwest of Horz; but, having no compass and no landmarks, I went, as I discovered later, a little too far to the west. Had I not done so we might have been saved some very harrowing experiences. Although, if my past life is any criterion, we would have found plenty of other adventures.

We had covered some two thousand five hundred haads of the four thousand we had to travel, or at least as nearly as I could compute it, with a minimum of untoward incidents. On two occasions we had been attacked by banths but had managed to kill them before they could harm us; and we had been attacked by a band of wild calots, but fortunately we had met no human beings—of all the creatures of Barsoom the most dangerous. For here, outside of your own country or the countries of your allies, every man is your enemy and bent upon destroying you; nor is it strange upon a dying world the natural resources of which have dwindled almost to the vanishing point and even air and water are only barely sufficient to meet the requirements of the present population.

The vast stretches of dead sea bottom, covered with its ocher vegetation, which we traversed were broken only occasionally by low hills. Here in shaded ravines we sometimes found edible roots and tubers. But for the most part we subsisted upon the milk-like sap of the mantalia bush, which grows on the dead sea bottom, though in no great profusion.

We had tried to keep track of the days, and it was on the thirty-seventh day that we encountered really serious trouble. It was the fourth zode, which is roughly about one P.M. Earth time, that we saw in the distance and to our left what I instantly recognized as a caravan of green Martians.

As no fate can be worse than falling into the hands of these cruel monsters, we hurried on in the hope of crossing their path before we were discovered. We took advantage of what cover the sea bottom afforded us, which was very little; oftentimes compelling us to worm our way along on our bellies, an art which I had learned from the Apaches of Arizona. I was in the lead, when I came upon a human skeleton. It was crumbling to dust, an indication that it must have lain there for many years, for so low is the humidity on Mars that disintegration of bony structures is extremely slow. Within fifty yards I came upon another skeleton and after that we saw many of them. It was a gruesome sight, and what it portended I could not guess. At first I thought that perhaps a battle had once been fought here, but when I saw that some of these skeletons were fresh and well preserved and that others had already started to disintegrate I realized that these men had died many years apart.

At last I felt that we had crossed the line of march of the caravan and that as soon as we had found a hiding place we would be comparatively safe, and just then I came to the edge of a yawning chasm.

Except for the Grand Canyon of the Colorado, I had never seen anything like it. It was a great rift valley that appeared to be about ten miles wide and perhaps two miles deep, extending for miles in either direction.

There were outcroppings of rock at the rim of the rift, and behind these we hid. Scattered about us were more human skeletons than we had seen before. Perhaps they were a warning; but at least they could not harm us, and so we turned our attention to the approaching caravan, which had now changed its direction a little and was coming straight toward us. Hoping against hope that they would again change their direction and pass us, we lay there watching them.

When I had been first miraculously transported to Mars I had been captured by a horde of green men, and I had lived with them for a long time; so that I learned to know their customs well. Therefore, I was quite positive that this caravan was making the quinquennial pilgrimage of the horde to its hidden incubator.

Each adult Martian female brings forth about thirteen eggs each year; and those which reach the correct size, weight and specific gravity are hidden in the recesses of some subterranean vault where the temperature is too low for incubation. Every year these eggs are carefully examined by a counsel of twenty chieftains, and all but about one hundred of the most perfect are destroyed out of each yearly supply. At the end of five years about five hundred almost perfect eggs have been chosen from the thousands brought forth. These are then placed in the almost air-tight incubators to be hatched by the sun's rays after a period of another five years.

All but about one per cent of the eggs hatch, and these are left behind when the horde departs from the incubator. If these eggs hatch, the fate of those abandoned little Martians is unknown. They are not wanted, as their offspring might inherit and transmit the tendency to prolonged incubation and thus upset the system which has been maintained for ages and which permits the adult Martians to figure the proper time for return to the incubator almost to an hour.

The incubators are built in remote fastnesses where there is little or no likelihood of their being discovered by other tribes. The result of such a catastrophe would mean no children in the community for another five years.

The green Martians' caravan is a gorgeous and barbaric thing to see. In this one were some two hundred and fifty enormous three wheeled chariots drawn by huge mastodonian animals known as zitidars, any one of which from their appearance might easily have drawn the entire train when fully loaded.

The chariots themselves were large, commodious and gorgeously decorated; in each was seated a female Martian loaded with ornaments of metal, with jewels and silks and furs; and upon the back of each of the zitidars a young Martian driver was perched on top of gorgeous trappings.

At the head of the caravan rode some two hundred warriors, five abreast; and a like number brought up the rear. About twenty-five or thirty out-riders flanked the chariots on either side.

The mounts of the warriors defy description in earthly words. They towered ten feet at the shoulder, had four legs on either side, a broad flat tail, larger at the tip than at the root, which they held straight out behind while running; a gaping mouth which splits the head from the snout to the long, massive neck.

Like their huge masters, they are entirely devoid of hair, but are a dark slate color and are exceedingly smooth and glossy. Their bellies are white and their legs shaded from the slate of the shoulders and hips to a vivid yellow at the feet. The feet themselves are heavily padded and nailless. Like the zitidars they wear neither bit nor bridle, but are guided entirely by telepathic means.

As we watched this truly magnificent and impressive cortege, it changed direction again; and I breathed a sigh of relief as I saw that they were going to pass us. Evidently, from the backs of their lofty mounts, they had seen the rift and were now moving parallel with it.

My relief was to be short-lived, for as the rear of the caravan was about to pass us one of the flankers spied us.

2

Instantly the fellow wheeled his thoat and, shouting to his companions, came galloping toward us. We sprang to our feet with drawn swords, expecting to die; but ready to sell our lives dearly.

A moment after we had gained our feet, Llana exclaimed, "Look! Here is a trail down into the valley."

I looked around. Sure enough, now that we were standing erect, I could see the head of a narrow, precipitous trail leading down over the edge of the cliff. If we could but reach it, we would be safe, for the great thoats and zitidars of the green men could not possibly negotiate it. It was very possible that the green men were not even aware of the presence of the rift before they had come suddenly upon it, and this is entirely possible; because they build their incubators in uninhabited and unexplored wildernesses sometimes as much as a thousand miles from their own stamping grounds.

As the three of us, Llana, Pan Dan Chee, and I, ran for the trail, I glanced over my shoulder and saw that the leading warrior was almost on top of us and that we could not all reach the trail. So I called to Pan Dan Chee to hurry down it with Llana. They both stopped and turned toward me.

"It is a command," I told them. Reluctantly they turned and continued on toward the end of the trail, while I wheeled and faced the warrior.

He had stopped his thoat and dismounted, evidently intent upon capturing me rather than killing me; but I had no mind to be captured for torture and eventual death. It was far better to die now.

He drew his long-sword as he came toward me and I did likewise. Had there not been six of his fellows galloping up on their huge thoats I should not have worried greatly, for with a sword I am a match for any green Martian that was ever hatched. Even their great size gives them no advantage. Perhaps it handicaps them, for their movements are slow and ponderous by comparison with my earthly agility; and though they are twice my size, I am fully as strong as they. The muscles of earthly man have not contended with the force of gravity since the dawn of humanity for nothing. It has developed and hardened muscles; because every move we make is contested by gravity.

My antagonist was so terribly cock-sure of himself, when facing such a seemingly puny creature as I, that he left himself wide open, as he charged down upon me like a wild bull.

I saw by the way he held his sword that he intended to strike me on the head with the flat of it, rendering me unconscious, so that he could more easily capture me; but when the sword fell I was not there; I had stepped to the right out of his way, and simultaneously I thrust for his heart. I would have punctured it, too, had not one of his four arms happened to swing against the point of my blade before it reached his body. As it was, I gave him a severe wound; and, roaring with rage, he turned and came at me again.

This time he was more careful; but it made no difference; he was doomed, for he was testing his skill against the best swordsman of two worlds.

The other six warriors were almost upon me now. This was no time for the sport of fencing. I feinted once, and ran him through the heart. Then, seeing that Llana was safe, I turned and ran along the edge of the rift; and the six green warriors did just what I had expected them to do. They had probably detached themselves from the rear guard for the sport of catching a red man for torture or for their savage games. Bunched close together they came after me, the nailless, padded feet of their ponderous mounts making no sound upon the ocher, moss-like vegetation of the dead sea bottom. Their spears couched, they came for me, each trying to make the kill or the capture. I felt much as a fox must feel at a fox hunt.

Suddenly I stopped, turned, and ran toward them. They must have thought that I had gone mad with fear, for they certainly couldn't have known what I had in mind and that I had run from them merely to lure them away from the head of the trail leading down into the valley. They were almost upon me when I leaped high into the air and completely over them. My great strength and agility and the lesser gravity of Mars had once again come to my aid in an emergency.

When I alighted, I dashed for the head of the trail. And when the warriors could stop their mounts they turned and raced after me, but they were too late. I can out-run any thoat that was ever foaled. The only trouble with me is that I am too proud to run; but, like the fellow that was too proud to fight, I sometimes have to, as in this case where the safety of others was at stake.

I reached the head of the trail in plenty of time and hurried down after Llana and Pan Dan Chee, whom I found waiting for me when I caught up with them.

As we descended, I looked up and saw the green warriors at the edge of the rift looking at us; and, guessing what would happen, I dragged Llana into the shelter of an overhanging ledge. Pan Dan Chee followed just as radium bullets commenced to explode close to us.

The rifles with which the green men of Mars are armed are of a white metal, stocked with wood; a very light and intensely hard growth much prized on Mars and entirely unknown to us denizens of Earth. The metal of the barrel is an alloy composed principally of aluminum and steel, which they have learned to temper to a hardness far exceeding that of the steel with which we are familiar. The weight of these rifles is comparatively little; and with the small caliber, explosive radium projectiles which they use and the great length of the barrel, they are deadly in the extreme and at ranges which would be unthinkable on Earth.

The projectiles which they use explode when they strike an object, for they have an opaque outer coating which is broken by the impact, exposing a glass cylinder, almost solid, in the forward end of which is a minute particle of radium powder.

(Editor's Note) I have used the word radium in describing this powder because in the light of recent discoveries on earth I believe it to be a mixture of which radium is the base. In Captain Carter's manuscripts it is mentioned always by the name used in the written language of Helium and is spelled in hieroglyphics which it would be difficult and useless to reproduce.

The moment the sunlight, even though diffused, strikes this powder it explodes with a violence which nothing can withstand. In night battles one notices the absence of these explosions, while the following morning will be filled at sunrise with the sharp detonations of exploding missiles fired the preceding night. As a rule, however, non-exploding projectiles are used after dark.

I felt it safer to remain where we were rather than to expose ourselves by attempting to descend, as I doubted very much that the huge green warriors would follow us down that steep declivity on foot, for the trail was too narrow for their great bodies and they hate going anywhere on foot.

After a few minutes I investigated and found that they apparently had departed. Then we started on down into the valley, not wishing to risk another encounter with that great horde of cruel and ruthless creatures.

3

The trail was steep and oftentimes dangerous for it zigzagged down the face of an almost perpendicular cliff. Occasionally on a ledge we would have to step over the skeleton of a man, and we passed three newly dead bodies in various stages of decomposition.

"What do you make of these skeletons and bodies?" asked Pan Dan Chee.

"I am puzzled," I replied; "there must be a great many more who died on the trail than those whose remains we have seen here. You will note that these all lie on ledges where the bodies could have lodged when they fell. Many more must have pitched to the foot of the cliff."

"But how do you suppose they met their death?" asked Llana.

"There might have been an epidemic of disease in the valley," suggested Pan Dan Chee, "and these poor devils died while trying to escape."

"I am sure I haven't the slightest idea of what the explanation can be," I replied. "You see the remains of harness on most of them, but no weapons. I am inclined to think that Pan Dan Chee is right in assuming that they were trying to escape, but whether from an epidemic of sickness or something else we may never know."

From our dizzy footing on that precarious trail we had an excellent view of the valley below. It was level and well watered and the monotony of the scarlet grass which grows on Mars where there is water, was broken by forests, the whole making an amazing sight for one familiar with this dying planet.

There are crops and trees and other vegetation along the canals; there are lawns and gardens in the cities where irrigation is available; but never have I seen a sight like this except in the Valley Dor at the South Pole, where lies the Lost Sea of Korus. For here there was not only a vast expanse of fertile valley but there were rivers and at least one lake which I could seen in the distance; and then Llana called our attention to a city, gleaming white, with lofty towers.

"What a beautiful city," she said. "I wonder what sort of people live there?"

"Probably somebody who would love nothing better than to slit our throats," I said.

"We Orovars are not like that," said Pan Dan Chee, "we hate to kill people. Why do all the other races on Mars hate each other so?"

"I don't think that it is hate that makes them want to kill each other," I said. "It is that is has become a custom. Since the drying up of the seas ages ago, survival has become more and more difficult; and in all those ages they have become so accustomed to battling for existence that now it has become second nature to kill all aliens."

"I'd still like to see the inside of that city," said Llana of Gathol.

"Your curiosity will probably never be satisfied," I said.

We stood for some time on a ledge looking down upon that beautiful valley, probably one of the most beautiful sights on all of Mars. We saw several herds of the small thoats used by the red Martians as riding animals and for food. There is a little difference in the saddle and butchering species, but at this distance we could not tell which these were. We saw game animals down there, too, and we who had been so long without good meat were tempted.

"Let's go down," said Llana; "we haven't seen any human beings and we don't need to go near the city; it is a long way off. I should like so much to see the beauties of that valley closer."

"And I would like to get some good red meat," I said.

"And I, too," said Pan Dan Chee.

"My better judgment tells me it would be a foolish thing to do," I said, "but if I had followed my better judgment always, my life would have been a very dull one."

"Anyway," said Llana, "we don't know that it is any more dangerous down on the floor of the valley than it was up on the edge of the rim. We certainly barely missed a lot of trouble up there, and it may still be hanging around."

I didn't think so; although I have known green Martians to hunt a couple of red men for days at a time. Anyway, the outcome of our discussion was that we continued on down to the floor of the valley.

Around the foot of the cliff, where the trail ended, there was a jumble of human bones and a couple of badly mangled bodies—poor devils who had either died on the trail above or fallen to their death here at the bottom. I wondered how and why.

Fortunately for us, the city was at such a distance that I was sure that no one could have seen us from there; and, knowing Martian customs, we had no intention of approaching it; nor would we have particularly cared to had it been safe, for the floor of the valley was so entrancingly beautiful in its natural state that the sights and sounds of a city would have proved a discordant note.

A short distance from us was a little river; and, beyond it, a forest came down to its edge. We crossed to the river on the scarlet sward, close-cropped by grazing herds and starred by many flowers of unearthly beauty.

A short distance down the river a herd of thoats was grazing. They were the beef variety, which is exceptionally good eating; and Pan Dan Chee suggested that we cross the river so that he could take advantage of the concealment of the forest to approach close enough to make a kill.

The river was simply alive with fish, and as we waded across I speared several with my long sword.

"At least we shall have fish for dinner," I said, "and if Pan Dan Chee is lucky, we shall have a steak."

"And in the forest I see fruits and nuts," said Llana. "What a banquet we shall have!"

"Wish me luck," said Pan Dan Chee, as he entered the forest to work his way down toward the thoats.

Llana and I were watching, but we did not see the young Orovaran again until he leaped from the forest and hurled something at the nearest thoat, a young bull. The beast screamed, ran a few feet, staggered and fell, while the rest of the herd galloped off.

"How did he do that?" asked Llana.

"I don't know," I said, "he did it so quickly that I couldn't see what it was he threw. It was certainly not a spear because he hasn't one, and if it had been his sword we could have seen it."

"It looked like a little stick," said Llana.

We saw Pan Dan Chee cutting steaks from his kill; and presently he was back with us, carrying enough meat for a dozen men.

"How did you kill that thoat?" demanded Llana.

"With my dagger," replied Pan Dan Chee.

"It was marvellous," I said, "but where did you learn it?"

"Dagger throwing is a form of sport in Horz. We are all good at it, but I happen to have won the Jeddak's trophy for the last three years; so I was pretty sure of my ground when I offered to get you a thoat, although I had never before used it to kill game. Very, very rarely is there a duel in Horz; and when there is, the contestants usually choose daggers, unless one of them is far more proficient than the other."

While Pan Dan Chee and I were making fire and cooking the fish and steaks, Llana gathered fruits and nuts; so that we had a delicious meal, and when night came we lay down on the soft sward and slept.

4

We slept late, for we had been very tired the night before. I speared some fresh fish, and we had fish and steaks and fruit and nuts again for breakfast. Then we started toward the trail that leads out of the valley.

"It is going to be an awful climb," said Pan Dan Chee.

"Oh, I wish we didn't have to make it," said Llana; "I hate to leave this beautiful spot."

My attention was suddenly attracted toward the lower end of the valley.

"Maybe you won't have to leave it, Llana," I said. "Look!"

Both she and Pan Dan Chee turned and looked in the direction I had indicated, to see two hundred warriors mounted on thoats. The men were ebony black, and I wondered if they could be the notorious Black Pirates of Barsoom that I had first met and fought many years ago at the South Pole —the people who called themselves the First Born.

They galloped up and surrounded us; their spears couched, ready for any emergency.

"Who are you?" demanded their leader. "What are you doing in the Valley of the First Born?"

"We came down the trail to avoid a horde of green men," I replied. "We were just leaving. We came in peace; we do not want war, but we are still three swords ready to give a good account of ourselves."

"You will have to come to Kamtol with us," said the leader.

"The city?" I asked. He nodded.

I whipped my sword from its scabbard.

"Stop!" he said. "We are two hundred; you are three. If you come to the city there would be at least a chance that you won't be killed; if you stay here and fight you will be killed."

I shrugged. "It is immaterial to me," I said. "Llana of Gathol wishes to see the city, and I would just as leave fight. Pan Dan Chee, what do you and Llana say?"

"I would like to see the city," said Llana, "but I will fight if you fight. Perhaps," she added, "they will not be unkind to us."

"You will have to give up your arms," said the leader.

I didn't like that and I hesitated.

"It is that or death," said the leader. "Come! I can't stand here all day."

Well, resistance was futile; and it seemed foolish to sacrifice our lives if there were the remotest hope that we might be well received in Kamtol, and so we were taken on the backs of three thoats behind their riders and started for the beautiful white city.

The ride to the city was uneventful, but it gave me an excellent opportunity to examine our captors more closely. They were unquestionably of the same race as Xodar, Dator of the First Born of Barsoom, to give him his full title, who had been first my enemy and then my friend during my strange adventures among the Holy Therns. They are an exceptionally handsome race, clean-limbed and powerful, with intelligent faces and features of such exquisite chiseling that Adonis himself might have envied them. I am a Virginian; and it may seem strange for me to say so, but their black skins, resembling polished ebony, add greatly to their beauty. The harness and metal of our captors was identical with that worn by the Black Pirates whose acquaintance I had made upon the Golden Cliffs above the Valley Dor.

My admiration of these people did not blind me to the fact that they are a cruel and ruthless race and that our life expectancy was reduced to a minimum by our capture.

Kamtol did not belie its promise. It was as beautiful on closer inspection as it had been at a distance. Its pure white outer wall is elaborately carved, as are the facades on many of its buildings. Graceful towers rise above its broad avenues, which, when we entered the city, were filled with people. Among the blacks, we saw a number of red men performing menial tasks. It was evident that they were slaves, and their presence suggested the fate which might await us.

I cannot say that I looked forward with any great amount of enthusiasm to the possibility that John Carter, Prince of Helium, Warlord of Mars, might become a street cleaner or a garbage collector. One thing that I noticed particularly in Kamtol was that the residences could not be raised on cylindrical columns, as is the case in most modern Martian cities, where assassination has been developed to a fine art and where assassins' guilds flourish openly, and their members swagger through the streets like gangsters once did in Chicago.

Heavily guarded, we were taken to a large building and there we were separated. I was taken to an apartment and seated in a chair with my back toward a strange looking machine, the face of which was covered with innumerable dials. A number of heavily insulated cables ran from various parts of the apparatus; metal bands at the ends of these cables were clamped about my wrists, my ankles, and my neck, the latter clamp pressing against the base of my skull; then something like a strait-jacket was buckled tightly around me, and I had a sensation as of countless needles touching my spine for almost its full length. I thought that I was to be electrocuted, but it seemed to me that they took a great deal of unnecessary pains to destroy me. A simple sword thrust would have done it much more quickly.

An officer, who was evidently in charge of the proceedings, came and stood in front of me. "You are about to be examined," he said, "you will answer all questions truthfully;" then he signalled to an attendant who threw a switch on the apparatus.

So I was not to be electrocuted, but examined. For what, I could not imagine. I felt a very gentle tingling throughout my entire body, and then they commenced to hurl questions at me.

There were six men. Sometimes they questioned me singly and sometimes all at once. At such times, of course, I could not answer very intelligently because I could not hear the questions fully. Sometimes they spoke soothingly to me, and again they shouted at me angrily; often they heaped insults upon me. They let me rest for a few moments, and then a slave entered the apartment with a tray of very tempting food which he offered to me. As I was about to take it, it was snatched away; and my tormentors laughed at me. They jabbed me with sharp instruments until the blood flowed, and then they rubbed the wounds with a burning caustic, after which they applied a salve that instantly relieved the pain. Again I rested and again food was offered me. When I made no move to attempt to take it, they insisted; and, much to my surprise, let me eat it.

By this time I had come to the conclusion that we had been captured by a race of sadistic maniacs, and what happened next assured me that I was right. My torturers all left the apartment. I sat there for several minutes wondering at the whole procedure and why they couldn't have tortured me without attaching me to that amazing contraption. I was facing a door in the opposite wall, and suddenly the door flew open and a huge banth leaped into the room with a horrid roar.

This, I thought, is the end, as the great carnivore came racing at me. As suddenly as he had entered the room, he came to a stop a few feet from me, and so instantly that he was thrown to the floor at my feet. It was then that I saw that he was secured by a chain just a little too short to permit him to reach me. I had had all the sensations of impending death—a most refined form of torture. However, if that had been their purpose they had failed, for I do not fear death.

The banth was dragged out of the apartment by his chain and the door closed; then the examining board re-entered smiling at me in the most kindly way.

"That is all," said the officer in charge; "the examination is over."

5

After the paraphernalia had been removed from me, I was turned over to my guard and taken to the pits, such as are to be found in every Martian city, ancient or modern. These labyrinthine corridors and chambers are used for storage purposes and for the incarceration of prisoners, their only other tenants being the repulsive ulsio.

I was chained to the wall in a large cell in which there was another prisoner, a red Martian; and it was not long until Llana of Gathol and Pan Dan Chee were brought in and chained near me.

"I see you survived the examination," I said.

"What in the world do they expect to learn from such an examination as that?" demanded Llana. "It was stupid and silly."

"Perhaps they wanted to find out if they could scare us to death," suggested Pan Dan Chee.

"I wonder how long they will keep us in these pits," said Llana.

"I have been here a year," said the red man. "Ocassionally I have been taken out and put to work with other slaves belonging to the jeddak, but until someone buys me I shall remain here."

"Buys you! What do you mean?" asked Pan Dan Chee.

"All prisoners belong to the jeddak," replied the red man, "but his nobles or officers may buy them if they wish another slave. I think he is holding me at too high a price, for a number of nobles have looked at me and said that they would like to have me."

He was silent for a moment and then he said, "You will pardon my curiosity, but two of you do not look like Barsoomians at all, and I am wondering from what part of the world you come. Only the woman is typical of Barsoom; both you men have white skin and one of you black hair and the other yellow."

"You have heard of the Orovars?" I asked.

"Certainly," he replied, "but they have been extinct for ages."

"Nevertheless, Pan Dan Chee here is an Orovar. There is a small colony of them that has survived in a deserted Orovar city."

And you?" he asked; "you are no Orovar, with that black hair."

"No," I said, "I am from another world—Jasoom."

"Oh," he exclaimed, "can it be that you are John Carter?"

"Yes; and you?"

"My name is Jad-han. I am from Amhor."

"Amhor?" I said. "I know a girl from Amhor. Her name is Janai."

"What do you know of Janai?" he demanded.

"You knew her?" I asked.

"She was my sister; she has been dead for years. While I was out of the country on a long trip, Jal Had, Prince of Amhor, employed Gantum Gur, the assassin, to kill my father because he objected to Jal Had as a suitor for Janai's hand. When I returned to Amhor, Janai had fled; and later I learned of her death. In order to escape assassination myself, I was forced to leave the city; and after wandering about for some time I was captured by the First Born. But tell me, what did you know of Janai?"

"I know that she is not dead," I replied. "She is mated with one of my most trusted officers and is safe in Helium."

Jad-han was overcome with happiness when he learned that his sister still lived. "Now," he said, "if I could escape from here and return to Amhor to avenge my father, I would die happy."

"Your father has been avenged," I told him. "Jal Had is dead."

"I am sorry that it was not given to me to kill him," said Jad-han.

"You have been here a year," I said, "and you must know something of the customs of the people. Can you tell us what fate may lie in store for us?"

"There are several possibilites," he replied. "You may be worked as slaves, in which event you will be treated badly, but may be permitted to live for years; or you may be saved solely for the games which are held in a great stadium. There you will fight with men or beasts for the edification of the First Born. On the other hand, you may be summarily executed at any moment. All depends upon the mental vagaries of Doxus, Jeddak of The First Born, who I think is a little mad."

"If the silly examination they gave us is any criterion," said Llana, "they are all mad."

"Don't be too sure of that," Jad-han advised. "If you realized the purpose of that examination, you would understand that it was never devised by any unsound mind. Did you see the dead men as you entered the valley?"

"Yes, but what have they to do with the examination?"

"They took that same examination; that is why they lie dead out there."

"I do not understand," I said. "Please explain."

"The machines to which you were connected recorded hundreds of your reflexes; and automatically recorded your own individual nerve index, which is unlike that of any other creature in the world.

"The master machine, which you did not see and never will, generates short wave vibrations which can be keyed exactly to your individual nerve index. When that is done you have such a severe paralytic stroke that you die almost instantly."

"But why all that just to destroy a few slaves?" demanded Pan Dan Chee.

"It is not for that alone," explained Jad-han. "Perhaps that was one of the initial purposes to prevent prisoners from escaping and spreading word of this beautiful valley on a dying planet. You can imagine that almost any country would wish to possess it. But it has another purpose; it keeps Doxus supreme. Every adult in the valley has had his nerve index recorded, and is at the mercy of his jeddak. You don't have to leave the valley to be exterminated. An enemy of the jeddak might be sitting in his own home some day, when the thing would find him out and destroy him. Doxus is the only adult in Kamtol whose index has not been recorded; and he and one other man, Myr-lo, are the only ones who know exactly where the master machine is located, or how to operate it. It is said to be very delicate and that it can be irreparably damaged in an instant—and can never be replaced."

"Why couldn't it be replaced?" asked Llana.

"The inventor of it is dead," replied Jad-han. "It is said that he hated Doxus because of the purpose to which the jeddak had put his invention and that Doxus had him assassinated through fear of him. Myr-lo, who succeeded him, has not the genius to design another such machine."

6

That night, after Llana had fallen asleep, Jad-han, Pan Dan Chee, and I were conversing in whispers; so as not to disturb her.

"It is too bad," said Jad-han, who had been looking at the sleeping girl; "it is too bad that she is so beautiful."

"What do you mean?" asked Pan Dan Chee.

"This afternoon you asked me what your fate might be; and I told you what the possibilities might be, but those were the possibilities for you two men. For the girl—" He looked sorrowfully at Llana and shook his head; he did not need to say more.

The next day a number of the First Born came down into our cell to examine us, as one might examine cattle that one purposed buying. Among them was one of the jeddak's officers, upon whom developed the duty of selling prisoners into slavery for the highest amounts he could obtain.

One of the nobles immediately took a fancy to Llana and made an offer for her. They haggled over the price for some time, but in the end the noble got her.

Pan Dan Chee and I were grief-stricken as they led Llana of Gathol away, for we knew that we should never see her again. Although her father is Jed of Gathol, in her veins flows the blood of Helium; and the women of Helium know how to act when an unkind Providence reserves for them the fate for which we knew Llana of Gathol was intended.

"Oh! to be chained to a wall and without a sword when a thing like this happens," exclaimed Pan Dan Chee.

"I know how you feel," I said; "but we are not dead yet, Pan Dan Chee; and our chance may come yet."

"If it does, we will make them pay," he said.

Two nobles were bidding for me, and at last I was knocked down to a dator named Xaxak. My fetters were removed, and the jeddak's agent warned me to be a good and docile slave.

Xaxak had a couple of warriors with him, and they walked on either side of me as we left the pits. I was the object of considerable curiosity, as we made our way toward Xaxak's palace, which stood near that of the jeddak. My white skin and gray eyes always arouse comment in cities where I am not known. Of course, I am bronzed by exposure to the sun, but even so my skin is not the copper red of the red men of Barsoom.

Before I was to be taken to the slaves' quarters of the palace, Xaxak questioned me. "What is your name?" he asked.

"Dotar Sojat," I replied. It is the name given me by the green Martians who captured me when I first came to Mars, being the names of the first two green Martians I had killed in duels; and is in the nature of an honorable title. A man with one name, an o-mad, is not considered very highly. I was always glad that they stopped with two names, for had I had to assume the name of every green Martian warrior I had killed in a duel it would have taken an hour to pronounce them all.

"Did you say dator?" asked Xaxak. "Don't tell me that you are a prince!"

"I said Dotar," I replied. I hadn't given my real name; because I had reason to believe that it was well known to the First Born, who had good reason to hate me for what I had done to them in the Valley Dor.

"Where are you from?" he asked.

"I have no country," I said; "I am a panthan."

As these soldiers of fortune have no fixed abode, wandering about from city to city offering their services and their swords to whomever will employ them, they are the only men who can go with impunity into almost any Martian city.

"Oh, a panthan," he said. "I suppose you think you are pretty good with a sword."

"I have met worse," I replied.

"If I thought you were any good, I would enter you in the lesser games," he said; "but you cost me a lot of money, and I'd hate to take the chance of your being killed."

"I don't think you need worry about that," I told him.

"You are pretty sure of yourself," he said. "Well, let's see what you can do. Take him out into the garden," he directed the two warriors. Xaxak followed us out to an open patch of sand.

"Give him your sword," he said to one of the warriors; and, to the other, "Engage him, Ptang; but not to the death;" then he turned to me. "It is not to the death, slave, you understand. I merely wish to see how good you are. Either one of you may draw blood, but don't kill."

Ptang, like all the other Black Pirates of Barsoom whom I have met, was an excellent swordsman—cool, quick, and deadly. He came toward me with a faint, supercilious smile on his lips.

"It is scarcely fair, my prince," he said to Xaxak, "to pit him against one of the best swordsmen in Kamtol."

"That is the only way in which I can tell whether he is any good at all, or not," replied Xaxak. "If he extends you, he will certainly be good enough to enter in the Lesser Games. He might even win his price back for me."

"We shall see," said Ptang, crossing swords with me.

Before he realized what was happening, I had pricked him in the shoulder. He looked very much surprised, and the smile left his lips.

"An accident," he said; "it will not occur again;" and then I pinked him in the other shoulder. Now, he made a fatal mistake; he became angry. While anger may stiffen a man's offense, it weakens his defense. I have seen it happen a thousand times, and when I am anxious to dispatch an antagonist quickly I always try to make him angry.

"Come, come! Ptang," said Xaxak; "can't you make a better showing than that against a slave?"

With that, Ptang came for me with blood in his eye, and I didn't see anything there that looked like a desire to pink— Ptang was out to kill me.

"Ptang!" snapped Xaxak; "don't kill him."

At that, I laughed; and drew blood from Ptang's breast. "Have you no real swordsmen in Kamtol?" I asked, tauntingly.

Xaxak and his other warrior were very quiet. I caught glimpses of their faces occasionally, and they looked a bit glum. Ptang was furious, and now he came for me like a mad bull with a cut that would have lopped off my head had it connected. However, it didn't connect; and I ran him through the muscles of his left arm.

"Hadn't we better stop," I asked Xaxak, "before your man bleeds to death?"

Xaxak did not reply; but I was getting bored with the whole affair and wanted to end it; so I drew Ptang into a lunge and sent his sword flying across the garden.

"Is that enough now?" I asked.

Xaxak nodded. "Yes," he said, "that is enough."

Ptang was one of the most surprised and crestfallen men I have ever seen. He just stood there staring at me, making no move to retrieve his blade. I felt very sorry for him.

"You have nothing to be ashamed of, Ptang," I told him. "You are a splendid swordsman, but what I did to you I can do to any man in Kamtol."

"I believe it," he said. "You may be a slave, but I am proud to have crossed swords with you. The world has never seen a better swordsman."

"I am convinced of that," said Xaxak, "and I can see where you are going to make a lot of money for me, Dotar Sojat."

7

Xaxak treated me much as a wealthy horse owner on Earth would treat a prospective Derby winner. I was quartered in the barracks of his personal guard, where I was treated as an equal. He detailed Ptang to see that I had the proper amount of exercise and sword play; and also, I presume, to see that I did not try to escape. And now my only concern was the fate of Llana of Gathol and Pan Dan Chee, of whose whereabouts and state I was totally ignorant.

Somewhat of a friendship developed between Ptang and myself. He admired my swordsmanship, and used to brag about it to the other warriors. At first they had been inclined to criticize and ridicule him because he had been bested by a slave; so I suggested that he offer to let his critics see if they could do any better with me.

"I can't do that," he said, "without Xaxak's permission; for if anything happened to you, I should be held responsible."

"Nothing will happen to me," I told him; "no one should know that better than you."

He smiled a bit ruefully. "You are right," he said, "but still I must ask Xaxak;" and this he did the next time that he saw the dator.

In order to win Ptang's greater friendship, I had been teaching him some of the finer points of swordsmanship which I had learned in two worlds and in a thousand duels and battles; but by no means did I teach him all of my tricks, nor could I impart to him the strength and agility which my earthly muscles give me on Mars.

Xaxak was watching us at swordplay when Ptang asked

him if I might take on some of his critics. Xaxak shook his head. "I am afraid that Dotar Sojat might be injured," he said.

"I will guarantee that I shall not be," I told him.

"Well," he said; "then I am afraid that you may kill some of my warriors."

"I promise not to. I will simply show them that they cannot last as long as Ptang did."

"It might be good sport," said Xaxak. "Who are those who criticized you, Ptang?"

Ptang gave him the names of five warriors who had been particularly venomous in their ridicule and criticism, and Xaxak immediately sent for them.

"I understand," said Xaxak, when they had assembled, "that you have condemned Ptang because he was bested in a duel with this slave. Do any of you think that you could do better than Ptang did? If so, here is your chance."

They assured him, almost in chorus, that they could do very much better.

"We shall see," he said, "but you must all understand that no one is to be killed and that you are to stop when I give the word. It is an order."

They assured him that they would not kill me, and then the first of them swaggered out to meet me. One after another, in rapid succession, I pinked each in the right shoulder and disarmed him.

I must say they took it very decently; all except one of them—a fellow named Ban-tor, who had been Ptang's most violent critic.

"He tricked me," he grumbled. "Let me at him again, my dator; and I will kill him." He was so angry that his voice trembled.

"No," said Xaxak; "he has drawn your blood and he has disarmed you, demonstrating that he is the better swordsman. If it were due to a trick, it was a trick of swordsmanship which you might do well to master before you attempt to kill Dotar Sojat."

The fellow was still scowling and grumbling as he walked away with the other four; and I realized that while all of these First Born were my nominal enemies, this fellow, Ban-tor, was an active one. However, I gave the matter little thought as I was too valuable to Xaxak for anybody to risk his displeasure by harming me; nor could I see that there was any way in which the fellow could injure me.

"Ban-tor has always disliked me," said Ptang, after they had all left us. "He dislikes me; because I have always bested him in swordsmanship and feats of strength; and, in addition to this, he is a natural born trouble maker. If it were not for the fact that he is related to Xaxak's wife, the dator would not have him around."

Since I have already compared myself to a prospective Derby winner, I might as well carry out the analogy by describing their Lesser Games as minor race meets. They are held about once a week in a stadium inside the city, and here the rich nobles pit their warriors or their slaves against those of other nobles in feats of strength, in boxing, in wrestling, and in dueling. Large sums of money are wagered, and the excitement runs high. The duels are not always to the death, the nobles deciding beforehand precisely upon what they will place their bets. Usually it is for first blood or disarming; but there is always at least one duel to the death, which might be compared to the feature race of a race meet, or the main event of a boxing tournament.

Kamtol has a population of about two hundred thousand, of which possibly five thousand are slaves. As I was allowed considerable freedom, I got around the city quite a bit; though Ptang always accompanied me, and I was so impressed with the scarcity of children that I asked Ptang what accounted for it.

"The Valley of the First Born will only comfortably support about two hundred thousand population," he replied; "so only sufficient children are permitted to replace the death losses. As you may have guessed, by looking at our people, the old and otherwise unfit are destroyed; so that we have about sixty-five thousand fighting men and about twice as many healthy women and children. There are two factions here, one of which maintains that the number of women should be greatly decreased; so that the number of fighting men may be increased, while the other faction insists that, as we are not menaced by any powerful enemies, sixty-five thousand fighting men are sufficient.

"Strange as it may seem, most of the women belong to the first faction; notwithstanding the fact that this faction which believes in decreasing the number of females would do so by permitting a far greater number of eggs to incubate, killing all the females which hatched and as many of the adult women as there were males in the hatching. This is probably due to the fact that each woman thinks that she is too desirable to be destroyed and that that fate will fall to some other woman. Doxus believes in maintaining the *status quo;* but some future jeddak may believe differently; and even Doxus may change his mind, which, confidentially, is most vacillating."

My fame as a swordsman soon spread among the sixty-five thousand fighting men of Kamtol, and opinion was most unevenly divided as to my ability. Perhaps a dozen men of Kamtol had seen my swordplay; and they were willing to back me against anyone; but all the remainder of the sixty-five thousand felt that they could best me in individual combat; for this is a race of fighting men, all extremely proud of their skill and their valor.

I was exercising in the garden with Ptang one day, when Xaxak came with another dator, whom he called Nastor. When Ptang saw them coming, he whistled. "I never saw Nastor here before," he said in a low tone of voice. "Xaxak has no use for him, and he hates Xaxak. Wait!" he exclaimed; "I have an idea why he is here. If they ask for swordplay, let me disarm you. I will tell you why, later."

"Very well," I said, "and I hope it will do you some good."

"It is not for me," he said; "it is for Dator Xaxak."

As the two approached us, I heard Nastor say, "So this is your great swordsman! I should like to wager that I have men who could best him any day."

"You have excellent men," said Xaxak; "still, I think my man would give a good account of himself. How much of a wager do you want to lay?"

"You have seen my men fight," said Nastor, "but I have never seen this fellow at work. I would like to see him in action; then I shall know whether to ask or give odds."

"Very well," said Xaxak, "that is fair enough," then he turned to us. "You will give the Dator Nastor an exhibition of your swordsmanship, Dotar Sojat; but not to the death—you understand?"

Ptang and I drew our swords and faced one another. "Don't forget what I asked of you," he said, and then we were at it.

I not only remembered what he had asked, but I now realized why he had asked it; and so I put up an exhibition of quite ordinary swordsmanship, just good enough to hold my own until I let Ptang disarm me.

"He is an excellent swordsman," said Nastor, knowing that he was lying, but not knowing that we knew it; "but I will bet even money that my man can kill him."

"You mean a duel to the death?" demanded Xaxak. "Then I shall demand odds; as I did not desire my man to fight to the death the first time he fought."

"I will give you two to one," said Nastor; "are those odds satisfactory?"

"Perfectly," said Xaxak. "How much do you wish to wager?"

"A thousand tanpi to your five hundred," replied Nastor. A tanpi is equivalent to about $1 in United States money.

"I want to make more than enough to feed my wife's sorak," replied Xaxak.

Now, a sorak is a little six-legged, cat-like animal, kept as a pet by many Martian women; so what Xaxak had said was equivalent to telling Nastor that we didn't care to fight for chicken feed. I could see that Xaxak was trying to anger Nastor; so that he would bet recklessly, and I knew then that he must have guessed that Ptang and I were putting on a show when I let Ptang disarm me so easily.

Nastor was scowling angrily. "I did not wish to rob you," he said; "but if you wish to throw your money away, you may name the amount of the wager."

"Just to make it interesting," said Xaxak, "I'll bet you fifty thousand tanpi against your hundred thousand."

This staggered Nastor for a moment; but he must have got to thinking how easily Ptang had disarmed me, for eventually he rose to the bait. "Done!" he said; "and I am sorry for both you and your man," with which polite hypocrisy he turned on his heel and left without another word.

Xaxak looked after him with a half smile on his lips; and when he had gone, turned to us. "I hope you were just playing a little game," he said, "for if you were not you may have lost me fifty thousand tanpi."

"You need not worry, my prince," said Ptang.

"I shall not worry unless Dotar Sojat worries," replied the dator.

"There is always a gamble in such an enterprise as this," I replied; "but I think that you got very much the best of the bargain, for the odds should have been the other way."

"At least you have more faith than I have," said Xaxak the dator.

8

Ptang told me that he had never known more interest to be displayed in a duel to the death than followed the announcement of the wager between Xaxak and Nastor. "No common warrior is to represent Nastor," he said. "He has persuaded a dator to fight for him, a man who is considered the best swordsman in Kamtol. His name is Nolat. I have never before known of a prince fighting a slave; but they say that Nolat owes Nastor a great deal of money and that Nastor will cancel the debt if Nolat wins, which Nolat is sure that he will—he is so sure that he has pledged his palace to raise money to bet upon himself."

"Not such a stupid thing for him to do, after all," I said; "for if he loses he won't need a palace."

Ptang laughed. "I hope he doesn't need it," he said; "but don't be over-confident, for he is rated the best swordsman among the First Born; and there are supposed to be no better swordsmen in all Barsoom."

Before the day arrived that I was to fight Nolat, Xaxak and Ptang grew more and more nervous; as did all of Xaxak's warriors, who seemed to feel a personal interest in me—that is, with the exception of Ban-tor, whose enmity I had aroused by disarming him.

Ban-tor had placed a number of wagers against me; and he kept bragging about this, insisting that I was no match for Nolat and that I should be killed in short order.

I slept in a small room by myself on old, discarded furs, as befitted a slave. My room connected with that occupied by Ptang; and had only one door, which opened into Ptang's room. It was on the second floor of the palace and overlooked the lower end of the garden.

The night before the encounter I was awakened by a noise in my room, and as I opened my eyes I saw a man leap out of the window with a sword in his hand; but, as neither of Mars' two moons was in the sky, it was not light enough for me to be sure that I could recognize him; yet there was something very familiar about him.

The next morning I told Ptang about my nocturnal visitor. Neither of us, however, could imagine why anyone would want to enter my room in stealth, as I had nothing to steal.

"It might have been an assassin who wanted to stop the fight," suggested Ptang.

"I doubt that," I said; "for he had plenty of opportunity to kill me, as I didn't awaken until he was leaping through the window."

"You missed nothing?" asked Ptang.

"I had nothing to miss," I replied, "except my harness and weapons, and I am wearing them now."

Ptang finally suggested that the fellow may have thought that a female slave slept in the room; and when he found out his error, took his departure; and with that we dropped the matter from our minds.

We went to the stadium about the fourth zode, and we went in style—in fact it was a regular pageant. There were Xaxak and his wife, with her female slaves, and Xaxak's officers and warriors. We were all mounted on gaily caparisoned thoats; pennants waved above us, and mounted trumpeters preceded us. Nastor was there with the same sort of retinue. We all paraded around the arena to the accompaniment of "Kaors!" and growls—the kaors were applause and the growls were boos. I received a great many more growls than kaors, for after all I was a slave pitted against a prince, a man of their own blood.

There were some wrestling and boxing matches and a number of duels for first blood only, but what the people were waiting for was the duel to the death. People are very much alike everywhere. On Earth, they go to boxing matches hoping for blood and a knockout; they go to the wrestling matches hoping to see someone thrown out of the ring and crippled; and when they go to automobile races they hope to see somebody killed. They will not admit these things, but without the element of danger and the risk of death these sports wouldn't draw a hatful of people.

At last the moment came for me to enter the arena, and I did so before a most distinguished audience. Doxus, Jeddak of the First Born, was there with his Jeddara. The loges and boxes were crowded with the nobility of Kamtol. It was a gorgeous spectacle; the harnesses of the men and women were resplendent with precious metals and jewels, and from every vantage point flew pennants and banners.

Nolat was escorted to the jeddak's box and presented; then to the box of Xaxak, where he bowed; and last of all to the box of Nastor, for whom he was fighting a stranger to the death.

I, being a slave, was not presented to the jeddak; but I was taken before Nastor; so that he could identify me as the individual against whom he had placed his wagers. It was, of course, a mere formality; but in accordance with the rules of the Games.

I had caught only a brief glimpse of Nastor's entourage as we had paraded around the arena; as they had been behind us; but now I got a good look at them, as I stood in the arena before Nastor, and I saw Llana of Gathol sitting there beside the dator. Now, indeed, would I kill Nastor's man!

Llana of Gathol gasped and started to speak to me; but I shook my head, for I was afraid she would call me by name, which might, here among the First Born, have been the equivalent of a death sentence. It was always a surprise to me that none of these men recognized me; for my white skin and gray eyes make me a marked man, and if any of them had been in the Valley Dor when I was there they must have remembered me. I was to learn later why none of these Black Pirates of Barsoom knew me.

"Why did you do that, slave?" demanded Nastor.

"Do what?" I asked.

"Shake your head," he replied.

"Perhaps I am nervous," I said.

"And well you may be, slave, for you are about to die," he snapped, nastily.

I was taken then to a point in the arena opposite the jeddak's box. Ptang was with me, as a sort of a second, I suppose. They let us stand there alone for several minutes, presumably to shake my nerves; then Nolat approached, accompanied by another noble dator. There was a fifth man; possibly he might have been called a referee; although he didn't have much to do besides giving the signal for the duel to commence.

Nolat was a large, powerful man; and built like a fighter. He was a very handsome man, but with a haughty, supercilious expression. Ptang had told me that we were supposed to salute each other with our swords before we engaged; and as soon as I got in position, I saluted; but Nolat merely sneered and said, "Come, slave! You are about to die."

"You made a mistake, Nolat," I said, as we engaged.

"What do you mean?" he demanded, lunging at me.

"You should have saluted your better," I said, parrying his lunge. "Now it will go harder with you—unless you would like to stop and salute me as you should have at first."

"Insolent calot!" he growled, and thrust viciously at me.

For reply, I cut a gash in his left cheek. "I told you you should have saluted," I mocked.

Nolat became furious then, and came at me with the evident intention of ending the encounter immediately. I sliced him along the other cheek, then; and a moment later I carved a bloody cross upon his left breast, a difficult maneuver requiring exceptional agility and skill, since his right side was always presented to me; or always should have been had he been quick enough to follow my foot work.

That audience was as silent as a tomb, except for the kaors from Xaxak's contingent. Nolat was bleeding profusely, and he had slowed down considerably.

Suddenly somebody shouted, "Death!" Then other voices took it up. They wanted the kill; and as it was quite evident that Nolat couldn't kill me, I assumed that they wished me to kill him. Instead, I disarmed him, sending his blade flying halfway across the arena. The referee ran after it; at last I had given him something to do.

I turned to Nolat's second. "I offer the man his life," I said in a tone of voice loud enough to have been heard in any part of the stadium.

Immediately there were shots of "Kaor!" and "Death!" The "Deaths" were in the majority.

"He offers you your life, Nolat," said the second.

"But the wagers must be paid precisely as though I had killed you," I said.

"It is to the death," said Nolat. "I shall fight."

Well, he was a brave man; and because of that I hated to kill him.

His sword was returned to him by now, and we fell to it again. This time Nolat did not smile nor sneer, and he had no nasty remarks to make to me. He was in deadly earnest, fighting for his life like a cornered rat. He was an excellent swordsman; but I do not think that he was the best swordsman among the First Born; for I had seen many of them fight before, and I could have named a dozen who could have killed him offhand.

I could have killed him myself any time that I had wished to, but somehow I couldn't bring myself to do it. It seemed a shame to kill such a good swordsman and such a brave man; so I pricked him a few times and disarmed him again. I did the same thing three more times; and then, while the referee was running after Nolat's sword again, I stepped to the jeddak's loge and saluted.

"What are you doing here, slave?" demanded an officer of the jeddak's guard.

"I come to ask for the life of Nolat," I replied. "He is a good swordsman and a brave man—and I am not a murderer; and it would be murder to kill him now."

"It is a strange request," said Doxus; "the duel was to the death; it must go on."

"I am a stranger here," I said, "but where I come from if a contestant can show fraud or chicanery he is awarded the decision without having to finish the contest."

"Do you mean to imply that there has been fraud or chicanery on the part of either the Dator Nastor or the Dator Nolat?" demanded Doxus.

"I mean to say that a man entered my room last night while I slept, took my sword, and left a shorter one in the scabbard. This sword is several inches shorter than Nolat's; I noticed it when we first engaged. It is not my sword, as Xaxak and Ptang can testify if they will examine it."

Doxus summoned Xaxak and Ptang and asked them if they could identify the sword. Xaxak said that he could only identify it as coming from his armory; that he did not know the sword that had been issued to me, but that Ptang did; then Doxus turned to Ptang.

"Is this the sword that was issued to the slave, Dotar Sojat?" he demanded.

"No; it is not," replied Ptang.

"Do you recognize it?"

"I do."

"To whom did it belong?"

"It is the sword of a warrior named Ban-tor," replied Ptang.

9

There was nothing for Doxus to do but award the contest
to me; and he also ordered that all bets be paid, just as
though I had killed Nolat. That didn't set very well with Nastor, nor did the fact that Doxus made him pay over to
Xaxak one hundred thousand tanpi in the jeddak's presence;
then he sent for Ban-tor.

Doxus was furious; for the First Born hold their honor as
fighting men very high, and the thing that had been done was
a blot upon the escutcheons of them all.

"Is this the man who entered your room last night?" he
asked me.

"It was dark; and I only saw his back; there was something familiar about the fellow, but I couldn't identify him
positively."

"Did you lay any wagers on this contest?" he asked Ban-
tor.

"A few little ones, Jeddak," replied the man.

"On whom?"

"On Nolat."

Doxus turned to one of his officers. "Summon all those
with whom Ban-tor wagered on this contest."

A slave was sent around the arena, shouting out the summons; and soon there were fifty warriors gathered before
Doxus' loge. Ban-tor appeared most unhappy; as, from each
of the fifty, Doxus gleaned the information that Ban-tor had
wagered large sums with each, in some instances giving extremely big odds.

"You thought that you were betting on a sure thing, didn't
you?" demanded Doxus.

"I thought that Nolat would win," replied Ban-tor; "there
is no better swordsman in Kamtol."

"And you were sure that he would win against an antagonist with a shorter sword. You are a disgrace; you have
dishonored the First Born. For punishment you will fight
now with Dotar Sojat;" then he turned to me. "You may
kill him; and before you engage him, I, myself, will see that

your sword is as long as his; although it would be only
fair were he to be compelled to fight with the shorter sword
he gave to you."

"I shall not kill him," I replied, "but I shall put a mark
upon him that he will carry through life to remind all men
that he is a knave."

As we started to take our places before the loge of the
jeddak, I heard bets being offered with odds as high as a
hundred to one that I would win, and later I learned that
even a thousand to one was offered without any takers; then,
as we faced one another, I heard Nastor shout, "I will lay no
wager, but I'll give Ban-tor fifty thousand tanpi if he kills
the slave." It appeared that the noble dator was wroth at
me.

Ban-tor was no mean antagonist; for he was not only a
good swordsman, but he was fighting for his life and fifty
thousand tanpi. He didn't try any rushing tactics this time;
but fought carefully, mostly on the defensive, waiting for me
to make one little false move that would give him an opening; but I do not make false moves. It was he who made
the false move; he thrust, following a feint, thinking to find
me off balance.

I am never off balance. My blade moved twice with the
swiftness of light, leaving an X cut deep in the center of
Ban-tor's forehead; then I disarmed him.

Without even glancing at him again, I walked to Doxus'
loge. "I am satisfied," I said. "To bear the scar of that cross
through life is punishment enough. To me, it would be worse
than death."

Doxus nodded assent; and then caused the trumpets to be
blown to announce that the Games were over, after which he
again turned to me.

"What country are you from?" he asked.

"I have no country; I am a panthan," I replied; "my
sword is for sale to the highest bidder."

"I shall buy you, and thereby acquire your sword also,"
said the jeddak. "What did you pay for this slave, Xaxak?"

"One hundred tanpi," replied my owner.

"You got him too cheap," said Doxus; "I shall give you
fifty tanpi for him." There is nothing like being a jeddak!

"It is my pleasure to present him to you," said Xaxak,
magnanimously; I had already netted him a hundred thousand tanpi, and he must have realized that it would be impossible ever to get another wager placed against me.

I welcomed this change of masters; because it would take
me into the palace of the jeddak, and I had been harbor-
ing a hare-brained scheme to pave the way for our eventual

escape, that could only be successful if I were to have entry to the palace—that is, if my deductions were correct.

So John Carter, Prince of Helium, Warlord of Barsoom, came into the palace of Doxus, Jeddak of the First Born, as a slave; but a slave with a reputation. The warriors of the jeddak's guard treated me with respect; I was given a decent room; and one of Doxus' trusted under-officers was made responsible for me, just as Ptang had been in the palace of Xaxak.

I was at something of a loss to know why Doxus had purchased me. He must have known that he couldn't arrange a money duel for me, for who would be fool enough to place a man or a wager against one who had made several of the best swordsmen of Kamtol look like novices?

The next day I found out. Doxus sent for me. He was alone in a small room when I was escorted in, and he immediately dismissed the warrior who had accompanied me.

"When you entered the valley," he commenced, "you saw many skeletons, did you not?"

"Yes," I replied.

"Those men died trying to escape," he said. "It would be impossible for you to succeed any better than they. I am telling you this so that you won't make the attempt. You might think that by killing me you might escape in the confusion which would ensue; but you could not; you can never escape from the Valley of the First Born. However, you may live on here in comfort, if you wish. All that you have to do is teach me the tricks of swordsmanship with which you bested the finest swordsman of all the First Born. I wish you to make me that, but I wish the instruction given in secret and no word of it ever to pass your lips on pain of instant death—and a most unpleasant death, I can assure you. What do you say?"

"I can promise the utmost discretion," I said, "but I cannot promise to make you the greatest swordsman among the First Born; the achievement of that will depend somewhat upon your own native ability. I will instruct you, however."

"You do not talk much like a poor panthan," he said. "You speak to me much as would a man who had been accustomed to speaking with jeddaks—and as an equal."

"You may have much to learn about being a swordsman," I said, "but I have even more to learn about being a slave."

He grunted at that, and then arose and told me to follow him. We passed through a little door behind the desk at which he had been sitting, and down a ramp which led to the pits below the palace. At the foot of the ramp we entered a large, well lighted room in which were filing cases, a couch, several benches, and a table strewn with writing materials and drawing instruments.

"This is a secret apartment," said Doxus. "Only one person other than myself has access to it. We shall not be disturbed here. This other man of whom I spoke is my most trusted servant. He may come in occasionally, but he will not divulge our little secret. Let us get to work. I can scarcely wait until the day that I shall cross swords with some of those egotistical nobles who think that they are really great swordsmen. Won't they be surprised!"

10

Now, I had no intention of revealing all of my tricks of swordsmanship to Doxus; although I might have as far as any danger to myself was concerned, for he could never equal me; because he could never match my strength or agility.

I had been practicing him in disarming an opponent, when a door opposite that from which we had entered the room opened; and a man came in. During the brief time that the door remained open, I saw beyond it a brilliantly lighted room; and caught a glimpse of what appeared to be an amazingly complicated machine. Its face was covered with dials, buttons, and other gadgets—all reminiscent of the machine to which I had been attached during the weird examination I had received upon entry to the city.

At sight of me, the newcomer looked surprised. Here was I, a total stranger and evidently a slave, facing the Jeddak of the First Born with a naked blade in my hand. Instantly, the fellow whipped out a radium pistol; but Doxus forestalled a tragedy.

"It is all right, Myr-lo," he said. "I am just taking some instruction in the finer points of swordsmanship from this slave. His name is Dotar Sojat; you will see him down here with me daily. What are you doing down here now? Anything wrong?"

"A slave escaped last night," said Myr-lo.

"You got him, of course?"

"Just now. He was about half way up the escarpment, I think."

"Good!" said Doxus. "Resume, Dotar Sojat."

I was so full of what I had just heard and seen and what I thought that it all connoted that I had hard work keeping my mind on my work; so that I inadvertently let Doxus prick me. He was as pleased as Punch.

"Wonderful!" he exclaimed. "In one lesson I have been so

improved that I have been able to touch you! Not even
Nolat could do that. We will stop now. I give you the freedom of the city. Do not go beyond the gates." He went to the
table and wrote for a minute; then he handed me what he
had written. "Take this," he said; "it will permit you to go
where you will in all public places and return to the palace."

He had written:

Dotar Sojat, the slave, is granted the freedom of the
palace and the city.

Doxus,
Jeddak.

As I returned to my quarters, I determined to let Doxus
prick me every day. I found Man-lat, the under-officer who
had been detailed to look after me, alone in his room, which
adjoined mine.

"Your duties are going to be lessened," I told him.

"What do you mean?" he asked.

I showed him the pass.

"Doxus must have taken a liking to you," he said. "I
never knew before of a slave being given that much freedom,
but don't try to escape."

"I know better than to try that. I saw the skeletons from
the top to the bottom of the escarpment."

"We call them Myr-lo's babies," said Man-lat; "he's so
proud of them."

"Who is Myr-lo?" I asked.

"Somebody you'll probably never see," replied Man-lat.
"He sticks to his pots and his kettles, his lathes and drills and
his drawing instruments."

"Does he live in the palace?" I asked.

"Nobody knows where he lives, unless it be the jeddak.
They say he has a secret apartment in the palace, but I don't
know about that. What I do know is that he's the most powerful man in Kamtol, next to Doxus; and that he has the
power of life and death over every man and woman in the
Valley of the First Born. Why, he could strike either one of
us dead right while we are sitting here talking; and we'd
never see what killed us."

I was even more convinced now than I had been before
that I had found what I had hoped to in that secret room
beneath the palace—but how to utilize the knowledge!

I immediately took advantage of my freedom to go out
into the city, only a part of which I had seen during the
short time that I had been out with Ptang. The guards at
the palace gate were as surprised when they read my pass as
Man-lat had been. Of course, pass or no pass, I was still an
enemy and a slave—a person to be viewed with suspicion

and contempt; but in my case the contempt was tempered by the knowledge that I had bested their best at swordsmanship. I doubt that you can realize in what high esteem a great swordsman is held everywhere on Mars. In his own country he is worshipped, as might be a Juan Belmonte in Spain or a Jack Dempsey in America.

I had not gone far from the palace, when I chanced to look up; and, to my surprise, saw a number of fliers dropping down toward the city. The First Born I had seen in the Valley Dor had all been flying men; but I had not before seen any fliers over the valley, and I had wondered.

Martian aeroplanes, being lighter than air, or in effect so; because of the utilization of that marvellous discovery, the ray of repulsion, which tends to push them away from the planet, can land vertically in a space but little larger in area than themselves; and I saw that the planes I was watching were coming down into the city at no great distance from the palace.

Fliers! I think that my heart beat a little faster at the sight of them. Fliers! a means of escape from the Valley of the First Born. It might take a great deal of scheming; and would certainly entail enormous risks; but if all went well with the other part of my plan, I would find a way—and a flier.

I made my way toward the point at which I had seen the fliers disappear behind the roofs of the buildings near me, and at last my search was rewarded. I came to an enormous building some three stories high, on the roof of which I could just see a part of a flier. Practically all hangars to Barsoom are on the roofs of buildings, usually to conserve space in crowded, walled cities; so I was not surprised to find a hangar in Kamtol thus located.

I approached the entrance to the building, determined to inspect it and some of the ships if I could get in. As I stepped through the entrance, a warrior barred my way with drawn sword.

"Where do you think you're going, slave?" he demanded. I showed him my pass.

He looked equally as surprised as the others had who had read it. "This says the freedom of the palace and the city," he said; "it doesn't say the freedom of the hangars."

"They're in the city, aren't they?" I demanded.

He shook his head. "They may be in the city, but *I* won't admit you. I'll call the officer."

He did so, and presently the officer appeared. "So!" he exclaimed, when he saw me; "you're the slave who could have killed Nolat, but spared his life. What do you want here?"

I handed him my pass. He read it carefully a couple of times. "It doesn't seem possible," he said, "but then your swordsmanship didn't seem possible either. It is hard for me to believe it yet. Why, Nolat was considered the best swordsman in Kamtol; and you made him look like an old woman with one leg. Why do you want to come in here?"

"I want to learn to fly," I said, naïvely.

He slapped his thighs and laughed at that. "Either you are foolish, or you think we First Born are, if you have an idea that we would teach a slave to fly."

"Well, I'd like to come in and look at the fliers anyway," I said. "That wouldn't do any harm. I've always been interested in them."

He thought a moment; then he said, "Nolat is my best friend; you might have killed him, but you refused. For that I am going to let you come in."

"Thank you," I said.

The first floor of the building was largely given over to shops where fliers were being built or repaired. The second and third floors were packed with fliers, mostly the small, swift ones for which the Black Pirates of Barsoom are noted. On the roof were four large battleships; and, parked under them, were a number of small fliers for which there was evidently no room on the floors below.

The building must have covered several acres; so there were an enormous number of planes hangared there. I could see them now, as I had seen them years before, swarming like angry mosquitoes over the Golden Cliffs of the Holy Therns; but what were they doing here? I had supposed that the First Born lived only in the Valley Dor, although the majority of Barsoomians still believe that they come from Thuria, the nearer moon. That theory I had seen refuted the time that Xodar, a Black Pirate, had nearly succumbed from lack of oxygen when I had flown too high while escaping from them, that time that Thuvia and I had escaped the Therns during their battle with the Black Pirates. If a man can't live without oxygen, he can't fly back and forth between Thuria and Barsoom in an open flier.

The officer had sent a warrior along with me, as a precaution against sabotage, I suppose; and I asked this fellow why I had seen no ships in the air since I had come, except the few I had seen this day.

"We fly mostly at night," he replied, "so that our enemies cannot see where we take off from, nor where we land. Those that you saw coming in a few minutes ago were visitors from Dor. That may mean that we are going to war, and I hope so. We haven't raided any cities for a long time. If it's to be a big raid, those from Dor and from Kamtol band together."

Some Black Pirates from the Valley Dor! Now, indeed, I might be recognized.

11

As I walked away from the hangar building, I turned and looked back, studying every detail of the architecture; then I walked around the entire building, which covered a whole square, with avenues on all four sides. Like nearly all Martian buildings, this one was highly ornamented with deep carvings. It stood in a rather poor section of the city, although not far from the palace; and was surrounded by small and modest homes. They were probably the homes of the artisans employed around the hangar. A little farther from the hangar a section of small shops began; and as I passed along, looking at the wares displayed, I saw something which brought me to a sudden stop, for it suggested a new accessory to my rapidly formulating plans for escape from the Valley of the First Born—from which none ever escaped. It is sometimes well not to be too greatly constrained by precedent.

I entered the shop and asked the proprietor the price of the article I wished. It was only three teepi, the equivalent of about thirty cents in United States money; but with the information came the realization that I had none of the money of the First Born.

The medium of exchange upon Mars is not dissimilar to our own, except that the coins are oval; and there are only three; the pi, pronounced pī; worth about one cent; the teepi, ten cents; and the tanpi, one dollar. These coins are oval; one of bronze, one of silver, and one of gold. Paper money is issued by individuals, much as we write a check, and is redeemed by the individual twice yearly. If a man issues more than he can redeem; the government pays his creditors in full; and the debtor works out the amount upon the farms, or in the mines, which are government owned.

I had with me money of Helium to the value of some fifty tanpi, and I asked the proprietor if he would accept a larger amount than the value of the article in foreign coin. As the value of the metal is equal to the value of the coin, he gladly accepted one dollar in gold for what was worth thirty cents in silver; and I placed my purchase in my pocket pouch and departed.

As I approached the palace, I saw a white-skinned man ahead of me carrying a heavy burden on his back. Now, as far as I knew, there was only one other white-skinned man in Kamtol; and that was Pan Dan Chee; so I hastened to overtake him.

Sure enough, it was the Orovar from Horz; and when I came up behind him and called him by name, he almost dropped his burden, so surprised was he.

"John Carter!" he exclaimed.

"Hush!" I cautioned; "my name is Dotar Sojat. If the First Born knew that John Carter was in Kamtol I hate to think what would happen to him. Tell me about yourself. What has happened to you since I last saw you?"

"I was purchased by Dator Nastor, who has the reputation of being the hardest master in Kamtol. He is also the meanest; he bought me only because he could buy me cheap, and he made them throw in Jad-han for good measure. He works us day and night, and feeds us very little—and poor food at that. Since he lost a hundred thousand tanpi to Xaxak, it has been almost like working for a maniac.

"By my first ancestor!" he exclaimed suddenly; "so it was you who defeated Nolat and caused Nastor to lose all that money! I didn't realize it until just now. They said the slave who won the contest was named Dotar Sojat, and that meant nothing to me until now—and I was a little slow in getting it, at that."

"Have you seen Llana of Gathol?" I asked him. "She was in Nastor's loge at the Games; so I presume she was purchased by him."

"Yes, but I have not seen her," replied Pan Dan Chee; "however, I have heard gossip in the slaves' quarters; and I am much worried by what is being whispered about the palace."

"What have you heard? I felt that she was in danger when I saw her in Nastor's loge. She is too beautiful to be safe."

"She was safe enough at first," said Pan Dan Chee, "as she was orginally purchased by Nastor's principal wife. Everything was comparatively well for her until Nastor got a good look at her at the Games; then he tried to buy her from his wife. But she, Van-tija, refused to sell. Nastor was furious, and told Van-tija that he would take Llana anyway; so Van-tija has locked her in an apartment at the top of the tower of her own part of the palace, and has placed her personal guards at the only entrance. There is the tower, there," he said, pointing; "perhaps Llana of Gathol is looking down at us now."

As I looked up at the tower, I saw that it rose above a

palace which stood directly across the large central plaza from that of the jeddak; and I saw something else—I saw the windows of Llana's apartments were not barred.

"Do you think that Llana is in any immediate danger?" I asked.

"Yes," he replied, "I do. It is rumored in the palace that Nastor is going to lead warriors to Van-tija's section of the palace and attempt to take the tower by storm."

"Then we have no time to lose, Pan Dan Chee. We must act tonight."

"But what can we two slaves do?" he demanded. "Even if we succeeded in getting Llana out of the tower, we could never escape from the Valley of the First Born. Do not forget the skeletons, John Carter."

"Trust me," I said, "and don't call me John Carter. Can you get out of the palace of Nastor after dark?"

"I think so; they are very lax; because assassination and theft are practically unknown here, and the secret machine of the jeddak makes escape from the valley impossible. I am quite sure that I can get out. In fact, I have been sent out on errands every night since I was purchased."

"Good!" I said. "Now listen carefully: Come out of the palace and loiter in the shadows near Nastor's palace at about twenty-five xats after the eighth zode.* Bring Jad-han with you, if he wishes to escape. If my plan succeeds, a flier will land here in the plaza near you; run for it and climb aboard. It will be piloted by a Black Pirate, but don't let that deter you. If you and Jad-han can arm yourselves, do so; there may be fighting. If the flier does not come, you will know that I have failed; and you can go back to your quarters and be no worse off. If I do not come, it will be because I am dead, or about to die."

"And Llana?" he asked. "What of her?"

"My plans all center around the rescue of Llana of Gathol," I assured him. "If I fail in that, I fail in all; for I will not leave without her."

"I wish you could tell me how you expect to accomplish the impossible," he said. "I should feel very much surer of the outcome, I know, if you would tell me at least something of your plans."

"Certainly," I said. "In the first place—"

"What are you two slaves doing loitering here?" demanded a gruff voice behind us. I turned to see a burly warrior at my shoulder. For answer, I showed him my pass from the jeddak.

* Midnight, Earth time.

Even after he read it, he looked as though he didn't believe it; but presently he handed it back to me and said, "That's all right for you, but how about this other one? Has he got a pass from the jeddak, too?"

"The fault is mine," I said. "I knew him before we were captured, and I stopped him to ask how he was faring. I am sure that if the jeddak knew, he would say that it was all right for me to talk with a friend. The jeddak has been very kind to me." I was trying to impress the fellow with the fact that his jeddak was very kindly disposed toward me. I think that I succeeded.

"Very well," he said, "but get on your way now—the Great Plaza is no place for slaves to visit with one another."

Pan Dan Chee picked up his burden and departed, and I was about to leave when the warrior detained me. "I saw you defeat Nolat and Ban-tor at the Games," he said. "We were talking about it a little while ago with some of our friends from the Valley Dor. They said that there was once a warrior came there who was just such a marvellous swordsman. His name was John Carter, *and he had a white skin and gray eyes!* Could your name, by any chance, be John Carter?"

"My name is Dotar Sojat," I replied.

"Our friends from the Valley Dor would like to get hold of John Carter," he said; and then, with a rather nasty little smile, he turned on his heel and left me.

12

Now indeed was the occasion for haste increased a hundredfold. If one man in Kamtol suspected that I might be John Carter, Prince of Helium, I should be lost by the morrow at the latest—perhaps before the morrow. Even as I entered the palace I feared arrest, but I reached my room without incident. Presently Man-lat came in; and at sight of him I expected the worst, for he had never visited me before. My sword was ready to leap from its scabbard, for I had determined to die fighting rather than let them arrest and disarm me. Even now, if Man-lat made a false move, I could kill him; and there might still be a chance that my plan could move on to successful fruition.

But Man-lat was in a friendly, almost jovial mood. "It is too bad that you are a slave," he said, "for there are going to be great doings in the palace tonight. Doxus is entertaining the visitors from Dor. There will be much to eat and much to drink, and there will be entertainment. Doxus will probably have you give an exhibition of sword play with one of our best swordsmen—not to the death, you understand, but just for first blood. Then there will be dancing by slave girls; the nobles will enter their most beautiful. Doxus has commanded Nastor to bring a new purchase of his whose beauty has been the talk of Kamtol since the last games. Yes, it is too bad that you are not a First Born; so that you might enjoy the evening to the full."

"I am sure I shall enjoy the evening," I said.

"How's that?" he demanded.

"Didn't you say that I was going to be there?"

"Oh, yes; but only as an entertainer. You will not eat nor drink with us, and you will not see the slave girls. It is really too bad that you are not a First Born; you would have been a credit to us."

"I feel that I am quite the equal of any of the First Born," I said, for I was pretty well fed up with their arrogance and conceit.

Man-lat looked at me in pained surprise. "You are presumptuous, slave," he said. "Do you not know that the First Born of Barsoom, sometimes known to you lesser creatures as The Black Pirates of Barsoom, are of the oldest race on the planet. We trace our lineage, unbroken, direct to the Tree of Life which flourished in the Valley Dor twenty-three million years ago.

"For countless ages the fruit of this tree underwent the gradual changes of evolution, passing by degrees from the true plant life to a combination of plant and animal. In the first stages of this phase, the fruit of the tree possessed only the power of independent muscular action, while the stem remained attached to the parent plant; later, a brain developed in the fruit; so that, hanging there by their long stems, they thought and moved as individuals.

"Then, with the development of perceptions, came a comparison of them; judgments were reached and compared, and thus reason and the power to reason were born upon Barsoom.

"Ages passed. Many forms of life came and went upon the Tree of Life, but still all were attached to the parent plant by stems of varying lengths. In time the fruit upon the tree consisted of tiny plant men, such as we now see reproduced in such huge dimensions in the Valley Dor; but still hanging to the limbs and branches of the Tree by the stems which grew from the tops of their heads.

"The buds from which the plant men blossomed resembled

large nuts about a sofad* in diameter, divided by double partition walls into four sections. In one section grew the plant man; in another a sixteen-legged worm; in the third the progenitor of the white ape; and in the fourth, the primeval black man of Barsoom.

"When the bud burst, the plant man remained dangling at the end of his stem; but the three other sections fell to the ground, where the efforts of their imprisoned occupants to escape sent them hopping about in all directions.

"Thus, as time went on, all Barsoom was covered by these imprisoned creatures. For countless ages they lived their long lives within their hard shells, hopping and skipping about the broad planet; falling into rivers, lakes, and seas to be still farther spread about the surface of the new world.

"Countless billions died before the first black man broke through his prison walls into the light of day. Prompted by curiosity, he broke open other shells; and the peopling of Barsoom commenced.

"The pure strain of the blood of this first black man has remained untainted by admixture with that of other creatures; but from the sixteen legged worm, the first white ape, and renegade black men has sprung every other form of life upon Barsoom."

I hoped he was through, for I had heard all this many times before; but, of course, I didn't dare tell him so. I wished he would go away—not that I could do anything until after dark, but I just wanted to be alone and re-plan every minutest detail of the night's work that lay before me.

At last he went; and at long last night came, but I must still remain inactive until about two hours before the time that I had told Pan Dan Chee to be prepared to climb aboard a flier piloted by a Black Pirate. I was betting that he was still puzzling over that.

The evening wore on. I heard sounds of revelry coming from the first floor of the palace through the garden upon which my window opened—the jeddak's banquet was in full swing. The zero hour was approaching—and then malign Fate struck. A warrior came, summoning me to the banquet hall!

I should have killed him and gone on about my business, but suddenly a spirit of bravado possessed me. I would face them all, let them see once more the greatest swordsman of two worlds, and let them realize, when I had escaped them, that I was greater in all ways than the greatest of the First Born. I knew it was foolish; but now I was following the

* 11.17 Earth inches.

warrior toward the banquet hall; the die was cast, and it was too late to turn back.

No one paid any attention to me as I entered the great room—I was only a slave. Four tables, forming a hollow square, were filled with men and women, gorgeously trapped. They were talking and laughing; and wine was flowing, and a small army of slaves was bearing more food and more wine. Some of the guests were already a little bit high, and it was evident that Doxus was holding his own with the best of them. He had his arm about his wife, on one side; but he was kissing another man's wife on the other.

The warrior who had fetched me went and whispered in the jeddak's ear, and Doxus banged a huge gong for silence. When they had quieted down, he spoke to them:"For long the First Born of the Valley Dor have boasted of their swordsmanship; and, in contests, I admit that they have proved that they possess some slight superiority over us; but I have in my palace a slave, a common slave, who can best the best swordsman from Dor. He is here now to give an exhibition of his marvellous ability in a contest with one of my nobles; not to the death, but for first blood only—unless there be one from Dor who believes that he can best this slave of mine."

A noble arose. "It is a challenge," he said. "Dator Zithad is the best swordsman here from Dor tonight; but if he will not meet a slave, I will for the honor of Dor. We have heard of this slave since we arrived in Kamtol, how he bested your best swordsmen; and I for one shall be glad to draw his blood."

Then Zithad arose, haughty and arrogant. "I have never sullied my sword with the blood of a slave," he said, "but I shall be glad to expunge the shame of Kamtol. Where is the knave?"

Zithad! He had been Dator of the Guards of Issus at the time of the revolt of the slaves and the overthrow of Issus. He had good reason to remember me and to hate me.

When we faced each other in the center of that hollow square in the banquet hall of Doxus, Jeddak of the First Born of Kamtol, he looked puzzled for a moment, and then stepped back. He opened his mouth to speak.

"So, you are afraid to meet a slave!" I taunted him. "Come! they want to see you spill my blood; let's not disappoint them." I touched him lightly with my point.

"Calot!" he growled, and came for me.

He was a better swordsman than Nolat, but I made a monkey of him. I backed him around the square, keeping him always on the defensive; but I drew no blood—yet. He

was furious—and he was afraid. The audience sat in breathless silence.

Suddenly he screamed: "Fools! Don't you know who this
slave is? He is—" Then I ran him through the heart.

Instantly pandemonium reigned. A hundred swords sprang
from their scabbards, but I waited to see no more—I'd seen
plenty! With drawn sword, I ran straight for the center of
one of the tables; a woman screamed. In a single bound I
cleared the table and the diners, and bolted through the
door behind them into the garden.

Of course, they were after me instantly; but I dodged into
the shrubbery, and made my way to a point beneath my
window at the lower end of the garden. It was scarcely a
fifteen foot jump to the sill; and a second later I had passed
through my room and down a ramp to the floor below.

It was dark, but I knew every inch of the way to my
goal. I had prepared for just some such eventuality. I reached
the room in which Doxus had first interviewed me, and passed
through the doorway behind the desk and down the ramp
to the secret chamber below.

I knew that no one would guess where I had gone; and
as Myr-lo was doubtless at the banquet, I should be able
to accomplish with ease that which I had come here to do.

As I opened the door into the larger room, Myr-lo arose
from the couch and faced me.

"What are you doing here, slave?" he demanded.

13

Here was a pretty pass! Everything seemed to be going
wrong; first, the summons to the banquet hall; then Zithad,
and now Myr-lo. I hated to do it, but there was no other
way.

"Draw!" I said. I am no murderer; so I couldn't kill him
unless he had a sword in his hand; but Myr-lo was not so
ethical—he reached for the radium pistol at his hip. Fatal
error! I crossed the intervening space in a single bound; and
ran Myr-lo, the inventor of Kamtol, through the heart.

Without even waiting to wipe the blood from my blade, I
ran into the smaller room. There was the master mechanism
that held two hundred thousand souls in thrall, the hideous
invention that had strewn the rim of the great rift with
mouldering skeletons.

I looked about and found a heavy piece of metal; then I
went for that insensate monster with all the strength and en-

thusiasm that I possess. In a few minutes it was an indescribable jumble of bent and broken parts—a total wreck.

Quickly I ran back into the next room, stripped Myr-lo's harness and weapons from his corpse and removed my own; then from my pocket pouch I took the article that I had purchased in the little shop. It was a jar of the ebony black cream with which the women of the First Born are wont to conceal the blemishes upon their glossy skins.

In ten minutes I was as black as the blackest Black Pirate that ever broke a shell. I donned Myr-lo's harness and weapons; and, except for my gray eyes, I was a noble of the First Born. I was glad now that Myr-lo had not been at the banquet, for his harness would help to pass me through the palace and out of it, an ordeal that I had not been looking forward to with much relish; for I had been wearing the harness of the commonest of common warriors, and I very much doubted that they passed in and out of the palace late at night without being questioned—and I had no answers.

I got through the palace without encountering anyone, and when I approached the gate I commenced to stagger. I wanted them to think that a slightly inebriated guest was leaving early. I held my breath as I approached the warriors on guard; but they only saluted me respectfully, and I passed out into the avenues of Kamtol.

My plan had been to climb the façade of the hangar building, which I could have done because of the deep carving of its ornamentation; but that would probably have meant a fight with the guard on the roof as I clambered over the cornice. Now, I determined to try another, if no less hazardous, plan.

I walked straight to the entrance. There was but a single warrior on guard there. I paid no attention to him, but strode in. He hesitated; then he saluted, and I passed on and up the ramp. He had been impressed by the gorgeous trappings of Myr-lo, the noble.

My greatest obstacle to overcome now was the guard on the roof, where I had no doubt but that I should find several warriors. It might be difficult to convince them that even a noble would go flying alone at this time of night, but when I reached the roof there was not a single warrior in sight.

It took me but a moment to find the flier I had selected for the adventure when I had been there before, and but another moment to climb to its controls and start the smooth, silent motor.

The night was dark; neither moon was in the sky, and for that I was thankful. I rose in a steep spiral until I was high above the city; then I headed for the tower of Nastor's palace where Llana of Gathol was imprisoned.

The black hull of the flier rendered me invisible, I was sure, from the avenues below on a dark night such as this; and I came to the tower with every assurance that my whole plan had worked out with amazing success, even in spite of the untoward incidents that had seemed about to wreck it in its initial stages.

As I drew slowly closer to the windows of Llana's apartment, I heard a woman's muffled scream and a man's voice raised in anger. A moment later the prow of my ship touched the wall just below the window; and, seizing the bow line, I leaped across the sill into the chamber, Myr-lo's sword in my hand.

Across the room, a man was forcing Llana of Gathol back upon a couch. She was striking at him, and he was cursing her.

"Enough!" I cried, and the man dropped Llana and turned toward me. It was Nastor, the dator.

"Who are you?" he demanded. "What are you doing here?"

"I am John Carter, Prince of Helium," I replied; "and I am here to kill you."

He had already drawn, and our swords crossed even as I spoke.

"Perhaps you will recall me better as Dotar Sojat, the slave who cost you one hundred thousand tanpi," I said; "the prince who is going to cost you your life."

He commenced to shout for the guard, and I heard the sound of running footsteps which seemed to be coming up a ramp outside the door. I saw that I must finish Nastor quickly; but he proved a better swordsman than I had expected, although the encounter quickly developed into a foot race about the chamber.

The guard was coming closer when Llana darted to the door and pushed a heavy bolt into place; and not a moment too soon, for almost immediately I heard pounding on the door and the shouts of the warriors outside; and then I tripped upon a fur that had fallen from the couch during the struggle between Llana and Nastor, and I went down upon my back. Instantly Nastor leaped for me to run me through the heart. My sword was pointed up toward him, but he had all the advantage. I was about to die.

Only Llana's quick wit saved me. She leaped for Nastor from the rear and seized him about the ankles. He pitched forward on top of me, and my sword went through his heart, two feet of the blade protruding from his back. It took all my strength to wrest it free.

"Come, Llana!" I said.

"Where to?" she asked. "The corridor is full of warriors."

"The window," I said. "Come!"

As I turned toward the window, I saw the end of my line, that I had dropped during the fight, disappear over the edge of the sill. My ship had drifted away, and we were trapped.

I ran to the window. Twenty-five feet away, and a few feet below the level of the sill, floated escape and freedom, floated life for Llana of Gathol, for Pan Dan Chee, for Jad-han, and for me.

There was but a single hope. I stepped to the sill, measured the distance again with my eyes—and jumped. That I am narrating this adventure must assure you that I landed on the deck of that flier. A moment later it was beside the sill again, and Llana was aboard.

"Pan Dan Chee!" she said. "What has become of him? It seems cruel to abandon him to his fate."

Pan Dan Chee would have been the happiest man in the world could he have known that her first thought was for him, but I knew that the chances were that she would snub or insult him the first opportunity she had—women are peculiar that way.

I dropped swiftly toward the plaza. "Where are you going?" demanded Llana. "Aren't you afraid we'll be captured down there?"

"I am going for Pan Dan Chee," I said, and a moment later I landed close to Nastor's palace, and two men dashed from the shadows toward the ship. They were Pan Dan Chee and Jad-han.

As soon as they were aboard, I rose swiftly; and headed for Gathol. I could feel Pan Dan Chee looking at me. Finally he could contain himself no longer. "Who are you?" he demanded; "and where is John Carter?"

"I am now Myr-lo, the inventor," I said; "a short time ago I was Dotar Sojat the slave; but always I am John Carter."

"We are all together again," he said, "and alive; but for how long? Have you forgotten the skeletons on the rim of the rift?"

"You need not worry," I assured him. "The mechanism that laid them there has been destroyed."

He turned to Llana. "Llana of Gathol," he said, "we have been through much together; and there is no telling what the future holds for us. Once again I lay my heart at your feet."

"You may pick it up," said Llana of Gathol; "I am tired and wish to sleep."

BOOK 3

ESCAPE ON MARS

1

THERE WERE four of us aboard the flier I had stolen from the hangar at Kamtol to effect our escape from The Valley of the First Born: Llana of Gathol; Pan Dan Chee of Horz; Jadhan, the brother of Janai of Amhor; and I, John Carter, Prince of Helium and Warlord of Barsoom.

It was one of those startlingly gorgeous Martian nights that fairly take one's breath away. In the thin air of the dying planet, every star stands out in scintillant magnificence against the velvet blackness of the firmament in splendor inconceivable to an inhabitant of Earth.

As we rose above the great rift valley, both of Mars' moons were visible, and Earth and Venus were in conjunction, affording us a spectacle of incomparable beauty. Cluros, the farther moon, moved in stately dignity across the vault of heaven but fourteen thousand miles away, while Thuria, but four thousand miles distant, hurtled through the night from horizon to horizon in less than four hours, casting ever changing shadows on the ground below us which produced the illusion of constant movement, as though the surface of Mars was covered by countless myriads of creeping, crawling things. I wish that I might convey to you some conception of the weird and startling strangeness of the scene and of its beauty; but, unfortunately, my powers of description are wholly inadequate. But perhaps some day you, too, will visit Mars.

As we rose above the rim of the mighty escarpment which bounds the valley, I set our course for Gathol and opened the throttle wide, for I anticipated possible pursuit; but, knowing the possibilities for speed of this type of flier, I was confident that, with the start we had, nothing in Kamtol could overhaul us if we had no bad luck.

Gathol is supposed by many to be the oldest inhabited city on Mars, and is one of the few that has retained its freedom; and that despite the fact that its ancient diamond mines are the richest known and, unlike practically all the other diamond fields, are today apparently as inexhaustible as ever.

In ancient times the city was built upon an island in

Throxeus, mightiest of the five oceans of old Barsoom. As the ocean receded, Gathol crept down the sides of the mountain, the summit of which was the island on which she had been built, until today she covers the slopes from summit to base, while the bowels of the great hill are honeycombed with the galleries of her mines.

Entirely surrounding Gathol is a great salt marsh, which protects it from invasion by land, while the rugged and oft-times vertical topography of the mountain renders the landing of hostile airships a precarious undertaking.

Gahan, the father of Llana, is jed of Gathol, which is very much more than just a single city, comprising, as it does, some one hundred forty thousand square miles, much of which is fine grazing land where run their great herds of throats and zitidars. It was to return Llana to her father and mother, Tara of Helium, that we had passed through so many harrowing adventures since we had left Horz. And now Llana was almost home; and I should soon be on my way to Helium and my incomparable Dejah Thoris, who must long since have given me up for dead.

Jad-han sat beside me at the controls, Llana slept, and Pan Dan Chee moped. Moping seems to be the natural state of all lovers. I felt sorry for Pan Dan Chee; and I could have relieved his depression by telling him that Llana's first words after I had rescued her from the tower of Nastor's palace had been of him—inquiring as to his welfare —but I didn't. I wished the man who won Llana of Gathol to win her by himself. If he gave up in despair while they both lived and she remained unmated; then he did not deserve her; so I let poor Pan Dan Chee suffer from the latest rebuff that Llana had inflicted upon him.

We approached Gathol shortly before dawn. Neither moon was in the sky, and it was comparatively dark. The city was dark, too; I saw not a single light. That was strange, and might forebode ill; for Martian cities are not ordinarily darkened except in times of war when they may be threatened by an enemy.

Llana came out of the tiny cabin and crouched on the deck beside me. "That looks ominous," she said.

"It does to me, too," I agreed; "and I'm going to stand off until daylight. I want to see what's going on before I attempt to land."

"Look over there," said Llana, pointing to the right of the black mass of the mountain; "see all those lights."

"The camp fires of the herdsmen, possibly," I suggested.

"There are too many of them," said Llana.

"They might also be the camp fires of warriors," said Jad-han.

"Here comes a flier," said Pan Dan Chee; "they have discovered us."

From below, a flier was approaching us rapidly. "A patrol flier doubtless," I said, but I opened the throttle and turned the flier's nose in the opposite direction. I didn't like the looks of things, and I wasn't going to let any ship approach until I could see its insigne. Then came a hail: "Who are you?"

"Who are you?" I demanded in return.

"Stop!" came the order; but I didn't stop; I was pulling away from him rapidly, as my ship was much the faster.

He fired then, but the shot went wide. Jad-han was at the stern gun. "Shall I let him have it?" he asked.

"No," I replied; "he may be Gatholian. Turn the searchlight on him, Pan Dan Chee; let's see if we can see his insigne."

Pan Dan Chee had never been on a ship before, nor ever seen a searchlight. The little remnant of the almost extinct race of Orovars, of which he was one, that hides away in ancient Horz, has neither ships nor searchlights; so Llana of Gathol came to his rescue, and presently the bow of the pursuing flier was brightly illuminated.

"I can't make out the insigne," said Llana, "but that is no ship of Gathol."

Another shot went wide of us, and I told Jad-han that he might fire. He did and missed. The enemy fired again; and I felt the projectile strike us, but it didn't explode. He had our range; so I started to zig zag, and his next two shots missed us. Jad-Han's also missed, and then we were struck again.

"Take the controls," I said to Llana, and I went back to the gun. "Hold her just as she is, Llana," I called, as I took careful aim. I was firing an explosive shell detonated by impact. It struck her full in the bow, entered the hull, and exploded. It tore open the whole front of the ship, which burst into flame and commenced to go down by the bow. At first she went slowly; and then she took the last long, swift dive—a flaming meteor that crashed into the salt marsh and was extinguished.

"That's that," said Llana of Gathol.

"I don't think it's all of that as far as we are concerned," I retorted; "we are losing altitude rapidly; one of his shots must have ripped open a buoyancy tank."

I took the controls and tried to keep her up; as, with

throttle wide open, I sought to pass that ring of camp fires before we were finally forced down.

2

That was a good little ship—staunch and swift, as are all the ships of The Black Pirates of Barsoom—and it carried us past the farthest camp fires before it finally settled to the ground just at dawn. We were close to a small forest of sorapus trees, and I thought it best to take shelter there until we could reconnoiter a bit.

"What luck!" exclaimed Llana, disgustedly, "and just when I was so sure that we were practically safe and sound in Gathol."

"What do we do now?" asked Pan Dan Chee.

"Our fate is in the hands of our ancestors," said Jad-han.

"But we won't leave it there," I assured them; "I feel that I am much more competent to direct my own fate than are my ancestors, who have been dead for many years. Furthermore, I am much more interested in it than they."

"I think perhaps you are on the right track there," said Llana, laughing, "although I wouldn't mind leaving my fate in the hands of my living ancestors—and now, just what is one of them going to do about it?"

"First I am going to find something to eat," I replied, "and then I am going to try to find out who were warming themselves at those fires last night; they might be friends, you know."

"I doubt it," said Llana; "but if they are friends, then Gathol is in the hands of enemies."

"We should know very shortly; and now you three remain here while I go and see if anything edible grows in this forest. Keep a good lookout."

I walked into the forest, looking for roots or herbs and that life giving plant, the mantalia, the milklike sap of which has saved me from death by thirst or starvation on many an occasion. But that forest seemed to be peculiarly barren of all forms of edible things, and I passed all the way through it and out upon the other side without finding anything that even a starving man would try to eat.

Beyond the forest, I saw some low hills; and that gave me renewed hope, as in some little ravine, where moisture might be held longest, I should doubtless find something worth taking back to my companions.

I had crossed about half the distance from the forest to the hills when I heard the unmistakable clank of metal and creaking of leather behind me; and, turning, saw some twenty red men mounted on riding thoats approaching me at a gallop, the nailless, padded feet of their mounts making no sound on the soft vegetation which covered the ground.

Facing them, I drew my sword; and they drew rein a few yards from me. "Are you men of Gathol?" I asked.

"Yes," replied one of them.

"Then I am a friend," I said.

The fellow laughed. "No Black Pirate of Barsoom is any friend of ours," he shot back.

For the moment I had forgotten the black pigment with which I had covered every inch of my face and body as a disguise to assist me in effecting my escape from The Black Pirates of the Valley of the First Born.

"I am not a Black Pirate," I said.

"Oh, no!" he cried; "then I suppose you are a white ape." At that they all laughed. "Come on now, sheathe your sword and come along with us. We'll let Gan Hor decide what is to be done with you, and I can tell you right now that Gan Hor doesn't like Black Pirates."

"Don't be a fool," I said; "I tell you I am no Black Pirate—this is just a disguise."

"Well," said the fellow, who thought he was something of a wit, "isn't it strange that you and I should meet?—I'm really a Black Pirate disguised as a red man." This simply convulsed his companions. When he could stop laughing at his own joke, he said, "Come on now, no more foolishness! Or do you want us to come and take you?"

"Come and take me!" I replied. In that, I made a mistake; but I was a little sore at being laughed at by these stupid fools.

They started circling me at a gallop; and as they did so, they uncoiled the ropes they use to catch thoats. They were whirling them about their heads now and shouting. Suddenly a dozen loops spun through the air at me simultaneously. It was a beautiful demonstration of roping, but I didn't really appreciate it at the moment. Those nooses settled around me from my neck to my heels, rendering me absolutely helpless as they yanked them taut; then the dozen whose ropes had ensnared me rode away all in the same direction, jerking me to the ground; nor did they stop there —they kept on going, dragging me along the ground.

My body rolled over and over in the soft ocher vegetation, and my captors kept riding faster and faster until their mounts were at a full run. It was a most undignified situation for a fighting man; it is like me that I thought first of the injury to my pride, rather than to the injury to my body—or the fact that much more of this would leave me but a bloody corpse at the ends of twelve rawhide ropes.

They must have dragged me half a mile before they finally stopped, and only the fact that the mosslike vegetation which carpets most of Mars *is* soft found me alive at the end of that experience.

The leader rode back to me, followed by the others. He took one look at me, and his eyes were wide. "By my first ancestor!" he exclaimed; "he is no Black Pirate—the black has rubbed off!"

I glanced at myself; sure enough, much of the pigment had been rubbed off against the vegetation through which I had been dragged, and my skin was now a mixture of black and white streaks smeared with blood.

The man dismounted; and, after disarming me, took the nooses from about me. "He isn't a Black Pirate and isn't even a red man," he said to his companions; "he's white and he has gray eyes. By my first ancestor, I don't believe he's a man at all. Can you stand up?"

I came to my feet. I was a little bit groggy, but I could stand. "I can stand," I said, "and if you want to find out whether or not I'm a man, give me back my sword and draw yours," and with that I slapped him in the face so hard that he fell down. I was so mad that I didn't care whether he killed me or not. He came to his feet cursing like a true pirate from the Spanish main.

"Give him his sword!" he shouted. "I was going to take him back to Gan Hor alive, but now I'll leave him here dead."

"You'd better take him back alive, Kor-an," advised one of his fellows. "We may have captured a spy; and if you kill him before Gan Hor can question him, it won't go so well for you."

"No man can strike me and live," shouted Kor-an; "where is his sword?"

One of them handed me my long sword, and I faced Kor-an. "To the death?" I asked.

"To the death!" replied Kor-an.

"I shall not kill you, Kor-an," I said; "and you cannot kill me, but I shall teach you a lesson that you will not soon forget." I spoke in a loud tone of voice, that the others might hear.

One of them laughed, and said, "You don't know who you're talking to, fellow. Kor-an is one of the finest swordsmen in Gathol. You will be dead in five minutes."

"In one," said Kor-an, and came for me.

I went to work on Kor-an then, after trying to estimate

roughly how many bleeding cuts and scratches I had on my body. He was a furious but clumsy fighter. In the first second I drew blood from his right breast; then I cut a long gash in his right thigh. Again and again I touched him, drawing blood from cuts or scratches. I could have killed him at any time, and he could touch me nowhere.

"It has been more than a minute, Kor-an," I said.

He did not reply; he was breathing heavily, and I could tell from his eyes that he was afraid. His companions sat in silence, watching every move.

Finally, after I had cut his body from forehead to toe, I stepped back, lowering my point. "Have you had enough, Kor-an?" I asked, "or do you want me to kill you?"

"I chose to fight to the death," he said, courageously; "it is your right to kill me—and I know that you can. I know that you could have killed me any time from the moment we crossed swords."

"I have no wish to kill a brave man," I said.

"Call the whole thing off," said one of the others; "you are up against the greatest swordsman anyone ever saw, Kor-an."

"No," said Kor-an, "I should be disgraced, if I stopped before I killed him or he killed me. Come!" He raised his point.

I dropped my sword to the ground and faced him. "You now have your chance to kill me," I told him.

"But that would be murder," he said; "I am no assassin."

"Neither am I, Kor-an; and if I ran you through, even while you carried your sword, I should be as much a murderer as you, were you to kill me now; for even with a sword in your hand you are as much unarmed against me as I am now against you."

"The man is right," spoke up one of the Gatholians. "Sheathe your sword, Kor-an; no one will hold it against you."

Kor-an looked at the others, and they all urged him to quit. He rammed his sword into its scabbard and mounted his thoat. "Get up behind me," he said to me. I mounted and they were off at a gallop.

3

After about half an hour they entered another grove of sorapus, and presently came to a cluster of the rude huts used by the warrior-herdsmen of Gathol. Here was the remainder of the troop to which my captors belonged. These herds-

men are the warriors of Gathol, being divided into regular
military units. This one was a utan of a hundred men commanded by a dwar, with two padwars, or lieutenants under
him. They remain on this duty for one month, which is
equivalent to about seventy days of Earth time; then they
are relieved and return to Gathol city.

Gan Hor, the dwar, was sitting in front of one of the shelters
playing jetan with a padwar when I was taken before him
by Kor-an. He looked us both up and down for a full minute. "In the name of Issus!" he exclaimed, "what have you
two been doing—playing with a herd of banths or a tribe of
white apes? And who is this? He is neither red nor black."

"A prisoner," said Kor-an; then he explained quite hon-
estly why we were in the condition we were.

Gan Hor scowled. "I'll take this matter up with you later,
Kor-an," he said; then he turned to me.

"I am the father of Tara of Helium," I said, "the princess
of your jed."

Gan Hor leaped to his feet, and Kor-an staggered as
though he had been struck; I thought he was going to fall.

"John Carter!" exclaimed Gan Hor. "The white skin, the
gray eyes, the swordsmanship of which Kor-an has told me.
I have never seen John Carter, but you could be no other;"
then he wheeled upon Kor-an. "And you dragged the Prince
of Helium, Warlord of Barsoom for half a mile at the ends
of your ropes!" He was almost screaming. "For that, you
die!"

"No," I said. "Kor-an and I have settled that between us;
he is to be punished no further."

These warrier-herdsmen of Gathol live much like our own
desert nomads, moving from place to place as the requirements of pasturage and the presence of water dictate. There
is no surface water in Gathol other than the moisture in the
salt marsh that encircles the city; but in certain places water
may be found by sinking wells, and in these spots they make
their camps, as here in the sorapus grove to which I had been
brought.

Gan Hor had water brought for me; and while I was
washing away the black pigment, the dirt, and the blood, I
told him that Llana of Gathol and two companions were not
far from the spot where Kor-an had captured me; and he
sent one of his padwars with a number of warriors and three
extra thoats to bring them in.

"And now," I said, "tell me what is happening to Gathol.
The fact that we were attacked last night, coupled with the
ring of camp fires encircling the city, suggests that Gathol is
besieged by an enemy."

"You are right," replied Gan Hor; "Gathol is surrounded by the troops of Hin Abtol, who styles himself Jeddak of Jeddaks of the North. He came here some time ago in an ancient and obsolete flier, but as he came in peace he was treated as an honored guest by Gahan. They say that he proved himself an egotistical braggart and an insufferable boor, and ended by demanding that Gahan give him Llana as a wife—he already had seven, he boasted.

"Of course, Gahan told him that Llana of Gathol would choose her own mate; and when Llana refused his proposition, he threatened to come back and take her by force. Then he went away, and the next day our Princess started out for Helium on a ship with twenty-five members of her personal guard. She never reached Helium, nor has she been seen or heard of since, until you just told me that she is alive and has returned to Gathol.

"But we soon heard from Hin Abtol. He came back with a large fleet of the most ancient and obsolete fliers that I have ever seen; some of his ships must be over a hundred years old. Hin Abtol came back, and he demanded the surrender of Gathol.

"His ships were crammed with warriors, thousands of whom leaped overboard and descended upon the city with equilibrimotors. There was fighting in the avenues and upon the roofs of buildings all of one day, but we eventually destroyed or made prisoners of all of them; so, finding that he could not take the city by storm, Hin Abtol laid siege to it.

"He has sent all but a few of his ships away, and we believe that they have returned to the frozen north for reinforcements. We who were on herd duty at the beginning of the investment are unable to return to the city, but we are continually harassing the warriors of Hin Abtol who are encamped upon the plain."

"So they are using equilibrimotors," I said; "it seems strange that any peoples from the frozen north should have these. They were absolutely unknown in Okar when I was there."

The equilibrimotor is an ingenious device for individual flying. It consists of a broad belt, not unlike the life belt used aboard passenger ships on Earth; the belt is filled with the eighth Barsoomian ray, or ray of propulsion, to a sufficient degree to equalize the pull of gravity and thus to maintain a person in equilibrium between that force and the opposite force exerted by the eighth ray. Attached to the back of the belt is a small radium motor, the controls for which are on the front of the belt; while rigidly attached to and projecting from the upper rim of the belt is a strong, light wing with small hand levers for quickly altering its position. I could understand that they might prove very effective for landing troops in an enemy city by night.

I had listened to Gan Hor with feelings of the deepest concern, for I knew that Gathol was not a powerful country and that a long and persistent siege must assuredly reduce it unless outside help came. Gathol depends for its food supplies upon the plains which comprise practically all of its territory. The far northwest corner of the country is cut by one of Barsoom's famous canals; and here the grains, and vegetables, and fruits which supply the city are raised; while upon her plains graze the herds that supply her with meat. And enemy surrounding the city would cut off all these supplies; and while Gahan doubtless had reserves stored in the city, they could not last indefinitely.

In discussing this with Gan Hor, I remarked that if I could get hold of a flier I'd return to Helium and bring a fleet of her mighty war ships and transports with guns and men enough to wipe Hin Abtol and his Panars off the face of Barsoom.

"Well," said Gan Hor, "your flier is here; it came with Hin Abtol's fleet. One of my men recognized it and your insigne upon it the moment he saw it; and we have all been wondering how Hin Abtol acquired it; but then, he has ships from a score of different nations, and has not bothered to remove their insignia."

"He found it in a courtyard in the deserted city of Horz," I explained; "and when he was attacked by green men, he made off in it with a couple of his warriors, leaving the others to be killed."

Just then the padwar who had gone to fetch Llana, Pan Dan Chee, and Jad-han returned with his detachment—and three riderless thoats!

"They were not there," he said; "though we searched everywhere, we could not find them; but there was blood on the ground where they had been."

4

So Llana of Gathol was lost to me again! That she had been captured by Hin Abtol's warriors, there seemed little doubt. I asked Gan Hor for a thoat, that I might ride out and examine the spot at which the party had been taken; and he not only acceded to my request, but accompanied me with a detachment of his warriors.

There had evidently been a fight at the place that I had left them; the vegetation was trampled, and there was blood upon it; but so resilient is this mosslike carpeting of the dead sea bottoms of Mars, that, except for the blood, the last traces of the encounter were fast disappearing; and there was no indication of the direction taken by Llana's captors.

"How far are their lines from here?" I asked Gan Hor.

"About nine haads," he replied—that is not quite three Earth miles.

"We might as well return to your camp," I said; "we haven't a sufficiently strong force to accomplish anything now. I shall return after dark."

"We can make a little raid on one of their encampments tonight," suggested Gan Hor.

"I shall go alone," I told him; "I have a plan."

"But it won't be safe," he objected. "I have a hundred men with whom I am constantly harassing them; we should be glad to ride with you."

"I am going only for information, Gan Hor; I can get that better alone."

We returned to camp, and with the help of one of Gan Hor's warriors I applied to my face and body the red pigment that I always carry with me for use when I find it necessary to disguise myself as a native born red man—a copper colored ointment such as had first been given me by the Ptor brothers of Zodanga many years ago.

After dark I set out on thoatback, accompanied by Gan Hor and a couple of his warriors; as I had accepted his offer of transportation to a point much nearer the Panar lines. Fortunately the heavens were temporarily moonless, and we came quite close to the enemy's first fires before I dismounted and bid my new friends goodby.

"Good luck!" said Gan Hor; "and you'll need it."

Kor-an was one of the warriors who had accompanied us. "I'd like to go with you, Prince," he said; "thus I might atone for the thing I did."

"If I could take anyone, I'd take you, Kor-an," I assured him. "Anyway, you have nothing to atone for; but if you want to do something for me, promise that you will fight always for Tara of Helium and Llana of Gathol."

"On my sword, I swear it," he said; and then I left them and made my way cautiously toward the Panar camp.

Once again, as upon so many other occasions, I used the tactics of another race of red warriors—the Apaches of our own Southwest—worming my way upon my belly closer and closer toward the lines of the enemy. I could see the forms of warriors clustered about their fires, and I could hear their voices and their rough laughter; and, as I drew nearer, the oaths and obscenities which seem to issue most naturally from the mouths of fighting men; and when a gust of wind blew from the camp toward me, I could even smell the sweat and the leather mingling with the acrid fumes of the smoke of their fires.

A sentry paced his post between me and the fires; when he came closest to me, I flattened myself upon the ground. I heard him yawn. When he was almost on top of me, I rose up before him; and before he could voice a warning cry, I seized him by the throat. Three times I drove my dagger into his heart. I hate to kill like that; but now there was no other way, and it was not for myself that I killed him—it was for Llana of Gathol, for Tara of Helium, and for Dejah Thoris, my beloved princess.

Just as I lowered his body to the ground, a warrior at a nearby fire arose and looked out toward us. "What was that?" he asked his fellows.

"The sentry," one of them replied; "there he is now." I was slowly pacing the post of the departed, hoping none would come to investigate.

"I could have sworn I saw two men scuffling there," said the first speaker.

"You are always seeing things," said a third.

I walked the post until they had ceased to discuss the matter and had turned their attention elsewhere; then I knelt beside the dead man and removed his harness and weapons, which I immediately donned. Now I was, to outward appearances anyway, a soldier of Hin Abtol, a Panar from some glazed, hothouse city of the frozen North.

Walking to the far end of my post, I left it and entered the camp at some distance from the group which included the warrior whose suspicions I had aroused. Although I passed close to another group of warriors, no one paid any attention to me. Other individuals were wandering around from fire to fire, and so my movements attracted no notice.

I must have walked fully a haad inside the lines away from my point of entry before I felt that it would be safe to stop and mix with the warriors. Finally I saw a lone warrior sitting beside a fire, and approached him.

"Kaor!" I said, using the universal greeting of Barsoom.

"Kaor!" he replied. "Sit down. I am a stranger here and have no friends in this dar." A dar is a unit of a thousand men, analogous to our Earthly regiment. "I just came down today with a fresh contingent from Pankor. It is good to move about and see the world again, after having been frozen in for fifty years."

"You haven't been away from Pankor for fifty years!" I exclaimed, guessing that Pankor was the name of the Arctic city from which he hailed, and hoping that I was guessing right.

"No," he said; "and you! How long were you frozen in?"

"I have never been to Pankor," I said; "I am a panthan who has just joined up with Hin Abtol's forces since they came south." I thought this the safest position to take, since I should be sure to arouse suspicion were I to claim familiarity with Pankor, when I had never been there.

"Well," said my companion, "you must be crazy."

"Why?" I asked.

"Nobody but a crazy man would put himself in the power of Hin Abtol. Well, you've done it; and now you'll be taken to Pankor after this war is over, unless you're lucky enough to be killed; and you'll be frozen in there until Hin Abtol needs you for another campaign. What's your name?"

"Dotor Sojat," I replied, falling back on that old time name the green Martian horde of Thark had given me so many years before.

"Mine is Em-tar; I am from Kobol."

"I thought you said you were from Pankor."

"I'm a Kobolian by birth," he explained. "Where are you from?"

"We panthans have no country," I reminded him.

"But you must have been born somewhere," he insisted.

"Perhaps the less said about that the better," I said, attempting a sly wink.

He laughed. "Sorry I asked," he said.

Sometimes, when a man has committed a political crime, a huge reward is offered for information concerning his whereabouts; so, as well as changing his name, he never divulges the name of his country. I let Em-tar think that I was a fugitive from justice.

"How do you think this campaign is going?" I asked.

"If Hin Abtol can starve them out, he may win," replied Em-tar; "but from what I have heard he could never take the city by storm. These Gatholians are great fighters, which is more than can be said for those who fight under Hin Abtol—our hearts aren't in it; we have no feeling of loyalty for Hin Abtol; but these Gatholians now, they're fighting for their homes and their jed; and they love 'em both. They say that Gahan's Princess is a daughter of The Warlord of Barsoom. Say, if he hears about this and brings a fleet and an army from Helium, we might just as well start digging our graves."

"Are we taking many prisoners?" I asked.

"Not many. Three were taken this morning; one of them was the daughter of Gahan, the Jed of Gathol; the other two were men."

"That's interesting," I said; "I wonder what Hin Abtol will do with the daughter of Gahan."

"That I wouldn't know," replied Em-tar, "but they say he's sent her off to Pankor already. You hear a lot of rumors in an army, though; and most of them are wrong."

"I suppose Hin Abtol has a big fleet of fliers," I said.

"He's got a lot of old junk, and not many men capable of flying what he has got."

"I'm a flier," I said.

"You'd better not let 'em know it, or they'll have you on board some old wreck," advised Em-tar.

"Where's their landing field here?"

"Down that way about a haad;" he pointed in the direction I had been going when I stopped to talk with him.

"Well, goodby, Em-tar," I said, rising.

"Where are you going?"

"To fly for Hin Abtol of Pankor," I said.

5

I made my way through the camp to where a number of fliers were lined up; it was an extremely ragged, unmilitary line, suggesting inefficiency; and the ships were the most surprising aggregation of obsolete relics I have ever seen; most of them were museum pieces.

Some warriors were sitting around fires nearby; and, assuming that they were attached to the flying service, I approached them.

"Where is the flying officer in command?" I asked.

"Over there," said one of the men, pointing at the largest ship on the line. "Why—do you want to see him?"

"Yes."

"Well, he's probably drunk."

"He *is* drunk," said another.

"What's his name?" I asked.

"Odwar Phor San," replied my informant. Odwar is about the same as general, or brigadier general. He commands ten thousand men in the army and a fleet in the navy.

"Thanks," I said; "I'll go over and see him."

"You wouldn't, if you knew him; he's as mean as an ulsio."

I walked over to the big ship. It was battered and weatherbeaten, and must have been at least fifty years old. A boarding ladder hung down amidships, and at its foot stood a warrior with drawn sword.

"What do you want?" he demanded.

"I have a message for Odwar Phor San," I said.

"Who is it from?"

"That is none of your business," I told him; "send word to the odwar that Dotor Sojat wishes to see him on an important matter."

The fellow saluted with mock elaborateness. "I didn't know we had a jedwar among us," he said. "Why didn't you tell me?"

Now, jedwar is the highest rank in a Barsoomian army or navy, other than that of jed or jeddak or Warlord, a rank created especially for me by the jeddaks of five empires. That warrior would have been surprised could he have known that he had conferred upon me a title far inferior to my own.

I laughed at his little joke, and said, "One never knows whom one is entertaining."

"If you really have a message for the old ulsio, I'll call the deck watch; but, by Issus, you'd better have a message of importance."

"I have," I assured him; and I spoke the truth, for it was of tremendous importance to me; so he hailed the deck watch and told him to tell the odwar that Dotor Sojat had come with an important message for him.

I waited about five minutes, and then I was summoned aboard and conducted to one of the cabins. A gross, slovenly man sat before a table on which was a large tankard and several heavy, metal goblets. He looked at me scowlingly out of bleary eyes.

"What does that son of a calot want now?" he demanded.

I guessed that he referred to a superior officer, and probably to Hin Abtol. Well, if he thought I bore a message from Hin Abtol, so much the better.

"I am to report to you as an experienced flier," I said.

"He sent you at this time of night to report to me as a flier?" he almost shouted at me.

"You have few experienced fliers," I said. "I am a panthan who has flown every type of ship in the navy of Helium. I gathered that you would be glad to get me before some other commander snapped me up. I am a navigator, and familiar with all modern instruments; but if you don't want me, I shall then be free to attach myself elsewhere."

He was befuddled by strong drink, or I'd probably never have gotten away with such a bluff. He pretended to be considering the matter seriously; and while he considered it, he poured himself another drink, which he swallowed in two or three gulps—what didn't run down his front. Then he filled another goblet and pushed it across the table toward me, slopping most of its contents on the table top.

"Have drink!" he said.

"Not now," I said; "I never drink when I am on duty."

"You're not on duty."

"I am always on duty; I may have to take a ship up at any moment."

He pondered this for several minutes with the assistance of another drink; then he filled another goblet and pushed it across the table toward me. "Have drink," he said.

I now had two full goblets in front of me; it was evident that Phor San had not noticed that I had failed to drink the first one.

"What ship shall I command?" I asked; I was promoting myself rapidly. Phor San paid no attention to my question, being engaged in what was now becoming a delicate and difficult operation—the pouring of another drink; most of it went on the table, from where it ran down into his lap.

"What ship did you say I was to command?" I demanded. He looked bewildered for a moment; then he tried to draw himself together with military dignity. "You will command the Dusar, Dwar," he said; then he filled another goblet and pushed it toward me. "Have drink, Dwar," he said. My promotion was confirmed.

I walked over to a desk covered with an untidy litter of papers, and searched until I found an official blank; on it I wrote:

To Dwar Dotor Sojat:
You will immediately take over command of ship Dusar.

By order of

Odwar Commanding

After finding a cloth and wiping the liquor from the table in front of him, I laid the order down and handed him a pen.

"You forgot to sign this, Odwar," I said. He was commencing to weave, and I saw that I must hurry.

"Sign what?" he demanded, reaching for the tankard.

I pushed it away from him, took his hand, and placed the pen point at the right place on the order blank. "Sign here," I ordered.

"Sign here," he repeated, and laboriously scrawled his name; then he fell forward on the table, asleep. I had been just in time.

I went on deck; both moons were now in the sky, Cluros just above the horizon, Thuria a little higher; by the time Cluros approached zenith, Thuria would have completed her orbit around Barsoom and passed him, so swift her flight through the heavens.

The deck watch approached me. "Where lies the Dusar?" I asked.

He pointed down the line. "About the fifth or sixth ship, I think," he said.

I went overside; and as I reached the ground, the sentry there asked, "Was the old ulsio as drunk as ever?"

"He was perfectly sober," I replied.

"Then some one had better send for the doctor," he said, "for he must be sick."

I walked along the line, and at the fifth ship I approached the sentry at the foot of its ladder. "Is this the Dusar?" I asked.

"Can't you read?" he demanded, impudently.

I look up then at the insigne on the ship's bow; it was the Dusar. "Can you read?" I asked, and held the order up in front of him.

He snapped to attention and saluted. "I couldn't tell by your metal," he said, sullenly. He was quite right; I was wearing the metal of a common warrior.

I looked the ship over. From the ground it hadn't a very promising appearance—just a disreputable, obsolete old hulk. Then I climbed the ladder and stepped to the deck of my new command; there was no boatswain's call to pipe the side; there was only one man on watch; and he was curled up on the deck, fast asleep.

I walked over and poked him with the toe of a sandal. "Wake up, there!" I ordered.

He opened an eye and looked up at me; then he leaped to his feet. "Who are you?" he demanded. "What are you doing here? What do you mean by kicking me in the ribs and waking me up?"

"One question at a time, my man," I said. "I shall answer your first question, and that will answer the others also." I held the order out to him.

As he took it, he said, "Don't call me my man, you—" But he stopped there; he had read the order. He saluted and handed the order back to me, but I noticed just the suggestion of a grin on his face.

"Why did you smile?" I asked.

"I was thinking that you probably got the softest job in Hin Abtol's navy," he said.

"What do you mean?"

"You won't have anything to do; the Dusar is out of commission—she won't fly."

So! Perhaps Odwar Phor San was not as drunk as I had thought him.

6

The deck of the Dusar was weatherbeaten and filthy; everything was in disorder, but what difference did that make if the ship wouldn't fly?

"How many officers and men comprise her complement?" I asked.

The fellow grinned and pointed to himself. "One," he said, "or, rather, two, now that you are here."

I asked him his name, and he said that it was Fo-nar. In the United States he would have been known as an ordinary seaman, but the Martian words for seaman and sailor are now as obsolete as the oceans with which they died, almost from the memory of man. All sailors and soldiers are known as *thans*, which I have always translated as *warriors*.

"Well, Fo-nar," I said; "let's have a look at our ship. What's wrong with her? Why won't she fly?"

"It's the engine, sir," he said; "it won't start any more."

"I'll have a look over the ship," I said, "and then we'll see if we can't do something about the engine."

I took Fo-nar with me and went below. Everything there was filthy and in disorder. "How long has she been out of commission?" I asked.

"About a month."

"You certainly couldn't have made all this mess by yourself in a month," I said.

"No, sir; she was always like this even when she was flying," he said.

"Who commanded her? Whoever he was, he should be cashiered for permitting a ship to get in this condition."

"He won't ever be cashiered, sir," said Fo-nar.

"Why?" I asked.

"Because he got drunk and fell overboard on our last flight," Fo-nar explained, with a grin.

I inspected the guns, there were eight of them, four on a side beside smaller bow and stern guns on deck; they all seemed to be in pretty fair condition, and there was plenty of ammunition. The bomb racks in the bilge were full, and there was a bomb trap forward and another aft.

There were quarters for twenty-five men and three officers,

a good galley, and plenty of provisions. If I had not seen Odwar Phor San, I could not have understood why all this material—guns, ammunition, provisions, and tackle—should have been left on a ship permanently out of commission. The ship appeared to me to be about ten years old—that is, after a careful inspection; superficially, it looked a hundred.

I told Fo-nar to go back on deck and go to sleep, if he wished to; and then I went into the dwar's cabin and lay down; I hadn't had much sleep the night before, and I was tired. It was daylight when I awoke, and I found Fo-nar in the galley getting his breakfast. I told him to prepare mine, and after we had both eaten I went to have a look at the engine.

It hurt me to go through that ship and see the condition its drunken skipper had permitted it to get into. I love these Barsoomian fliers, and I have been in the navy of Helium for so many years that ships have acquired almost human personalities for me. I have designed them; I have superintended their construction; I have developed new ideas in equipment, engines, and armament; and several standard flying and navigating instruments are of my invention. If there is anything I don't know about a modern Martian flier; then nobody else knows it.

I found tools and practically dismantled the engine, checking every part. While I was doing this, I had Fo-nar start cleaning up the ship. I told him to start with my cabin and then tackle the galley next. It would have taken one man a month or more to put the Dusar in even fair condition, but at least we would make a start.

I hadn't been working on the engine half an hour before I found what was wrong with it—just dirt! Every feed line was clogged; and that marvellous, concentrated, Martian fuel could not reach the motor.

I was appalled by the evidence of such stupidity and inefficiency, though not entirely surprised; drunken commanders and Barsoomian fliers just don't go together. In the navy of Helium, no officer drinks while on board ship or on duty; and not one of them drinks to excess at any time.

If an officer were ever drunk on board his ship, the crew would see to it that he was never drunk again; they know that their lives are in the hands of their officers, and they don't purpose trusting them to a drunken man—they simply push the officer overboard. It is such a well established custom, or used to be before drinking on the part of officers practically ceased, that no action was ever taken against the warrior who took discipline into his own hands, even though the act were witnessed by officers. I rather surmised that this time honored custom had had something to do with the deplorable accident that had robbed the Dusar of her former commander.

The day was practically gone by the time I had cleaned every part of the engine thoroughly and reassembled it; then I started it; and the sweet, almost noiseless and vibrationless, hum of it was music to my ears. I had a ship—a ship that would fly!

One man can operate such a ship, but of course he can't fight it. Where, however, could I get men? I didn't want just any men; I wanted good fighting men who would just as lief fight against Hin Abtol as not.

Pondering this problem, I went to my cabin to clean up; it looked spick-and-span. Fo-nar had done a good job; he had also laid out the harness and metal of a dwar—doubtless the property of the late commander. Bathed and properly garbed, I felt like a new man as I stepped out onto the upper deck. Fo-nar snapped to attention and saluted.

"Fo-nar," I said, "are you a Panar?"

"I should say not," he replied with some asperity. "I am from Jahar originally, but now I have no country—I am a panthan."

"You were there during the reign of Tul Axtar?" I asked.

"Yes," he replied; "it was on his account that I became an exile—I tried to kill him, and I got caught; I just barely escaped with my life. I cannot go back so long as he is alive."

"You can go back, then," I said; "Tul Axtar is dead."

"How do you know, sir?"

"I know the man who killed him."

"Just my luck!" exclaimed Fo-nar; "now that I might go back, I can't."

"Why can't you?"

"For the same reason, sir, that where ever you are from you'll never go back, unless you are from Panar, which I doubt."

"No, I am not from Panar," I said; "but what makes you think I won't go back to my own country?"

"Because no one upon whom Hin Abtol gets his hands ever escapes, other than through death."

7

"Oh, come, Fo-nar," I said; "that is ridiculous. What is to prevent either one of us from deserting?"

"If we deserted here," he replied, "we would immediately be picked up by the Gatholians and killed; after this campaign is over, we will not make a landing until we reach Panar; and from Panar there is no escape. Hin Abtol's ships never stop at a friendly city, where one might find an opportunity to escape; for there are no cities friendly to Hin Abtol. He attacks every city that he believes he can take, sacks it, and flies away with all the loot he can gather and with as many prisoners as his ships will carry—mostly men; they say he has a million now, and that he plans eventually to conquer Helium and then all of Barsoom. He took me prisoner when he sacked Raxar on his way down from Panar to Gathol; I was serving there in the army of the jed."

"You would like to return to Jahar?" I asked.

"Certainly," he replied. "My mate is there, if she still lives; I have been gone twenty years."

"You feel no loyalty toward Hin Abtol?"

"Absolutely none," he replied; "why?"

"I think I can tell you. I have the same power that all Barsoomians have of being able to read the mind of another when he happens to be off guard; and a couple of times, Fo-nar, your subconscious mind has dropped its guard and permitted me to read your thoughts; I have learned several things about you. One is that you are constantly wondering about me—who I am and whether I am to be trusted. For another thing, I have learned that you despise the Panars. I also discovered that you were no common warrior in Jahar, but a dwar in the jeddak's service—you were thinking about that when you first saw me in the metal and harness of a dwar."

Fo-nar smiled. "You read well," he said; "I must be more careful. You read much better than I do, or else you guard your thoughts more jealously than I; for I have not been able to obtain even the slightest inkling of what is passing in your mind."

"No man has ever been able to read my mind," I said, "and that is very strange, too, and quite inexplicable. The Martians have developed mind reading to a point where it is a fine art, but none has ever been able to read my mind. Perhaps that is because it is the mind of an Earth man, and may account for the fact that telepathy has not advanced far on our planet.

"You are fortunate," said Fo-nar; "but please go on and tell me what you started to."

"Well," I said, "in the first place, I have repaired the engine—the Dusar can now fly."

"Good!" exclaimed Fo-nar. "I said you were no Panar; they are the stupidest people in the world. No Panar could ever have repaired it; all they can do is let things go to wrack and ruin. Go on."

"Now we need a crew. Can we find from fifteen to twenty-five men whom we can trust and who can fight—men who will follow me anywhere I lead them to win their freedom from Hin Abtol?"

"I can find you all the men you need," replied Fo-nar.

"Get busy then," I said; "you are now First Padwar of the Dusar."

"I am getting up in the world again," said Fo-nar, laughing. "I'll start out immediately, but don't expect a miracle —it may take a little time to find the right men."

"Have them report to the ship after dark, and tell them to be sure that no one sees them. What can we do about that sentry at the foot of the ladder?"

"The one who was on duty when you came aboard is all right," said Fo-nar; "he'll come with us. He's on from the eighth to the ninth zodes, and I'll tell the men to come at that time."

"Good luck, padwar!" I said, as he went overside.

The remainder of the day dragged slowly. I spent some time in my cabin looking through the ship's papers. Barsoomian ships keep a log just as Earth ships do, and I occupied several hours looking through the log of the Dusar. The ship had been captured four years before while on a scientific expedition to the Arctic, since then, under Panar commanders, the log had been very poorly kept. Some times there were no entries for a week, and those that were made were unprofessional and sloppy; the more I learned about the Panars the less I liked them—and to think that the creature who ruled them aspired to conquer a world!

About the end of the seventh zode Fo-nar returned. "I had much better luck than I anticipated," he said; "every man I approached knew three or four he could vouch for; so it didn't take long to get twenty-five. I think, too, that I have just the man for Second Padwar. He was a padwar in the army of Helium, and has served on many of her ships."

"What is his name?" I asked. "I have known many men from Helium."

"He is Tan Hadron of Hastor," replied Fo-nar.

Tan Hadron of Hastor! Why, he was one of my finest officers. What ill luck could have brought him to the navy of Hin Abtol?

"Tan Hadron of Hastor," I said aloud; "the name sounds a little familiar; it is possible that I knew him." I did not wish anyone to know that I was John Carter, Prince of Helium; for if it became known, and I was captured, Hin Abtol could have wrested an enormous ransom from Tardos Mors, Jeddak of Helium and grandfather of my mate, Dejah Thoris.

Immediately after the eighth zode, warriors commenced to come aboard the Dusar. I had instructed Fo-nar to immediately send them below to their quarters, for I feared that too much life on the deck of the Dusar might attract attention; I had also told him to send Tan Hadron to my cabin as soon as he came aboard.

About half after the eighth zode someone scratched on my door; and when I bade him enter, Tan Hadron stepped into the cabin. My red skin and Panar harness deceived him, and he did not recognize me.

"I am Tan Hadron of Hastor," he said; "Padwar Fo-nar instructed me to report to you."

"You are not a Panar?" I asked.

He stiffened. "I am a Heliumite from the city of Hastor," he said, proudly.

"Where is Hastor?" I asked.

He looked surprised at such ignorance. "It lies directly south of Greater Helium, sir; about five hundred haads. You will pardon me," he added, "but I understood from Padwar Fo-nar that you knew many men from Helium, and so I imagined that you had visited the empire; in fact he gave me to understand that you had served in our navy."

"That is neither here nor there," I said. "Fo-nar has recommended you for the post of Second Padwar aboard the Dusar. You will have to serve me faithfully and follow where ever I lead; your reward will consist of your freedom from Hin Abtol."

I could see that he was a little bit skeptical about the whole proposition now that he had met me—a man who had never heard of Hastor couldn't amount to much; but he touched the hilt of his sword and said that he would follow me loyally.

"Is that all, sir?" he asked.

"Yes," I said; "for the time being. After the men are all aboard I shall have them mustered below deck, and at that time I shall name the officers; please be there."

He saluted, and turned to go.

"Oh, by the way," I called to him, "how is Tavia?"

At that he wheeled about as though he had been shot, and his eyes went wide. "What do you know of Tavia, sir?" he demanded. Tavia is his mate.

"I know that she is a very lovely girl, and that I can't understand why you are not back in Hastor with her; or are you stationed in Helium now?"

He came a little closer, and looked at me intently. As a

matter of fact, the light was not very good in my cabin, or he would have recognized me sooner. Finally his jaw dropped, and then he unbuckled his sword and threw it at my feet. "John Carter!" he exclaimed.

"Not so loud, Hadron," I cautioned; "no one here knows who I am; and no one must, but you."

"You had a good time with me, didn't you, sir?" he laughed.

"It has been some time since I have had anything to laugh about," I said; "so I hope you will forgive me; now tell me about yourself and how you got into this predicament."

"Perhaps half the navy of Helium is looking for Llana of Gathol and you," he said. "Rumors of the whereabouts of one or the other of you have come from all parts of Barsoom. Like many another officer I was scouting for you or Llana in a one man flier. I had bad luck, sir; and here I am. One of Hin Abtol's ships shot me down, and then landed and captured me."

"Llana of Gathol and I, with two companions, were also shot down by one of Hin Abtol's ships," I told him. "While I was searching for food, they were captured, presumably by some of Hin Abtol's warriors, as we landed behind their lines. We must try to ascertain, if possible, where Llana is; then we can plan intelligently. Possibly some of our recruits may have information; see what you can find out."

He saluted and left my cabin. It was good to know that I had such a man as Tan Hadron of Hastor as one of my lieutenants.

8

Shortly after Tan Hadron left my cabin, Fo-nar entered to report that all but one of the recruits had reported and that he had the men putting the flier in shipshape condition. He seemed a little bit worried about something, and I asked him what it was.

"It's about this warrior who hasn't reported," he replied. "The man who persuaded him to join up is worried, too. He said he hadn't known him long, but since he came aboard the *Dusar* he's met a couple of men who know the fellow well; and they say he's an ulsio."

"Well, there's nothing we can do about it now," I said. "If this man talks and arouses suspicion, we may have to take off in a hurry. Have you assigned each man to his station?"

"Tan Hadron is doing that now," he replied. "I think we have found a splendid officer in that man."

"I am sure of it," I agreed. "Be sure that four men are detailed to cut the cables instantly, if it becomes necessary for us to make a quick getaway."

When on the ground, the larger Martian fliers are moored to four deadmen, one on either side at the bow and one on either side at the stern. Unless a ship is to return to the same anchorage, these deadmen are dug up and taken aboard before she takes off. In the event of forced departure, such as I anticipated might be necessary in our case, the cables attached to the deadmen are often cut.

Fo-nar hadn't been gone from my cabin five minutes before he came hurrying in again. "I guess we're in for it, sir," he said; "Odwar Phor San is coming aboard! That missing recruit is with him; he must have reported all he knew to Phor San."

"When the odwar comes aboard, bring him down to my cabin; and then order the men to their stations; see that the four men you have detailed for that duty stand by the mooring cables with axes; ask Tan Hadron to start the engine and stand by to take off; post a man outside my cabin door to pass the word to take off when I give the signal; I'll clap my hands twice."

Fo-nar was gone only a couple of minutes before he returned. "He won't come below," he reported; "he's storming around up there like a mad thoat, demanding to have the man brought on deck who gave orders to recruit a crew for the Dusar."

"Is Tan Hadron at the controls ready to start the engine?" I asked.

"He is," replied Fo-nar.

"He will start them, then, as soon as I come on deck; at the same time post your men at the mooring cables; tell them what the signal will be."

I waited a couple of minutes after Fo-nar had left; then I went on deck. Phor San was stamping up and down, evidently in a terrible rage; he was also a little drunk.

I walked up to him and saluted. "Did you send for me, sir?" I asked.

"Who are you?" he demanded.

"Dwar commanding the Dusar, sir," I replied.

"Who said so?" he yelled. "Who assigned you to this ship? Who assigned you to any ship?"

"You did, sir."

"I?" he screamed. "I never saw you before. You are under arrest. Arrest him!" He turned to a warrior at his elbow

—my missing recruit, as I suspected—and started to speak to him again.

"Wait a minute," I said; "look at this; here's a written order over your own signature assigning me to the command of the Dusar." I held the order up where he could read it in the bright light of Mars' two moons.

He looked surprised and a little crestfallen for just a moment; then he blustered, "It's a forgery! Anyway, it didn't give you authority to recruit warriors for the ship." He was weakening.

"What good is a fighting ship without warriors?" I demanded.

"You don't need warriors on a ship that won't fly, you idiot," he came back. "You thought you were pretty cute, getting me to sign that order; but I was a little cuter—I knew the Dusar wouldn't fly."

"Well, then, why all the fuss, sir?" I asked.

"Because you're plotting something; I don't know what, but I'm going to find out—getting men aboard this ship secretly at night! I rescind that order, and I place you under arrest."

I had hoped to get him off the ship peaceably, for I wanted to make sure of Llana's whereabouts before taking off. One man had told me that he had heard that she was on a ship bound for Pankor, but that was not definite. I also wished to know if Hin Abtol was with her.

"Very well, Phor San," I said; "now let me tell you something. I am in command of this ship, and I intend to stay in command. I'll give you and this rat here three seconds to get over the side, for the Dusar will take off in three seconds," and then I clapped my hands twice.

Phor San laughed a sneering laugh. "I told you it wouldn't fly," he said; "now come along! If you won't come quietly, you'll be taken;" he pointed overside. I looked, and saw a strong detachment of warriors marching toward the Dusar; at the same time, the Dusar rose from the ground.

Phor San stood in front of me, gloating. "What are you going to do now?" he demanded.

"Take you for a little ride, Phor San," I replied, and pointed overside.

He took one look, and then ran to the rail. His warriors were looking up at him in futile bewilderment. Phor San shouted to the padwar commanding them, "Order the Okar to pursue and take this ship!" The Okar was his flagship.

"Perhaps you'd like to come down to my cabin and have a little drink," I suggested, the liquor of the former commander being still there. "You go with him," I ordered the recruit who had betrayed us; "you will find liquor in one of the cab-

inets;" then I went to the bridge. On the way, I sent a warrior to summon Fo-nar. I told Tan Hadron to circle above
the line of ships; and when Fo-nar reported, I gave him his
orders, and he went below.

"We can't let them take to the air," I told Tan Hadron;
"this is not a fast ship, and if several of them overhauled us
we wouldn't have a chance."

Following my orders, Tan Hadron flew low toward the first
ship on the line; it was the Okar, and she was about to take
off. I signalled down to Fo-nar, and an instant later there was
a terrific explosion aboard the Okar—our first bomb had
made a clean hit! Slowly we moved down the line, dropping
our bombs; but before we had reached the middle of it, ships
at the lower end were taking off and projectiles were bursting
around us from the ground batteries.

"It's time we got out of here," I said to Tan Hadron. He
opened the throttle wide then, and the Dusar rose rapidly in
a zig zag course.

Our own guns were answering the ground batteries, and
evidently very effectively, for we were not hit once. I felt that
we had come out of the affair so far very fortunately. We
hadn't disabled as many ships as I had hoped that we might,
and there were already several in the air which would doubtless pursue us; I could see one ship on our tail already, but
she was out of range and apparently not gaining on us rapidly, if at all.

I told Tan Hadron to set his course due North, and then
I sent for Fo-nar and told him to muster all hands on deck;
I wanted a chance to look over my crew and explain what
our expedition involved. There was time for this now, while
no ships were within range of us, which might not be true in
a short time.

The men came piling up from below and from their stations on deck. They were, for the most part, a hardbitten lot,
veterans, I should say, of many a campaign. As I looked
them over, I could see that they were sizing me up; they
were probably wondering more about me than I was about
them, for I was quite sure what they would do if they
thought they could get the upper hand of me—I'd "fall" overboard, and they would take over the ship; then they'd quarrel
among themselves as to what they would do with it and
where they would fly it; in the end, half a dozen of the hardiest would survive, make for the nearest city, sell the Dusar,
and have a wild orgy—if they didn't wreck her before.

I asked each man his name and his past experience; there
were, among the twenty-three, eleven panthans and twelve
assassins; and they had fought all over the world. Seven of

the panthans were from Helium, or had served in the Helium navy. I knew that these men were accustomed to discipline. The assassins were from various cities, scattered all over Barsoom. I didn't need to ask them, to be quite sure that each had incurred the wrath of his Guild and been forced to flee in order to escape assassination himself; they were a tough lot.

"We are flying to Pankor," I told them, "in search of the daughter of the jed of Gathol, who has been abducted by Hin Abtol. There may be a great deal of fighting before we get her; if we succeed and live, we will fly to Helium; there I shall turn the ship over to you, and you can do what you please with it."

"You're not flying me to Pankor," said one of the assassins; "I've been there for twenty-five years, and I'm not going back."

This was insubordination verging on mutiny. In a well disciplined navy, it would have been a very simple thing to handle; but here, where there was no higher authority than I, I had to take a very different course from a commander with a powerful government behind him. I stepped up to the man and slapped him as I had slapped Kor-an; and, like Kor-an, he went down.

"You're flying wherever I fly you," I said; "I'll have no insubordination on this ship."

He leaped to his feet and whipped out his sword, and there was nothing for me to do but draw also.

"The penalty for this, you understand, is death," I said, "—unless you sheathe your sword immediately."

"I'll sheathe it in your belly, you calot!" he cried, making a terrific lunge at me, which I parried easily and then ran him through the right shoulder. I knew that I would have to kill him, for the discipline of the ship and perhaps the fate of Llana of Gathol might hinge on this question of my supremacy and my authority; but first I must give an exhibition of swordplay that would definitely assure the other members of the crew that the lethal thrust was no accident, as they might have thought had I killed him at once.

So I played with him as a cat plays with a mouse, until the other members of the crew, who had stood silent and scowling at first, commenced to ridicule him.

"I thought you were going to sheathe your sword in his belly," taunted one.

"Why don't you kill him, Gan-ho?" demanded another. "I thought you were such a great swordsman."

"I can tell you one thing," said a third: "you are not going to fly to Pankor, or anywhere else. Goodby, Gan-ho! you are dead."

Just to show the other men how easily I could do it, I disarmed Gan-ho, sending his blade rattling across the deck. He stood for a moment glaring at me like a mad beast; then he turned and ran across the deck and dove over the rail. I was glad that I did not have to kill him.

I turned to the men gathered before me. "Is there any other who will not fly to Pankor?" I asked, and waited for a reply.

Several of them grinned sheepishly; and there was much scuffing of sandals on the deck, but no one replied.

"I had you mustered here to tell where we were flying and why; also that Fo-nar is First Padwar, Tan Hadron is Second Padwar, and I am your Dwar—we are to be obeyed. Return to your stations."

9

Shortly after the men dispersed, Phor San and his satellite appeared on deck; they were both drunk. Phor San came toward me and stopped in front of me waving an erratic finger at me. He stunk of the liquor he had been drinking.

"In the name of Hin Abtol, Jeddak of Jeddaks of the North," he declaimed, "I order you to turn over the command of this ship to me, or suffer the full consequences of your crime of mutiny."

I saw the men on deck eyeing the two banefully. "You'd better go below," I said; "you might fall overboard."

Phor San turned to some of the crew members. "I am Odwar Phor San," he announced, "commander of the fleet; put this man in irons and return the ship to the air field!"

"I think you have gone far enough, Phor San," I said; "if you continue, I shall have to assume that you are attempting to incite my crew to mutiny, and act accordingly. Go below!"

"You trying to give me orders on one of my ships?" he demanded. "I'll have you understand that I am Phor San—"

"Commander of the fleet," I finished for him, "Here," I said to a couple of warriors standing near, "take these two below, and if they don't behave themselves, tie them up."

Fuming and blustering, Phor San was dragged below. His companion went quietly; I guess he knew what was good for him.

The one ship was still hanging onto our tail and not gaining perceptibly, but there were two just behind her which were overhauling both of us.

"That doesn't look so good," I said to Tan Hadron, who was standing at my side.

"Let's show them something," he said.

"What, for instance?" I asked.

"Do you remember that maneuver of yours the last time Helium was attacked by an enemy fleet, where you got the flag ship and two other ships that thought you were running from them?"

"All right," I said, "we'll try it." Then I sent for Fo-nar and gave him full instructions. While we were talking, I heard a series of piercing screams, gradually diminishing in the distance; but my mind was so occupied with this other matter, that I scarcely gave them a thought. Presently I got an "all's ready" report from Fo-nar, and told Tan Hadron to go ahead with the maneuver.

The Dusar was going full speed ahead against a strong head wind, and when he brought her about she sped toward the oncoming ships like a racing thoat. Two of them were in position to open up on us when we came within range; however, they commenced firing too soon. We quite properly held our fire until it was effective. We were all firing our bow guns—the only ones that could be brought to bear; and no one was doing much damage.

As we drew closer to the leading ship, I saw considerable confusion on her deck; I imagine they thought we were going to ram them. Just then our gunner succeeded in putting her bow gun out of commission, which was fortunate indeed for us; then Tan Hadron elevated the Dusar's nose, and we rose above the leading ship. As we passed over her, there was a terrific explosion on her deck and she burst into flame. Tan Hadron turned to port so fast that the Dusar lay over on her side, and we on deck had to hang to anything we could get hold of to keep from going overboard; by this maneuver, he crossed over the second ship; and the bombers in the bilge of the Dusar dropped a heavy bomb on her deck. With the detonation of the bomb, she turned completely over, and then plummeted toward the ground, four thousand feet below. The explosion must have burst all her buoyancy tanks.

Only one ship now remained in our immediate vicinity; and as we made for her, she turned tail and ran, followed by the cheers of our men. We now resumed our course toward the north, the enemy having abandoned the chase.

The first ship was still burning, and I directed Tan Hadron to approach her to learn if any of the crew remained alive. As we came closer, I saw that she was hanging bow down,

the whole after part of the ship being in flames. The bow
was not burning, and I saw a number of men clinging to
holds upon the tilted deck.

My bow gunner thought that I was going to finish them off,
and trained his piece on them; but I stopped him just in
time; then I hailed them. "Can you get at your boarding
harness?" I shouted.

"Yes," came back the answer.

"I'll pull in below you and take you off," I called, and
in about fifteen minutes we had taken off the five survivors
one of which was a Panar padwar.

They were surprised that I hadn't either finished them off
when I had them at such a disadvantage, or let them hang
there and burn. The padwar was sure that we had some
ulterior motive in taking them off the burning ship, and asked
me how I intended to have them killed.

"I don't intend to kill you at all," I said, "unless I have
to."

My own men were quite as surprised as the prisoners;
but I heard one of them say, "The Dwar's been in the
Helium navy—they don't kill prisoners of war in Helium."
Well, they don't kill them in all Martian countries, except
that most do kill their prisoners if they find it difficult or
impossible to take them home into slavery without endan-
gering their own ships.

"What are you going to do with us?" asked the padwar.

"I'll either land as soon as it is convenient, and set you
free; or I'll let you enlist and come with us. You must understand, however, that I am at war with Hin Abtol."

All five decided to cast their lot with us, and I turned
them over to Fo-nar to assign them to watches and prescribe
their duties. My men were gathered amidships discussing the
engagement; they were as proud as peacocks.

"We destroyed two ships and put a third to flight without
suffering a casualty," one was saying.

"That's the kind of a Dwar to fly under," said another. "I
knew he was all right when I saw him handle Gan-ho. I
tell you there's a man to fight for."

After overhearing this conversation and a lot more like it,
I felt much more assured as to the possible success of the
venture, for with a disloyal crew anything may happen except
success.

A little later, as I was crossing the deck, I saw one of the
warriors who had taken Phor San and his companion below;
and I hailed him and asked him if the prisoners were all
right.

"I am sorry to report, sir," he said, "that they both fell overboard."

"How could they fall overboard when they were below?" I demanded.

"They fell through the after bomb trap, sir," he said, without cracking a smile.

10

Naturally I was a little suspicious of the dependability of Gor-don, the Panar padwar we had taken off the disabled Panar ship. He was the only Panar aboard the Dusar, and the only person aboard who might conceivably owe any allegiance to Hin Abtol. I cautioned Fo-nar and Tan Hadron to keep an eye on the fellow, although I really couldn't imagine how he could harm us.

As we approached the North Polar region, it was necessary to issue the warm fur clothing which the Dusar carried in her stores—the white fur of Apts for the warriors, and the black and yellow striped fur of orluks for the three officers; and to issue additional sleeping furs to all.

I was quite restless that night with a perfectly baseless premonition of impending disaster, and about the 9th zode (1:12 A.M. E.T.) I arose and went on deck. Fo-nar was at the wheel, for as yet I didn't know any of the common warriors of the crew well enough to trust them with this important duty.

There was a group of men amidships, whispering among themselves. As they were not members of the watch, they had no business there at that time of night; and I was walking toward them to order them below, when I saw three men scuffling farther aft. This infraction of discipline requiring more immediate attention than the gathering on the deck, I walked quickly toward the three men, arriving just as two of them were about to hurl the third over the rail.

I seized the two by their collars and dragged them back; they dropped their victim and turned on me; but when they recognized me, they hesitated.

"The Panar was falling overboard," said one of the men, rather impudently.

Sure enough, the third man was Gor-don, the Panar. He had had a mighty close call. "Go below, to my cabin," I told him; "I will talk with you there later."

"He won't talk too much, if he knows what's good for him," one of the men who had tried to throw him overboard shouted after him as he walked away.

"What is the meaning of this?" I demanded of the two men, whom I recognized as assassins.

"It means that we don't want any Panars aboard this ship," replied one.

"Go to your quarters," I ordered; "I'll attend to you later." It was my intention to immediately have them put in irons.

They hesitated; one of them moved closer to me. There is only one way to handle a situation like that—be first. I swung a right to the fellow's chin, and as he went down I whipped out my sword and faced them.

"I'll run you both through if you lay a hand on a weapon," I told them, and they knew that I meant it. I made them stand against the rail then, with their backs toward me, and disarmed them. "Now go below," I said.

As they walked away, I saw the men in the group amidships watching us, and as I approached them they moved away and went below before I could order them to do so. I went forward and told Fo-nar of what had happened, cautioning him to be constantly on the lookout for trouble.

"I am going below to talk to Panar," I said; "I have an idea that there was more to this than just the wish to throw him overboard; then I'll have a talk with some of the men. I'm going to rouse Tan Hadron first and instruct him to have those two assassins put in irons at once. I'll be back on deck shortly; the three of us will have to keep a close watch from now on. Those men weren't on deck at this hour in the night just to get fresh air."

I went below then and awakened Tan Hadron, telling him what had occurred on deck and ordering him to take a detail of men and put the two assassins in irons; after that, I went to my cabin. Gor-don arose from a bench and saluted as I entered.

"May I thank you, sir," he said, "for saving my life."

"Was it because you are a Panar that they were going to throw you overboard?" I asked.

"No, sir, it was not," he replied. "The men are planning to take over the ship—they are afraid to go to Pankor—and they tried to get me to join with them, as none of them can navigate a ship and I can; they intended killing you and the two padwars. I refused to join them, and tried to dissaude them; then they became afraid that I would report their plans to you, as I intended doing; so they were going to throw me overboard. You saved my life, sir, when you took me off that burning ship; and I am glad to offer it in the defense of yours—and you're going to need all the defense you can get; the men are determined to take over the ship, though they are divided on the question of killing you."

"They seemed very contented to serve under me immediately after our engagement with your three ships," I said; "I wonder what could have changed them."

"Fear of Hin Abtol as the ship drew nearer to Pankor," replied Gor-don; "they are terrified at the thought that they might be frozen in there again for years."

"Pankor must be a terrible place," I said.

"For them, it would be," he replied.

I saw to it that he was armed, and then I told him to follow me on deck. There would be at least four of us, and I hoped that some of the crew might be loyal. Tan Hadron of Hastor and I could give a good account of ourselves; as to Fo-nar and Gor-don, I did not know.

"Come!" I said to the Panar, and then I opened my cabin door and stepped into the arms of a dozen men, waiting there, who fell upon me and bore me to the deck before I could strike a blow in defense; they disarmed both the Panar and me and bound our hands behind our backs. It was all done very expeditiously and quietly; the plan had been admirably worked out, and it won my approbation—anyone who can take John Carter as easily as that deserves praise.

They took us on deck, and I could not but notice that many of them still treated me with deference. Those who immediately surrounded me were all panthans. On deck, I saw that both Fo-nar and Tan Hadron were prisoners.

The men surrounded us, and discussed our fate. "Overboard with the four of them!" cried an assassin.

"Don't be a fool," said one of the panthans; "we can't navigate the ship without at least one of them."

"Keep one of them, then; and throw the others over the rail—over with the dwar first!"

"No!" said another panthan; "he is a great fighting man, a good commander who led us to victory; I will fight before I will see him killed."

"And I!" shouted several others in unison.

"What do you want to do with them, then?" demanded still another assassin. "Do you want to take them along so that we'll all have our heads lopped off at the first city we stop at where they can report us to the authorities?"

"Keep two to pilot the ship," said a man who had not spoken before; "and ground the other two, if you don't want to kill them."

Several of the assassins were still for killing us; but the others prevailed, and they had Tan Hadron bring the Dusar to ground. Here, as they put us off the ship, Gor-don and I, they gave us back our weapons over the protest of several of the assassins.

As I stood there on the snow and ice of the Arctic and saw the Dusar rise in the air and head toward the south, I thought that it might have been kinder had they killed us.

11

North of us rose a range of rocky hills, their wind swept granite summits, flecked with patches of snow and ice, showed above their snow covered slopes like the backbone of some dead monster. To the south stretched rough, snow covered terrain as far as the eye could reach—to the north, a frozen wilderness and death; to the south, a frozen wilderness and death. There seemed no alternative.

But it was the south that called me. I could struggle on until death claimed me, but I would never give up while life remained.

"I suppose we might as well be moving," I said to Gor-don, as I started toward the south.

"Where are you going?" he asked; "only death lies in that direction for a man on foot."

"I know that," I replied; "death lies in any direction we may go."

The Panar smiled. "Pankor lies just beyond those hills," he said. "I have hunted here many times on this side of them; we can be in Pankor in a couple of hours."

I shrugged. "It doesn't make much difference to me," I said, "as I shall probably be killed in Pankor;" and I started off again, but this time toward the north.

"You can come into Pankor safely," said Gor-don, "but you will have to come as my slave. It is not as I would have it, sir; but it is the only way in which you will be safe."

"I understand," I said, "and I thank you."

"We shall have to say that I took you prisoner; that the crew of my ship mutinied and grounded us," he explained.

"It is a good story, and at least founded on fact," I said. "But, tell me: will I ever be able to escape from Pankor?"

"If I get another ship, you will," he promised. "I am al-lowed a slave on board, and I'll take you along; the rest we shall have to leave to fate; though I can assure you that it is no easy thing to escape from Hin Abtol's navy."

"You are being very generous," I said.

"I owe you my life, sir."

Life is strange. How could I have guessed a few hours before that my life would be in the hands of one of Hin Abtol's officers, and safe? If ever a man was quickly rewarded for a good deed, it was I now for the rescuing of those poor devils from the burning ship.

Gor-don led the way with confidence over that trackless waste to a narrow gorge that split the hills. One unfamiliar with its location could have passed along the foot of the hills within a hundred yards of its mouth without ever seeing it, for its ice- and snow-covered walls blended with the surrounding snow to hide it most effectively.

It was rough going in that gorge. Snow covered broken ice and rocks, so that we were constantly stumbling and often falling. Transverse fissures crossing the gorge formed a labyrinth of corridors in which a man might be quickly lost. Gor-don told me this was the only pass through the hills, and that if an enemy ever got into it he would freeze to death before he found his way out again.

We had plodded on for about half an hour, when, at a turn, our way was blocked by one of the most terrible creatures that inhabit Mars. It was an apt, a huge, white furred creature with six limbs, four of which, short and heavy, carry it swiftly over the snow and ice; while the other two, growing forward from its shoulders on either side of its long, powerful neck, terminate in white, hairless hands, with which it seizes and holds its prey.

Its head and mouth are more nearly similar in appearance to those of a hippopotamus than to any other earthly animal, except that from the sides of the upper jawbone two mighty horns curve slightly downward toward the front.

Its two huge eyes inspire one's greatest curiosity. They extend in two vast oval patches from the center of the top of the cranium down either side of the head to below the roots of the horns, so that these weapons really protrude from the lower part of the eyes, which are composed of several thousand ocelli each.

This eye structure has always seemed remarkable to me in a beast whose haunts were on a glaring field of ice and snow, and though I found upon minute examination of the eyes of several that Thuvan Dihn and I killed, that time that we passed through the carrion caves, that each ocellus is furnished with its own lid, and that the animal can, at will, close as many of the facets of its huge eyes as it wishes, yet I am sure that nature has thus equipped him because much of his life is spent in dark, subterranean recesses.

The moment that the creature saw us, it charged; and Gordon and I whipped out our radium pistols simultaneously, and commenced firing. We could hear the bullets exploding in its carcass and see great chunks of flesh and bone being torn away, but still it came on. One of my bullets found a thousand faceted eye and exploded there, tearing the eye away. For just a moment the creature hesitated and wavered; then it came on again. It was right on top of us now, and our bullets were tearing into its vitals. How it could continue to live, I cannot understand; but it did, and it reached out and seized Gor-don with its two horrible, white, hairless hands and dragged him toward its massive jaws.

I was on its blind side; and realizing that our bullets would not bring death in time to save Gor-don, I drew my long-sword; and, grasping the hilt in both hands, swung it from low behind my right shoulder and brought the keen blade down onto the beast's long neck. Just as the jaws were about to close on Gor-don, the apt's head rolled upon the icy floor of the gorge; but its mighty fingers still clung to the Panar, and I had to hack them off with my short sword before the man was freed.

"That was a close call," I said.

"Once again you have saved my life," said Gor-don; "how can I ever repay you?"

"By helping me find Llana of Gathol, if she is in Pankor," I told him.

"If she is in Pankor, I'll not only help you find her; but I'll help you get her away, if it is humanly possible to do so," he replied. "I am an officer in Hin Abtol's navy," he continued, "but I feel no loyalty toward him. He is a tyrant, hated by all; how he has been able to rule us for more than a hundred years, without being found by the assassin's dagger or poison, is a miracle."

As we talked, we continued on through the gorge; and presently came out upon a snow covered plain upon which rose one of those amazing, glass covered, hot-house cities of Barsoom's North Polar region.

"Pankor," said Gor-don; presently he turned and looked at me and commenced to laugh.

"What is it?" I asked.

"Your metal," he said; "you are wearing the insigne of a dwar in Hin Abtol's service; it might appear strange that you, a dwar, are the prisoner and slave of a padwar."

"That might be difficult to explain," I said, as I removed the insigne and threw it aside.

At the city gate, it was our good fortune to find one of Gor-don's acquaintances in command of the guard. He heard Gor-don's story with interest and permitted us to enter, paying no attention whatever to me.

Pankor was much like Kadabra, the capital city of Okar, only much smaller. Though the country around it and up to its walls was clothed in snow and ice, none lay upon the great crystal dome which roofed the entire city; and beneath the dome a pleasant, springlike atmosphere prevailed. Its avenues were covered with the sod of the mosslike ocher vegetation which clothes the dead sea bottoms of the red planet, and bordered by well kept lawns of crimson Barsoomian grass. Along these avenues sped the noiseless traffic of light and airy ground fliers with which I had become familiar in Marentina and Kadabra long years before.

The broad tires of these unique fliers are but rubberlike gas bags filled with the eighth Barsoomian ray, or ray of propulsion—that remarkable discovery of the Martians that has made possible the great fleets of mighty airships that render the red man of the outer world supreme. It is this ray which propels the inherent and reflected light of suns and planets off into space, and when confined gives to Martian craft their airy buoyancy.

Hailing a public flier, Gor-don and I were driven to his home, I sitting with the driver, as befitted a slave. Here he was warmly greeted by his mother, father, and sister; and I was conducted to the slaves' quarters by a servant. It was not long, however, before Gor-don sent for me; and when the servant who had brought me had departed, Gor-don explained to me that he had told his parents and his sister that I had saved his life, and that they wished to express their gratitude. They were most appreciative.

"You shall be my son's personal guard," said the father, "and we shall not look upon you here in this home as a slave. He tells me that in your own country you are a noble." Gor-don had either guessed at that, or made up the story for effect; as I certainly had told him nothing of my status at home. I wondered how much more he had told them; I did not wish too many people to know of my search for Llana. When next we were alone, I asked him; and he assured me that he had told them nothing.

"I trust them perfectly," he said, "but the affair is not mine to speak of." At least there was one decent Panar; I presume that I had come to judge them all by Hin Abtol.

Gor-don furnished me with harness and insignia which definitely marked me as a slave of his household and rendered it safe for me to go about the city, which I was anxious to do on the chance that I might pick up some word regarding Llana; for Gor-don had told me that in the market place, where slaves gathered to buy and sell for their owners, all the gossip of the city was discussed daily.

"*If it has happened or is going to happen, the market place knows it,*" is an old saying here," he told me; and I found this to be true.

As Gor-don's bodyguard, I was permitted to wear weapons, the insignia on my harness so denoting. I was glad of this, as I feel lost without arms—much as an Earth man would feel walking down the street without his pants.

The day after we arrived, I went alone to the market place.

12

I got into conversations with a number of slaves, but I didn't learn anything of value to me; however, being there, put me in the way of learning something that was of value to me. I was talking with another slave, when we saw an officer coming through the market place, touching first one slave and then another, who immediately fell in behind him.

"If he touches you, don't ask any questions; but go along," said the slave with whom I was talking and whom I had told I was a newcomer to Pankor.

Well, the officer did tap me on the shoulder as he passed; and I fell in behind him with fifteen or twenty other slaves. He led us out of the market place and along an avenue of poorer shops, to the city wall. Here, beside a small gate, was a shed in which was a stock of apt-fur suits. After we had each donned one of these, in accordance with the officer's instructions, he unlocked the small gate and led us out of the city into the bitter cold of the Arctic, where such a sight met my eyes as I hope I may never see again. On row after row of racks which extended as far as I could see hung frozen human corpses, thousands upon thousands of them hanging by their feet, swinging in the biting wind.

Each corpse was encased in ice, a transparent shroud through which their dead eyes stared pleadingly, reproachfully, accusingly, horribly. Some faces wore frozen grins, mocking Fate with bared teeth.

The officer had us cut down twenty of the bodies, and the thought of the purpose for which they seemed obviously intended almost nauseated me. As I looked upon those endless lines of corpses hanging heads down, I was reminded of winter scenes before the butcher shops of northern cities in my native country, where the bodies of ox and bear and deer hung, frozen, for the gourmet to inspect.

It took the combined strength of two red men to lift and carry one of these ice encrusted bodies; and as the officer had tapped an odd number of slaves, I was left without a partner to carry a corpse with me; so I waited for orders.

The officer saw me standing idle, and called to me. "Hey,

you!" he cried; "don't loaf around doing nothing; drag one of them over to the gate."

I stooped and lifted one of the bodies to my shoulder, carrying it alone to the gate. I could see that the officer was astounded, for what I had done would have been an impossible feat of strength for a Martian. As a matter of fact, it was not at all remarkable that I was able to do it; because my unusually great strength, combined with the lesser gravity of Mars, made it relatively easy for me.

All the time I was carrying my grisly burden, I was thinking of the roast we had had at the meal I had eaten at Gordon's house—and wondering! Was it possible that civilized human beings could be so depraved? It seemed incredible of such people as Gordon and his family. His sister was a really beautiful girl. Could she—? I shuddered at the implication.

We carried the corpses into a large building across the avenue from the little gate. Here were row upon row and tier upon tier of ersite topped tables; and when, at the officer's direction, we laid the bodies upon some of them, the place looked like a morgue.

Presently a number of men entered the room; they carried heavy knives. These are the butchers, I thought. They attached hoses to hydrants, and each one of them stood over a corpse and sprayed it with warm water, at the same time chipping away the ice with his knife. It took some little time.

When the first corpse was entirely released from its icy winding sheet I wanted to look away, but I couldn't—I was fascinated by the horror of it as I waited to see the butcher wield his knife; but he didn't. Instead, he kept on spraying the body with warm water, occasionally massaging it. Finally, he took a hypodermic syringe from his pocket pouch and injected something into the arm of the cadaver; then the most horrifying thing of all occurred: the corpse rolled its head to and fro and opened its eyes!

"Stand by, slaves!" commanded the officer; "some of them may be a little wild at first—be ready to seize them."

The first corpse sat up and looked around, as others of them showed signs of life. Soon they were all either sitting up or standing staring about them in a confused sort of way. Now they were each given the harness of a slave; and when a detachment of warriors came to take charge of them, we other slaves were dismissed. Now I recalled and understood that oft repeated reference of the warriors of Hin Abtol to being "frozen in." I had thought that they merely meant being confined in an Arctic city surrounded by ice and snow.

As I was leaving the building, the officer accosted me. "Who are you, slave?" he demanded.

"I am the slave and bodyguard of Padwar Gor-don," I replied.

"You are a very strong man," he said; "what country are you from?"

"Virginia," I replied.

"I never heard of it; where is it?"

"Just south of Maryland."

"Well, never mind—let's see how strong you are; can you lift one end of that ersite table alone?"

"I don't know."

"Try it," he ordered.

I picked up the entire table and held it above my head. "Incredible!" exclaimed the officer. The warriors were standing looking at me in open mouthed astonishment.

"What is your name?" demanded the officer.

"Dotor Sojat."

"Very good," he said; "you may go now."

When I returned to Gor-don's home, he told me that he had become apprehensive because of my long absence. "Where have you been all this time?" he asked. "I was worried."

"Thawing out corpses," I told him, laughing. "Before I saw them start coming to life, I thought you Panars ate them. Tell me; what is the idea?"

"It is a part of Hin Abtol's mad scheme to conquer all of Barsoom and make himself Jeddak of Jeddaks and Warlord of Barsoom. He has heard of the famous John Carter, who holds these titles; and he is envious. He has been at the preserving of human beings by freezing for fully a hundred years. At first it was only a plan by which he might have great numbers of slaves available at any time without the expense of feeding them while they were idle. After he heard of John Carter and the enormous wealth of Helium and several other empires, this grandiose scheme of conquest commenced taking form.

"He had to have a fleet; and as no one in Pankor knew how to build airships, he had to acquire them by trickery and theft. A few crossed the ice barrier from some of the northern cities: these were lured to land by signals of friendship and welcome: then their crews were captured and all but one or two of them frozen in. Those who were not had promised to train Panars in the handling of the ships. It has been a very slow process of acquiring a navy; but he has supplemented it by visiting several of the northern cities, pretending friendship, and then stealing a ship or two, just as he pretended friendship for Gahan of Gathol and then stole his daughter.

"His present attack on Gathol is merely a practice campaign to give his officers and warriors experience and perhaps at the same time acquire a few more ships."

"How many of those frozen men has he?" I asked.

"He has accumulated fully a million in the last hundred years," replied Gor-don; "a very formidable army, if he had the ships to transport them."

On this dying planet, the population of which has been steadily decreasing for probably a million years, an army of a million warriors would indeed be formidable; but led by Hin Abtol and officered by Panars, *two* million disloyal warriors would be no great menace to such a power as Helium.

"I am afraid Hin Abtol's dream will never come true," I said.

"I hope not. Very few Panars are in sympathy with it. Life here is easy, and we are content to be left alone and leave others alone. By the way, did you learn anything about the whereabouts of Llana of Gathol while you were away?"

"Not a thing; did you?"

"No," he replied; "but I haven't made any direct inquiries yet. I am waiting until I can talk with some of my friends who are stationed in the palace. I do know, however, that Hin Abtol has returned from Gathol and is in his palace."

As we talked, a slave came to announce that an officer had come from the Jeddak and wished to speak to Gor-don.

"Bring him here," said my master; and a moment later a gorgeously trapped man entered the room, by which time I was standing behind Gor-don's chair, as a well trained slave and bodyguard should do.

The two men greeted each other by name and title; and then the visitor said, "You have a slave named Dotor Sojat?"

"Yes," replied Gor-don; "my personal bodyguard, here."

The officer looked at me. "You are the slave who lifted the ersite table alone today in the resuscitating house?" he inquired.

"Yes."

He turned again to Gor-don. "The Jeddak will honor you by accepting this slave as a gift," he said.

Gor-don bowed. "It is a great pleasure as well as an honor to present the slave, Dotor Sojat, to my jeddak," he said; and then, as the officer looked away from him to glance again at me, Gor-don winked at me. He knew how anxious I had been to get into the palace of Hin Abtol.

Like a dutiful slave, I left the home of Gor-don, the padwar, and followed the jeddak's officer to the palace of the jeddak.

A high wall encloses the grounds where stands the palace of Hin Abtol in the city of Pankor at the top of the world, and guards pace this wall night and day. At the gates are a full utan of a hundred men; and within, at the grand entrance to the palace itself, is another utan. No wonder that it has been difficult to assassinate Hin Abtol, self-styled Jeddak of Jeddaks of the North.

At one side of the palace, on an open scarlet sward, I saw something which made me start with astonishment—it was my own flier! It was the flier that Hin Abtol had stolen from me in the deserted city of Horz; and now, as I learned later, he had it on exhibition here as proof of his great courage and ability. He bragged that he had taken it single handed from The Warlord of Barsoom after defeating him in a duel. The fact that there could be no doubt but that it was my personal flier lent color to the story; my insigne was there for everyone to read, plain upon the bow. They must have towed it through one of the gates; and then flown it to its present resting place; as, of course, no airship could land inside Pankor's great dome.

I was left in the guardroom just inside the entrance to the palace, where some of the warriors of the guard were loafing; two of them were playing Jetan, the Martian chess game, while others played Yano. They had all risen when the officer entered the room with me; and when he left I sat down on a bench at one side, as the others seated themselves and resumed their games.

One of them looked over at me, and scowled. "Stand up, slave!" he ordered. "Don't you know better than to sit in the presence of Panar warriors?"

"If you can prove that you are a better man than I?" I said, "I'll stand." I was in no mood to take anything like that meekly; as a matter of fact, I was pretty well fed up on being a slave.

The warrior leaped to his feet. "Oh, insolent, too!" he said; "well, I'll teach you a lesson."

"You'd better go slow there, Ul-to," warned one of his companions; "I think this fellow was sent for by the jeddak. If you muss him up, Hin Abtol may not like it."

"Well, he's got to be taught a lesson," snarled Ul-to; "if there's one thing I can't stand, it's an impudent slave," and he came toward me. I did not rise, and he grabbed me by the harness and attempted to drag me to my feet; at the same time, he struck at me.

I parried his blow, and seized hold of his harness; then I stood up and lifted him above my head. I held him there for a moment, and then I tossed him across the room. "That will teach you," I called to him, "to be more respectful to your betters."

Some of the other guardsmen were scowling at me angrily; but many were laughing at Ul-to, who now scrambled to his feet, whipped out his long-sword, and came for me. They had not yet disarmed me; and I drew mine; but before we could engage, a couple of Ul-to's companions seized him and held him. He was cursing and struggling to free himself and get at me, when the officer of the guard, evidently attracted by the disturbance, entered the room.

When he heard what had happened, he turned angrily on me. "You ought to be flogged," he said, "for insulting and attacking a Panar warrior."

"Perhaps you would like to try to flog me," I said.

At that, he turned purple and almost jumped up and down, he was so furious. "Seize him!" he shouted to the warriors, "and give him a good beating."

They all started toward me, and I drew my sword. I was standing with my back to a wall, and there would have been several dead Panars scattered about that room in a few minutes if the officer who had brought me there had not come in just then.

"What's the meaning of this?" he demanded.

The guard officer explained, making me appear wholly in the wrong.

"He lies," I said to the officer; "I was attacked without provocation."

He turned to the guard officer. "I don't know who started this," he said, "but it's a good thing for your neck that nothing happened to this man;" then he disarmed me and told me to follow him.

He led me out of the palace again and to the side of the building where my flier stood. I noticed that it was not moored, there being no danger of winds beneath that great dome; and I wished that it were out in the open so that I could fly it away if I were able to find Llana of Gathol; it would have been a Heaven sent opportunity for escape had it not been for that enclosing dome.

He took me out to the center of an expanse of well kept lawn, facing a number of people who had gathered beside the building. There were both men and women, and more were coming from the palace. At last there was a fanfare of trumpets; and the Jeddak came, accompanied by courtiers and women.

In the meantime, a large man had come out on the lawn beside me; he was a warrior wearing metal that denoted him a member of Hin Abtol's bodyguard.

"The Jeddak has heard tales of your great strength," said the officer who had brought me there, "and he wishes to see a demonstration of it. Rab-zov, here, is supposed to be the strongest man in Pankor—"

"I *am* the strongest man in Pankor, sir," interrupted Rab-zov; "I am the strongest man on Barsoom."

"He must be pretty strong," I said. "What is he going to do to me?"

"You are going to wrestle to amuse the Jeddak and his court. Rab-zov will demonstrate how easily he can throw you to the ground and hold you there. Are you ready, Rab-zov?"

Rab-zov said he was ready, and the officer signed us to start. Rab-zov swaggered toward me, taking occasional quick glances at the audience to see if all were looking at him. They were; looking at him and admiring his great bulk.

"Come on, fellow!" said Rab-zov; "put up the best fight you can; I want to make it interesting for the Jeddak."

"I shall hope to make it interesting for you, Rab-zov," I said.

He laughed loudly at that. "You won't feel so much like joking when I'm through with you," he said.

"Come on, wind bag!" I cried; "you talk too much."

He was leaning forward, reaching for a hold, when I seized one of his wrists, turned quickly and threw him over my shoulder. I purposely let him fall hard, and he was still a little groggy when he came to his feet. I was waiting, very close; and I seized him by the harness and lifted him over my head; then I commenced to whirl with him. He was absolutely helpless; and when I thought he was befuddled enough, I carried him over and threw him down heavily in front of Hin Abtol. Rab-zov was down—and out.

"Have you no strong men in Pankor?" I asked him, and then I saw Llana of Gathol standing beside the Jeddak. Almost with the suddenness of a revelation a mad scheme came to me.

"Perhaps I had better send two men against you," said Hin Abtol, rather good-naturedly; he had evidently enjoyed the spectacle.

"Why not a swordsman?" I asked. "I am quite good with a sword," and I wanted a sword very much right then—I needed a sword to carry out my plan.

"'Do you want to be killed, slave?" demanded Hin Abtol; "I have the best swordsmen in the world in my guard."

"Bring out your best, then," I said; "I may surprise him —and somebody else," and I looked straight at Llana of Gathol, and winked. Then, for the first time, she recognized me through my disguise.

"Who were you winking at?" demanded Hin Abtol, looking around.

"Something got in my eye," I said.

Hin Abtol spoke to an officer standing near him. "Who is the best swordsman in the guard?" he asked.

"There is none better than Ul-to," replied the officer.

"Fetch him!"

So! I was to cross swords with my old friend, Ul-to. That would please him—for a few moments.

They brought Ul-to; and when he found that he was to fight me, he beamed all over. "Now, slave," he said, "I will teach you that lesson that I promised you."

"Again?" I asked.

"It will be different this time," he said.

We crossed swords.

"To the death!" I said.

"To the death, slave!" replied Ul-to.

I fought on the defensive mostly at first, seeking to work my man around in the position in which I wanted him; and when I had him there, I pressed him; and he fell back. I kept backing him toward the audience, and to make him more amenable to my directions, I started carving him—just a little. I wanted him to acquire respect for my point and my ability. Soon he was covered with blood, and I was forcing him to go wherever I wished him.

I backed him into the crowd, which fell back; and then I caught Llana's eye, and motioned her with my head to step to one side; then I pressed close to her. "At the kill," I whispered, "run for the flier and start the engine."

I backed Ul-to away from the crowd then, and I saw Llana following, as though she was so much interested in the duel that she did not realize what she was doing.

"Now! Llana!" I whispered, and I saw her walking slowly backward toward the flier.

In order to attract the crowd's attention from Llana, I pressed Ul-to to one side with such an exhibition of swordplay as I knew would hold every eye; then I turned him around and had him almost running backward, carrying me nearer my ship.

Suddenly I heard Hin Abtol cry, "The girl! Get her! She's gone aboard that flier!"

As they started forward, I ran Ul-to through the heart and turned and ran for my ship. At my heels came a dozen warriors with drawn swords. The one who started first, and who was faster than the others, overtook me just as I had to pause a moment at the side of the flier to make assurance doubly sure that she was not moored in any way. I wheeled and parried a vicious cut; my blade moved once more with the swiftness of light, and the warrior's head rolled from his shoulders.

"Let her go!" I cried to Llana, as I leaped to the deck. As the ship rose, I hastened to the controls, and took over.

"Where are we going, John Carter?" asked Llana.

"To Gathol," I replied.

She looked up at the dome above us. "How——?" she started, but she saw that I had turned the nose of the flier upward at an angle of forty-five degrees and opened the throttle—that was her answer.

The little ship, as sweet and fast a flier as I have ever flown, was streaking through the warm air of Pankor at tremendous speed. We both huddled close to the deck of the little cockpit—and hoped.

The flier shuddered to the terrific impact; broken glass showered in every direction—and then we were out in the cold, clear air of the Arctic.

I levelled off then, and headed for Gathol at full speed; there was danger of our freezing to death if we didn't get into a warmer climate soon, for we had no furs.

"What became of Pan Dan Chee and Jad-han?" I asked.

"I haven't seen them since we were all captured in Gathol," replied Llana. "Poor Pan Dan Chee; he fought for me, and he was badly wounded; I am afraid that I shall never see him again," and there were tears in her voice.

I greatly deplored the probable fate of Pan Dan Chee and Jad-han, but at least Llana of Gathol was at last safe. Or was this a masterpiece of overstatement? She was at least safe from Hin Abtol, but what lay in the future? Immediately she was in danger of freezing to death should any mishap delay our flight before we reached a warmer latitude, and there were innumerable other hazards in the crossing of the wastelands of this dying planet.

But, being an incorrigible optimist, I still felt that Llana was safe; and so did she. Perhaps because no conceivable danger could have been greater than that which had threatened her while she lay in the power of Hin Abtol.

Presently I noticed that she was laughing, and I asked her what amused her. "More than any other man on Barsoom, Hin Abtol feared you," she said, "and he had you in his power and did not know it. And he pitted against you, the greatest swordsman of two worlds, a clumsy oaf, when he might have loosed upon you a full utan and destroyed you. Though he would doubtless have lost half his utan. I only pray that some day he may know the opportunity he missed when he permitted John Carter, Warlord of Barsoom to escape him."

"Yes," I said, "it is amusing. So is that hole we left in the roof of his hothouse city; but I am afraid that Hin Abtol's sense of humor will not be equal to the task of appreciating it."

We sped swiftly toward the south and warmer climes, happy in our miraculous escape from the tyrant of Panar; and, fortunately, unaware of what lay in our future.

Llana of Gathol was safe—but for how long? When would we see Gathol again, or Helium?

BOOK 4

INVISIBLE MEN OF MARS

1

YES, LLANA of Gathol was safe at last. I had brought her from captivity in the Arctic city of Pankor, stolen her from under the very nose of Hin Abtol, the self-styled Jeddak of Jeddaks of the North; and we were speeding through the thin air of dying Mars in my own fast flier toward Gathol. I was very contented with what I had achieved, but I was also very cold.

"You said that you were taking me to Gathol," said Llana, after we had left Pankor far behind. "Nothing would make me happier than to return to my father, my mother, and my native city; but how may we hope to make a landing there while Gathol is surrounded by the warriors of Hin Abtol?"

"The Panars are a stupid, inefficient lot," I replied; "most of Hin Abtol's warriors are unwilling conscripts who have no heart in waging war for their tyrannical master. These poor frozen men only endure it because they know there is no escape and prefer life and consciousness to being returned to Pankor and frozen in again until Hin Abtol needs their swords for a future war."

" 'Frozen men'!" ejaculated Llana; "what do you mean by that?"

"You heard nothing of them while you were a prisoner in Pankor?" I asked, surprised.

"Nothing," Llana assured me; "tell me about them."

"Just outside the walls of the hot-house city there are rows upon rows of racks in the biting cold and bitter wind of the North Polar region. On these racks, like beef in a cold storage warehouse, thousands of warriors hang by their feet, frozen solid and in a state of suspended animation. They are captives whom he had taken on numerous raids during a period of fully a hundred years. I have talked with some who had been frozen in over fifty years.

"I was in the resuscitating room when a number of them were thawed out; after a few minutes they don't seem to be any worse for their experience, but the whole idea is revolting."

"Why does he do it?" demanded Llana. "Why thousands of them?"

"Better say thousands upon thousands," I said; "one slave told me that there were at least a million. Hin Abtol dreams of conquering all of Barsoom with them."

"How grotesque!" exclaimed Llana.

"Were it not for the navy of Helium, he might go far along the road toward the goal of his grandiose ambition; and you may thank your revered ancestors, Llana, that there is a navy of Helium. After I return you to Gathol, I shall fly to Helium and organize an expedition to write finis to Hin Abtol's dreams."

"I wish that before you do that we might try to find out what has become of Pan Dan Chee and Jad-han," said Llana; "the Panars separated us shortly after we were captured."

"They may have been taken to Pankor and frozen in," I suggested.

"Oh, no!" exclaimed Llana; "that would be too terrible."

"You are very fond of Pan Dan Chee, aren't you?" I asked.

"He has been a very good friend," she replied, a little stiffly. The stubborn minx wouldn't admit that she was in love with him—and possibly she wasn't; you never can tell anything about a woman. She had treated him abominably when they were together; but when they were separated and he was in danger, she had evinced the greatest concern for his safety.

"I don't know how we can learn anything about his fate," I said, "unless we can inquire directly of the Panars; and that might prove rather dangerous. I should like to know what has become of them and Tan Hadron of Hastor as well."

"Tan Hadron of Hastor? Where is he?"

"The last I saw of him, he was on board the Dusar, the

Panar ship I stole from their line outside Gathol; and he was the prisoner of the mutinous crew that took it from me. There were a lot of assassins among them, and these were determined to kill Tan Hadron as soon as he had taken the ship to whatever destination they had decided upon; you see, none of the crew knew anything about navigation."

"Tan Hadron of Hastor," said Llana again; "his mother was a royal princess of Gathol and Tan Hadron himself one of the greatest fighting men of Barsoom."

"A splendid officer," I added.

"Steps must be taken to save him, too."

"If it is not too late," I said; "and the only chance of saving any of them lies in my reaching Helium in time to bring a fleet to Gathol before Hin Abtol succeeds in reducing it, and then on to Pankor, if we do not find these three among Hin Abtol's prisoners at Gathol."

"Perhaps we had better fly direct to Helium," suggested Llana. "A fleet from Helium could accomplish something, while we two, alone, might accomplish no more than getting ourselves captured again by the Panars—and it would go hard with you, John Carter, if Hin Abtol ever got his hands on you again, after what you did in Pankor today." She laughed. "I shall never forget what you did to Rab-zov, 'the strongest man in Pankor.' "

"Neither will Rab-zov," I said.

"Nor Hin Abtol. And the hole you made in the glass dome covering the city, when you drove the flier right through it! I'll wager they all had chills before they got that patched up. No, Hin Abtol will never forget you."

"But he never knew who I really was," I reminded Llana; "with my disguise removed, I was no longer a red man; and he might never guess that he had once had John Carter in his power."

"The results would be the same as far as you are concerned," said Llana; "I think it would be death in either event."

Before we had come far from Pankor I decided that our wisest course would be to proceed directly to Helium and enlist the aid of Tardos Mors, the jeddak. While I hold the titles of Jeddak of Jeddaks and Warlord of Barsoom, conferred upon me by the jeddaks of five nations, I have always considered them largely honorary, and have never presumed to exercise the authority implicit in them, except in times of war when even the great Jeddak of Helium has graciously served under me.

Having reached the decision to fly to Helium rather than Gathol, I turned toward the southeast. Before us lay a jour-

ney half the distance around the planet, and we were absolutely without water or provisions. Soon the towers and
stately ruins of Horz were visible, reminding us both of the
circumstances under which we had met Pan Dan Chee, and
I thought that Llana looked down a little sadly on that long
dead city from which her lost lover had been self-exiled because of us. It was here that she had escaped from Hin Abtol, and it was here that Hin Abtol had stolen this very flier
of mine that I had found and recovered in his Polar capital.
Yes, Horz held many memories for both of us; and I was
glad when it lay behind us, this dead monument to a dead
past.

Far ahead lay Dusar where water and provisions might
be obtained, but the friendliness of Dusar was open to question. It had not been so many years since Carthoris, the
Prince of Helium, had almost been done to death there by
Astok, son of Nutus, the jeddak of Dusar; and there had
been no intercourse between Helium and Dusar since that
time. Beyond Dusar was no friendly city all the way to Helium.

I decided to give Dusar a wide berth, and in doing so we
flew over country with which I was entirely unfamiliar. It
was a hilly country; and in the long, deep valley I saw one
of those rarest of all sights on Mars, a splendid forest. Now,
to me a forest means fruits and nuts and, perhaps, game
animals; and we were hungry. There would doubtless be
mantilia plants too, the sap of which would quench our thirst;
and so I decided to land. My best judgment told me that it
was a risky thing to do, and subsequent events proved that
my judgment was wholly correct.

2

I landed on level ground close to the forest, and telling
Llana to remain aboard the flier ready to take off at a moment's notice, I went in search of food. The forest consisted
principally of skeel, sorapus, and sompus trees. The first two
are hardwood trees bearing large, delicious nuts, while the
sompus trees were loaded with a citrus-like fruit with a thin
red rind. The pulp of this fruit, called somp, is not unlike
grapefruit, though much sweeter. It is considered a great delicacy among Barsoomians, and is cultivated along many of the
canals. I had never seen any, however, as large as these, growing wild; nor had I ever seen trees on Mars of the size of
many of those growing in this hidden forest.

I had gathered as much of the fruit and as many nuts as

I could carry, when I heard Llana calling me. There was a note of excitement and urgency in her voice, and I dropped all that I had gathered and ran in the direction of the flier. Just before I came out of the forest I heard her scream; and as I emerged, the flier rose from the ground. I ran toward it as fast as I can run, and that is extremely fast under the conditions of lesser gravity which prevail on Mars. I took forty or fifty feet in a leap, and then I sprang fully thirty feet into the air in an effort to seize the rail of the flier. One hand touched the gunwale; but my fingers didn't quite close over the rail, and I slipped back and fell to the ground. However, I had had a glimpse of the deck of the flier, and what I saw there filled me with astonishment and, for some reason, imparted that strange sensation to my scalp as though each separate hair were standing erect—Llana lay on the deck absolutely alone, and there was no one at the controls!

"A noble endeavor," said a voice behind me; "you can certainly jump."

I wheeled about, my hand flying to the hilt of my sword. There was no one there! I looked toward the forest; there was no sign of living thing about me. From behind me came a laugh—a taunting, provocative laugh. Again I wheeled. As far as I could see there was only the peaceful Martian landscape. Above me, the flier circled and disappeared beyond the forest—flown with no human hand at the controls by some sinister force which I could not fathom.

"Well," said a voice, again behind me, "we might as well be on our way. You realize, I presume, that you are our prisoner."

"I realize nothing of the sort," I retorted. "If you want to take me, come and get me—come out in the open like men; if you are men."

"Resistance will be futile," said the voice; "there are twenty of us and only one of you."

"Who are you?" I demanded.

"Oh, pardon me," said the voice, "I should have introduced myself. I am Pnoxus, son of Ptantus, jeddak of Invak; and whom have I had the honor of capturing?"

"You haven't had the honor of capturing me yet," I said. I didn't like that voice—it was too oily and polite.

"You are most unco-operative," said the voice named Pnoxus. "I should hate to have to adopt unpleasant methods with you." The voice was not so sweet now; there was just a faint ring of steel in it.

"I don't know where you're hiding," I said; "but if you'll

come out, all twenty of you, I'll give you a taste of steel. I have had enough of this foolishness."

"And I've had enough," snapped the voice. Somehow it sounded like a bear trap to me—all the oily sweetness had gone out of it. "Take him, men!"

I looked quickly around for the men, but I was still alone —just I and a voice were there. At least that is what I thought until hands seized my ankles and jerked my feet from beneath me. I fell flat on my face, and what felt like half a dozen heavy men leaped on my back and half a dozen hands ripped my sword from my grasp and more hands relieved me of my other weapons. Then unseen hands tied my own behind my back and others fastened a rope around my neck, and the voice said, "Get up!"

I got up. "If you come without resistance," said the voice named Pnoxus, "it will be much easier for you and for my men. Some of them are quite short tempered, and if you make it difficult for them you may not get to Invak alive."

"I will come," I said, "but where? For the rest, I can wait."

"You will be led," said Pnoxus, "and see that you follow where you're led. You've already given me enough trouble."

"You won't know what trouble is until I can see you," I retorted.

"Don't threaten; you have already stored up enough trouble for yourself."

"What became of the girl who was with me?" I demanded.

"I took a fancy to her," said Pnoxus, "and had one of my men, who can fly a ship, take her on to Invak."

I cannot tell you what an eerie experience it was being led through that forest by men that I could not see and being talked to by a voice that had no body; but when I realized that I was probably being taken to the place that Llana of Gathol had been taken, I was content, nay, anxious, to follow docilely where I was led.

I could see the rope leading from my neck out in front of me; it fell away in a gentle curve as a rule and then gradually vanished, vignette-like; sometimes it straightened out suddenly, and then I would feel a jerk at the back of my neck; but by following that ghostly rope-end as it wound among the trees of the forest and watching the bight carefully, so as to anticipate a forthcoming jerk by the straightening of the curve, I learned to avoid trouble.

In front of me and behind I continually heard voices berating other voices: "Sense where you're going, you blundering idiot," or, "Stop stepping on my heels, you fool," or

"Who do you think you're bumping into, son-of-a-calot!" The voices seemed to be constantly getting in one another's way. Serious as I felt my situation might be, I could not help but be amused.

Presently I felt an arm brush against mine, or at least it felt like an arm, the warm flesh of a bare arm; it would touch me for an instant only to be taken away immediately, and then it would touch me again in a measured cadence, as might the arms of two men walking out of step side by side; and then a voice spoke close beside me, and I knew that a voice was walking with me.

"We are coming to a bad place," said the voice; "you had better take my arm."

I groped out with my right hand and found an arm that I could not see. I grasped what felt like an upper arm, and as I did so *my right hand disappeared!* Now, my right arm ended at the wrist, or at least it appeared to do so; but I could feel my fingers clutching that arm that I could not see. It was a most eerie sensation. I do not like situations that I cannot understand.

Almost immediately we came to an open place in the forest, where no trees grew. The ground was covered with tiny hummocks, and when I stepped on it it sank down a few inches. It was like walking on coil springs covered with turf.

"I'll guide you," said the voice at my side. "If you should get off the trail here alone you'd be swallowed up. The worst that can happen to you now would be to get one leg in it, for I can pull you out before it gets a good hold on you."

"Thank you," I said; "it is very decent of you."

"Think nothing of it," replied the voice. "I feel sorry for you; I am always sorry for strangers whom Fate misguides into the forest of Invak. We have another name for it which, I think, better describes it— The Forest of Lost Men."

"It is really so bad to fall into the hands of your people?" I asked.

"I am afraid that it is," replied the voice; "there is no escape."

I had heard that one before; so it didn't impress me greatly. The lesser peoples of Barsoom are great braggarts; they always have the best swordsmen, the finest cities, the most outstanding culture; and once you fall into their hands, you are always doomed to death or a life of slavery—you can never escape them.

"May I ask you a question?" I inquired.

"Certainly," said the voice.

"Are you always only a voice?"

A hand, I suppose it was his right hand, seized my arm and squeezed it with powerful, though invisible, fingers; and whatever it was that walked beside me chuckled. "Does that feel like only a voice?" it asked.

"A stentorian voice," I said. "You seem to have the physical attributes of a flesh and blood man; have you a name?"

"Most assuredly; it is Kandus; and yours?" he asked politely.

"Dotar Sojat," I told him, falling back upon my well-worn pseudonym.

We had now successfully crossed the bog, or whatever it was; and I removed my hand from Kandus's arm. Immediately I was wholly visible again, but Kandus remained only a voice. Again I walked alone, I and a rope sticking out in front of me and apparently defying the law of gravity. Even the fact that I surmised that the other end of it was fastened to a voice did not serve to make it seem right; it was a most indecent way for a rope to behave.

" 'Dotar Sojat,' " repeated Kandus; "it sounds more like a green man's name."

"You are familiar with the green men?" I asked.

"Oh, yes; there is a horde which occasionally frequents the dead sea bottoms beyond the forest; but they have learned to give us a wide berth. Notwithstanding their great size and strength, we have a distinct advantage over them. As a matter of fact, I believe that they are very much afraid of us."

"I can well imagine so; it is not easy to fight voices; there is nothing one may get one's sword into."

Kandus laughed. "I suppose you would like to get your sword into me," he said.

"Absolutely not," I said; "you have been very decent to me, but I don't like that voice which calls itself Pnoxus. I wouldn't mind crossing swords with it."

"Not so loud," cautioned Kandus. "You must remember that he is the jeddak's son. We all have to be very nice to Pnoxus—no matter what we may privately think of him."

I judged from that that Pnoxus was not popular. It is really amazing how quickly one may judge a person by his voice; this had never been so forcibly impressed upon me before. Now, I had disliked the Pnoxus voice from the first, even when it was soft and oily, perhaps because of that; but I had liked the voice named Kandus—it was the voice of a man's man, open and without guile; a good voice.

"Where are you from, Dotar Sojat?" asked Kandus.

"From Virginia," I said.

"That is a city of which I have never heard. In what country is it?"

"It is in the United States of America," I replied, "but you never heard of that either."

"No," he admitted; "that must be a far country."

"It is a far country," I assured him, "some forty-three million miles from here."

"You can talk as tall as you jump," he said. "I don't mind your joking with me," he added, "but I wouldn't get funny with Pnoxus, nor with Ptantus, the jeddak, if I were you; neither one of them has a sense of humor."

"But I was not joking," I insisted. "You have seen Jasoom in the heavens at night?"

"Of course," he replied.

"Well, that is the world I come from; it is called Earth there, and Barsoom is known as Mars."

"You look and talk like an honorable man," said Kandus; "and, while I don't understand, I am inclined to believe; however, you'd better pick out some place on Barsoom as your home when anyone else in Invak questions you; and you may soon be questioned—here we are at the gates of the city now."

3

Invak! The city in the Forest of Lost Men. At first only a gate was visible, so thickly set were the trees that hid the city wall—the trees and the vines that covered the wall.

I heard a voice challenge as we approached the gate, and I heard Pnoxus' voice reply, "It is Pnoxus, the prince, with twenty warriors and a prisoner."

"Let one advance and give the countersign," said the voice.

I was astonished that the guard at the gate couldn't recognize the jeddak's son, nor any of the twenty warriors with him. I suppose that one of the voices advanced and whispered the countersign, for presently a voice said, "Enter, Pnoxus, with your twenty warriors and your prisoner."

Immediately the gates swung open, and beyond I saw a lighted corridor and people moving about within it; then my rope tightened and I moved forward toward the gate; and ahead of me, one by one, armed men suddenly appeared just beyond the threshold of the gateway; one after another they appeared as though materialized from thin air and continued on along the lighted corridor. I approached the gate apparently alone, but as I stepped across the threshold there was a warrior at my side where the voice of Kandus had walked.

I looked at the warrior, and my evident amazement must have been written large upon my face, for the warrior grinned. I glanced behind me and saw warrior after warrior materialize into a flesh and blood man the moment that he crossed the threshold. I had walked through the forest accompanied only by voices, but now ten warriors walked ahead of me and nine behind and one at my side.

"Are you Kandus?" I asked this one.

"Certainly," he said.

"How do you do it?" I exclaimed.

"It is very simple, but it is the secret of the Invaks," he replied. "I may tell you, however, that we are invisible in daylight, or rather when we are not illuminated by these special lamps which light our city. If you will notice the construction of the city as we proceed, you will see that we take full advantage of our only opportunity for visibility."

"Why should you care whether other people can see you or not?" I asked. "Is it not sufficient that you can see them and yourselves?"

"Unfortunately, there is the hitch," he said. "We can see you, but we can't see each other any more than you can see us."

So that accounted for the grumbling and cursing I had heard upon the march through the forest—the warriors had been getting in each other's way because they couldn't see one another any more than I could see them.

"You have certainly achieved invisibility," I said, "or are you hatched invisible from invisible eggs?"

"No," he replied, "we are quite normal people; but we have learned to make ourselves invisible."

Just then I saw an open courtyard ahead of us, and as the warriors passed out of the lighted corridor into it they disappeared. When Kandus and I stepped out, I was walking alone again. It was most uncanny.

The city was spotted with these courtyards which gave ventilation to the city which was, otherwise, entirely roofed and artificially lighted by the amazing lights which gave complete visibility to its inhabitants. In every courtyard grew spreading trees, and upon the city's roof vines had been trained to grow; so that, built as it was in the center of the Forest of Lost Men, it was almost as invisible from either the ground or the air as were its people themselves.

Finally we halted in a large courtyard in which were many trees wherein iron rings were set with chains attached to them, and here invisible hands snapped around one of my ankles a shakle that was fastened to the end of one of these chains.

Presently a voice whispered in my ear, "I will try to help you, for I have rather taken a liking to you—you've got to admire a man who can jump thirty feet into the air; and you've got to be interested in a man who says he comes from another world forty-three million miles from Barsoom."

It was Kandus. I felt that I was fortunate in having even the suggestion of a friend here, but I wondered what good it would do me. After all, Kandus was not the jeddak; and my fate would probably rest in the hands of Ptantus.

I could hear voices crossing and recrossing the courtyard. I could see people come down the corridors or streets and then fade into nothingness as they stepped out into the courtyard. I could see the backs of men and women appear quite as suddenly in the entrances to the streets as they left the courtyard. On several occasions voices stopped beside my tree and discussed me. They commented upon my light skin and gray eyes. One voice mentioned the great leap into the air that one of my captors had recounted to its owner.

Once a delicate perfume stopped near me, and a sweet voice said, "The poor man, and he is so handsome!"

"Don't be a fool, Rojas," growled a masculine voice. "He is an enemy, and anyway he's not very good-looking."

"I think he is very good-looking," insisted the sweet voice, "and how do you know he's an enemy?"

"I was not an enemy when I brought my ship down beside the forest," I said, "but the treatment I have received is fast making one of me."

"There, you see," said the sweet voice; "he was not an enemy. What is your name, poor man?"

"My name is Dotar Sojat, but I am not a 'poor man,'" I replied with a laugh.

"That may be what you think," said the masculine voice. "Come on, Rojas, before you make any bigger fool of yourself."

"If you'll give me a sword and come out of your cowardly invisibility, I'll make a fool of you, calot," I said.

An invisible, but very material, toe kicked me in the groin. "Keep your place, slave!" growled the voice.

I lunged forward and, by chance, got my hands on the fellow; and then I held him by his harness for just long enough to feel for his face, and when I had located it I handed him a right upper-cut that must have knocked him half way across the courtyard.

"That," I said, "will teach you not to kick a man who can't see you."

"Did Motus kick you?" cried the sweet voice, only it wasn't so sweet now; it was an angry voice, a shocked voice. "You looked as though you were hitting him—I hope you did."

"I did," I said, "and you had better see if there is a doctor in the house."

"Where are you, Motus?" cried the girl.

There was no response; Motus must have gone out like a light. Pretty soon I heard some lurid profanity, and a man's voice saying, "Who are you, lying around here in the courtyard?" Some voice had evidently stumbled over Motus.

"That must be Motus," I said in the general direction from which the girl's voice had last come. "You'd better have him carried in."

"He can lie there until he rots, for all I care," replied the voice as it trailed away. Almost immediately I saw the slim figure of a girl materialize in the entrance to one of the streets. I could tell from her back that she was an angry girl, and if her back were any criterion she was a beautiful girl— anyway, she had had a beautiful voice and a good heart. Perhaps these Invaks weren't such bad people after all.

4

"That was a beauty that you handed Motus," said a voice behind me.

I wasn't going to bother even to turn around. What was the use of turning around and seeing no one there? But when the voice said, "I'll bet he's out for a week, the dirty Invak calot," I did turn around, for I knew no Invak had made a remark like that.

Chained to a tree near me, I saw another red man (it is strange that I should always think of myself as a red man here on Barsoom; and yet, perhaps, not so strange after all. Except for my color, I *am* a red man—a red man in thought and feeling to the marrow of my bones. I no longer ever think of myself as a Virginian, so ingrained has become my love for this world of my adoption.)

"Well, where did *you* come from?" I demanded. "Are you one of the invisibles?"

"I am not," replied the man. "I have been here all along. When you were first brought I must have been asleep behind my tree, but the people stopping to comment on you awoke me. I heard you tell the girl that your name is Dotar Sojat. That is a strange name for a red man. Mine is Ptor Fak; I am from Zodanga."

Ptor Fak! I recalled him now; he was one of the three Ptor brothers who had befriended me that time that I had wished to enter Zodanga in search of Dejah Thoris. At first I hesitated to tell him who I really was; but then, knowing him to be an honorable man, I was about to when he suddenly exclaimed, "By the mother of the nearer moon! Those eyes, that skin!"

"S-h-h!" I cautioned. "I don't know the nature of these people yet, and so I thought it wiser to be Dotar Sojat."

"If you're not Dotar Sojat, who are you?" demanded a voice at my elbow. That's the trouble with this invisibility business —a man can sneak up on you and eavesdrop, and you haven't the slightest idea that there is anyone near you.

"I am the Sultan of Swat," I said, that being the first name that popped into my head.

"What's a sultan?" demanded the voice.

"A jeddak of jeddaks," I replied.

"In what country?"

"In Swat."

"I never heard of Swat," said the voice.

"Well, now that it's out, you had better tell your jeddak that he's got a sultan chained up here in his back yard."

The voice must have gone away, for I heard it no more. Ptor Fak was laughing. "I can see that things are going to brighten up a bit now that you are here," he said. "My deepest reverence for whichever one of your ancestors gave you a sense of humor. This is the first laugh I have had since they got me."

"How long have you been here?"

"Several months. I was trying out a new motor that we have developed in Zodanga and was trying to establish a record for a circumnavigation of Barsoom at the Equator, and of course this place had to be on the Equator and right under me when my motor quit. How did you get here?"

"I had just escaped from Pankor with Llana, daughter of Gahan of Gathol, and we were on our way to Helium to bring back a fleet to teach Hin Abtol a lesson. We had neither food nor water on our flier; so I landed beside this forest to get some. While I was in the forest, one of these Invaks, invisible of course to Llana, climbed aboard the flier and took off with her; and twenty more of them jumped on me and took me prisoner."

"A girl was with you! That is too bad. They may kill us, but they'll keep her."

"Pnoxus said that he had taken a fancy to her," I said, bitterly.

"Pnoxus is a calot and the son of a calot and the grandson of a calot," said Ptor Fak, illuminatingly. Nothing could have evaluated Pnoxus more concisely.

"What will they do with us?" I asked. "Will we have any

opportunity to escape that might also give me an opportunity to take Llana away?"

"Well, as long as they keep you chained to a tree, you can't escape; and that's what they've done with me ever since I've been here. I think they intend to use us in some sort of Games, but just what they are I don't know. Look!" he exclaimed, pointing and laughing.

I looked in the direction he indicated and saw two men carrying the limp form of a third down one of the streets.

"That must be Motus," said Ptor Fak. "I am afraid that may get you into trouble," he added, suddenly sobered.

"Whatever trouble it gets me into, it was worth it," I said. "Think of kicking a blind man, and that's what it amounted to. The girl was as mad about it as I; she must be a good sort. Rojas—that's rather a pretty name."

"The name of a noblewoman," said Ptor Fak.

"You know her?" I asked.

"No, but you can tell by the endings of their names whether or not they are noble and by the beginnings and endings of their names if they're royal. The names of the noblemen end in us and the names of noblewomen in as. The names of royalty end the same way but always begin with two consonants, like Pnoxus and Ptantus."

"Then Motus is a nobleman," I said.

"Yes; that is what is going to make it bad for you."

"Tell me," I said; "how do they make themselves invisible?"

"They have developed something that gives them invisibility for perhaps a day; it is something they take internally— a large pill. I understand that they take one every morning, so as to be sure that they will be invisible if they have to go outside the city. You see it takes about an hour for the stuff to work, and if the city were attacked by an enemy they'd be in a bad way if they had to go out and fight while visible."

"What enemies can they have around here?" I asked. "Kandus told me that even the green men are afraid of them."

"There is another city in the forest inhabited by an offshoot of this tribe," explained Ptor Fak; "it is called Onvak, and its people also possess the secret of invisibility. Occasionally the Onvaks come and attack Invak, or lie in wait for the Invak hunting parties when they go out into the forest."

"I should think it might be rather difficult to fight a battle in which one could see neither foe nor friend," I suggested.

"Yes; I understand that there's never very much damage done, though occasionally they capture a prisoner. The last battle they had the Invaks took two prisoners, and when they got them into the city they discovered that they were both their own men. The never know how many of their own people they kill; they just go slashing about them with their swords, and Issus help whoever gets in the way."

Just as Ptor Fak finished speaking I felt hands doing something to the shackles about my ankles and presently they were unlocked and removed.

"Come, slave," said the voice. Then someone took me by the arm and led me toward the entrance to one of the streets.

The moment we entered I could see a warrior at my side and there were others in front and behind me. They conducted me along this street through two other courtyards in which, of course, they immediately became invisible and I seemed to be walking alone with only the presure of a hand upon my arm to indicate that I was not. They took me to a large room in which a number of people were standing about in front of and on either side of a desk at which there sat a scowling, fierce visaged man.

I was led up to the desk and halted there and the man behind it surveyed me in silence for several seconds. His harness was extremely elaborate, the leather being beautifully carved and studded with precious stones. The hilt of his sword which I could just see above the desk was apparently of gold and it too was studded with those rare and beautiful gems of Barsoom which defy description in words of earthly origin. Encircling his brow was a diadem of carved leather upon the front of which the Barsoomian hieroglyphs which spelled jeddak were emblazoned in precious stones. So this was Ptantus, jeddak of Invak. I felt that Llana and I could not have fallen into much worse hands.

5

Ptantus looked at me so ferociously that I was sure he was attempting to frighten me. It seems to be a way that tyrants and bullies have of attempting to break down the morale of a victim before they destroy him; but I was not greatly impressed; and, impelled by a rather foolish desire to annoy him, I stopped looking at him. I guess that got his goat for he thumped the desk with his fist and leaned forward across it.

"Slave!" he almost roared at me, "pay attention to me."

"You haven't said anything yet," I reminded him. "When you say anything worth listening to I shall listen, but you don't have to yell at me."

He turned angrily to an officer. "Don't ever dare to bring a prisoner before me again," he said, "until he has been instructed how to behave in the presence of a jeddak."

"I know how to behave in the presence of a jeddak," I told him, "I have been in the presence of some of the greatest jeddaks on Barsoom, and I treat a jeddak just as I treat any other man—as he deserves. If he is a nobleman at heart he has my deference, if he is a boor he does not."

The inference was clear, and Ptantus colored. "Enough of your insolence," he said. "I understand that you are a troublesome fellow, that you gave Pnoxus, the prince, a great deal of trouble after your capture and that you struck and badly injured one of my nobles."

"That man may have a title," I said, "but he is no noble; he kicked me while he was invisible—it was the same as kicking a blind man."

"That is right," said a girlish voice a little way behind me and at one side. I turned and looked. It was Rojas.

"You saw this thing done, Rojas?" demanded Ptantus.

"Yes, Motus insulted me; and this man, Dotar Sojat, berated him for it. Then Motus kicked him."

"Is this true, Motus?" asked Ptantus, turning his head and looking past me on the other side. I turned and glanced in that direction and saw Motus with his face swathed in bandages; he was a sorry looking sight.

"I gave the slave what he deserves," he growled; "he is an insolent fellow."

"I quite agree with you," said Ptantus, "and he shall die when the time comes. But I did not summon him here to conduct a trial. I, the jeddak, reach my decisions without testimony or advice. I sent for him because an officer said he could leap thirty feet into the air; and if he can do that it may be worth keeping him a while for my amusement."

I couldn't help but smile a little at that for it had been my ability to jump that had probably preserved my life upon my advent to Barsoom so many years ago, when I had been captured by the green hordes of Thark, and Tars Tarkas had ordered me to *sak* for the edification of Lorquas Ptomel, the jed, and now it was going to give me at least a short reprieve from death.

"Why do you smile?" demanded Ptantus. "Do you see anything funny in that? Now jump, and be quick about it."

I looked up at the ceiling. It was only about fifteen feet from the floor. "That would be only a hop," I said.

"Well hop then," said Ptantus.

I turned and looked behind me. For about twenty feet between me and the doorway men and women were crowded thickly together. Thanking my great agility and the lesser gravity of Mars, I easily jumped completely over them. I could have made a bolt for the door then, leaped to the roof of the city and made my escape; and I should have done it had it not been that Llana of Gathol was still a prisoner here.

Exclamations of surprise filled the room at this, to them, marvelous feat of agility; and when I leaped back again there was almost a ripple of applause.

"What else can you do?" demanded Ptantus.

"I can make a fool out of Motus with a sword," I said, "as well as with my fists, if he will meet me under the lights where I can see him."

Ptantus actually laughed. "I think I shall let you do that sometime when I am through with you," he said, "for Motus will most certainly kill you. There is probably not a better swordsman on all Barsoom than the noble Motus."

"I shall be delighted to let him try it," I said, "and I can promise you that I shall still be able to jump after I have killed Motus. But, if you really want to see some jumping," I continued, "take me and the girl who was captured with me out into the forest, and we will show you something worthwhile." If I could only get outside the gates with Llana I knew that we should be able to get away, for I could outdistance any of them even if I had to carry her.

"Take him back and lock him up," said Ptantus; "I have seen and heard enough for today;" so they took me back into the courtyard and chained me to my tree.

"Well," said Ptor Fak, after he thought the guards had left, "how did you get along?"

I told him all that had transpired in the jeddak's presence; and he said he hoped that I would get a chance to meet Motus, as Ptor Fak well knew my reputation as a swordsman.

After dark that night, a voice came out and sat down beside me. It was Kandus.

"It's a good thing you jumped for Ptantus today," he said, "the old devil thought Pnoxus had been lying to him and after it had been demonstrated that you could not jump Ptantus was going to have you destroyed immediately in a very unpleasant way he has of dealing with those who have aroused his anger or resentment."

"I hope I can keep on amusing him for a while," I said.

"The end will be the same eventually," said Kandus, "but if there is anything I can do to make your captivity easier for you I shall be glad to do it."

"It would relieve my mind if you could tell me what has become of the girl who was captured at the same time that I was."

"She is confined in the quarters of the female slaves. It's over on that side of the city beyond the palace," and he nodded in that direction.

"What do you think is going to happen to her?" I asked.

"Ptantus and Pnoxus are quarreling about her," he replied; "they are always quarreling about something; they hate each other. Because Pnoxus wants her Ptantus doesn't want him to have her; and so, for the time being at least, she is safe. I must go now," he added a moment later, and I could tell from the direction of his voice that he had arisen. "If there is anything I can do for you be sure to let me know."

"If you could bring me a piece of wire," I said, "I would appreciate it."

"What do you want of wire?" he asked.

"Just to pass the time," I said; "I bend them around in different shapes and make little figures of them to amuse myself. I am not accustomed to being chained to a tree, and time is going to hang very heavy on my hands."

"Certainly," he said, "I'll be glad to bring you a piece of wire; I'll be back with it in just a moment, and until then good-by."

"You are fortunate to have made a friend here," said Ptor Fak; "I've been here several months and I haven't made one."

"I think it was my jumping," I said; "it has served me in good stead before and in many ways."

It was not long before Kandus returned with the wire. I thanked him and he left immediately.

It was night now and both moons were in the sky. Their soft light illuminated the courtyard, while the swift flight of Thuria across the vault of heaven swept the shadows of the trees into constantly changing movement across the scarlet sward, turned purple now in the moonlight.

Ptor Fak's chain and mine were sufficiently long to just permit us to sit side by side, and I could see that his curiosity was aroused by my request for a piece of wire by the fact that he kept watching it in my hand. Finally he could contain himself no longer. "What are you going to do with that wire?" he asked.

"You'd be surprised," I said; and then I paused for I felt a presence near me, "at the clever things one may do with a piece of wire."

6

Were I to live here in Invak the rest of my life I am sure I could never accustom myself to these uncanny presences, or to the knowledge that someone might always be standing close to me listening to everything that I said to Ptor Fak.

Presently I felt a soft hand upon my arm, and then that same sweet voice that I had heard before said, "It is Rojas."

"I am glad that you came," I said. "I wished an opportunity to thank you for the testimony you gave in my behalf before Ptantus today."

"I'm afraid it didn't do you much good," she replied; "Ptantus doesn't like me."

"Why should he dislike you?" I asked.

"Pnoxus wanted me as his mate and I refused him; so, though Ptantus doesn't like Pnoxus, his pride was hurt; and he has been venting his spleen on my family ever since." She moved closer to me, I could feel the warmth of her arm against mine as she leaned against me. "Dotar Sojat," she said, "I wish that you were an Invak so that you might remain here in safety."

"That is very sweet of you, Rojas," I said, "but I am afraid that Fate has ordained it otherwise."

The soft arm stole up around my shoulders. The delicate perfume which had first announced her presence to me that afternoon, filled my nostrils and I could feel her warm breath upon my cheek. "Would you like to stay here, Dotar Sojat," she paused, "—with me?"

The situation was becoming embarrassing. Even Ptor Fak was embarrassed and there were no soft invisible arms about his neck. I knew that he was embarrassed because he had moved away from us the full length of his chain. Of course he couldn't see Rojas any more than I could but he must have heard her words; and, being a gentleman, he had removed himself as far as possible; and now he sat there with his back toward us. Being made love to by a beautiful girl in a moonlit garden may be romantic, but if the girl is wholly invisible it is like being made love to by a ghost; though I can assure you that Rojas didn't feel like a ghost at all.

"You have not answered me, Dotar Sojat," she said.

I have never loved but one woman—my incomparable Dejah Thoris; nor do I, like some men, run around pretending love for other women. So, as you say in America, I was on the spot. They say that all is fair in love and war; and as far as I was concerned I, personally, was definitely at war with Invak. Here was an enemy girl whose loyalty I could win or whose bitter hatred I could incur by my reply. Had I had only myself to consider I should not have hesitated; but the fate of Llana of Gathol outweighted all other considerations, and so I temporized.

"No matter how much I should like to be with you always, Rojas," I said, "I know that is impossible. I shall be here only subject to the whims of your jeddak and then death will separate us forever."

"Oh, no, Dotar Sojat," she cried, drawing my cheek close to hers, "you must not die—for I love you."

"But Rojas," I expostulated, "how can you love a man whom you have known for only a few hours and seen but for a few minutes?"

"I knew that I loved you the moment that I set eyes upon you," she replied, "and I've seen you for a great many more than a few minutes. I have been almost contantly in the courtyard since I first saw you, watching you. I know every changing expression of your face. I have seen the light of anger, and of humor, and of friendship in your eyes. Had I known you all my life I could not know you better. Kiss me, Dotar Sojat," she conclued. And, then I did something for which I shall probably always be ashamed. I took Rojas in my arms and kissed her.

Did you ever hold a ghost in your arms and kiss her? It humiliates me to admit that it was not an unpleasant experience. But Rojas clung to me so tightly and for so long that I was covered with confusion and embarrassment.

"Oh, that we could be always thus," sighed Rojas.

Personally I thought that however pleasant, it might be a little inconvenient. However, I said, "Perhaps you will come often again, Rojas, before I die."

"Oh, don't speak of death," she cried.

"But you know yourself that Ptantus will have me killed—unless I escape."

"Escape!" She scarcely breathed the word.

"But I suppose there will be no escape for me," I added, and I tried not to sound too hopeful.

"Escape," she said again, "Escape! ah if I could but go with you."

"Why not?" I asked. I had gone this far and I felt that I might as well go all the way if by so doing I could release Llana of Gathol from captivity.

"Yes, why not?" repeated Rojas, "but how?"

"If I could become invisible," I suggested.

She thought that over for a moment and then said, "It

would be treason. It would mean death, a horrible death, were I apprehended."

"I couldn't ask that of you," I said, and I felt like a hypocrite for that I knew that I could ask it of her if I thought that she would do it. I would willingly have sacrificed the life of every person in Invak, including my own, if thereby I could have liberated Llana of Gathol. I was desperate, and when a man is desperate he will resort to any means to win his point.

"I am most unhappy here," said Rojas, in a quite natural and human attempt at self-justification. "Of course, if we were successful," continued Rojas, "it wouldn't make any difference who knew what I had done because they could never find us again. We would both be invisible, and together we could make our way to your country." She was planning it all out splendidly.

"Do you know where the flier is that brought the girl prisoner?" I asked.

"Yes, it was landed on the roof of the city."

"That will simplify matters greatly," I said. "If we all become invisible we can reach it and escape with ease."

"What do you mean 'all'?" she demanded.

"Why I want to take Ptor Fak with me," I said, "and Llana of Gathol who was captured the same time I was."

Rojas froze instantly and her arms dropped from about me. "Not the girl," she said.

"But, Rojas, I must save her," I insisted. There was no reply. I waited a moment and then I said, "Rojas!" but she did not answer, and a moment later I saw her slim back materialize in the entrance to one of the streets opposite me. A slim back surmounted by a defiantly held head. That back radiated feminine fury.

7

After Rojas left I was plunged almost into the depths of despair. Had she but waited I could have explained everything and the four of us might have escaped. I will admit that I have never been able to fathom the ways of women, but I felt that Rojas would never return. I presume that my conviction was influenced by those lines from The Mourning Bride, "Heaven has no rage like love to hatred turned, nor hell a fury like a woman scorned."

However, I did not give up hope entirely—I never do. Instead of repining, I went to work on the lock of my shackle with the bit of wire that Kandus had brought me. Ptor Fak moved over to watch me. I sat facing my tree, close to it, and bending over my work; and Ptor Fak leaned close and bent over it too. We were trying to hide from preying eyes the thing that I was attempting to do; and as it was now late at night we hoped that there would be no one in the court-yard other than ourselves.

At last I found the combination and after that it took me only a few seconds to unlock Ptor Fak's shackle. Then a voice behind us spoke.

"What are you doing?" it demanded; "why are you not asleep?"

"How can we sleep with people constantly annoying us?" I asked, hiding the wire beneath me.

"Stand up," said the voice, and as we stood up the shackles fell away from our ankles.

"I thought so," said the voice. Then I saw the piece of wire rise from the gr und and disappear. "You are very clever, but I don't think Ptantus will appreicate your clever-ness when he hears about this. I shall set a guard to watch you two constantly hereafter."

"Everything is going wrong," I said to Ptor Fak a moment later, after I saw a warrior enter one of the streets, hoping that it was he who had spoken to us and that there were no others around.

"It seems hopeless, doesn't it?" said Ptor Fak.

"No," I snapped, "not while I still live."

The following afternoon Kandus' voice came and sat down beside me. "How goes it?" he asked.

"Terrible," I said.

"How is that?" he asked.

"I can't tell you," I said, "because there is probably a guard standing right here listening to everything that I say."

"There is no one here but us," said Kandus.

"How do you know?" I asked; "your people are as invisible to you as they are to me."

"We learn to sense the presence of others," he explained; "just how, I can't tell you."

"How you do it is immaterial," I said, "as long as you are sure there is no one here listening to us. I will be perfectly frank with you, I succeeded in removing Ptor Fak's shackle and my own. Someone caught me at it and took the piece of wire away from me." I did not tell Kandus that I had broken the wire he had given me in two and that I still had the other half of it in my pocket pouch. There is no use in telling even a friend everything that you know.

"How in the world could you have hoped to escape even if you could remove your shackles?" he asked.

"It was only the first step," I told him. "We really had no plan, but we knew that we certainly could not escape as long as we were shackled."

Kandus laughed. "There is something in that," he said, and then he was silent for a moment. "The girl who was captured with you," he said presently.

"What of her?" I asked.

"Ptanus has given her to Motus," he replies; "it was all done very suddenly. Why, no one seems to know, because Ptantus hasn't any particular love for Motus."

If Kandus didn't know why, I thought that I did. I saw Rojas's hand and a green-eyed devil in it—jealousy is a heartless monster. "Will you do something more for me, Kandus?" I asked.

"Gladly, if I can," he replied.

"It may seem like a very silly request," I said, "but please don't ask me to explain. I want you to go to Rojas and tell her that Llana of Gathol, the girl that Ptantus has given to Motus, is the daughter of my daughter." It may seem strange to you denizens of earth that Rojas could have become infatuated with a grandfather, but you must remember that Mars is not Earth and that I am unlike all other Earth-men. I do not know how old I am. I recall no childhood. It seems to me that have just always been, and I have always been the same. I look now as I did when I fought with the Confederate army during the Civil War—a man of about thirty. And here on Barsoom, where the natural span of life is around a thousand years and people do not commence to show the ravages of old age until just shortly before dissolution, differences in age do not count. You might fall in love with a beautiful girl on Barsoom; and, as far as appearances were concerned, she might be seventeen or she might be seven hundred.

"Of course I don't understand," said Kandus, "but I'll do what you ask."

"And now another favor," I said. "Ptantus half promised me that he would let me duel with Motus and he assured me that Motus would kill me. Is there any possible way of arranging for that duel to be fought today?"

"He will kill you," said Kandus.

"That is not what I asked," I said.

"I don't know how it could be done," said Kandus.

"Now if Ptantus has any sporting blood," I suggested, "and likes to lay a wager now and then, you bet him that if Motus will fight me while Motus is still visible, that he cannot kill me but that I can kill him whenever I choose."

"But you can't do it," said Kandus. "Motus is the best

swordsman on Barsoom. You would be killed and I should lose my money."

"How can I convince you?" I said. "I know that I can kill Motus in a fight. If I had anything of value, I would give it to you as security for your wager."

"I have something of value," said Ptor Fak, "and I would wager it and everything that I could scrape together on Dotar Sojat." He reached into his pocket pouch and drew froth a gorgeous jewelled medallion. "This," he said to Kandus, "is worth a jeddak's ransom—take it as security and place its value on Dotar Sojat."

A second later the medallion disappeared in thin air, and we knew that Kandus had reached out his hand and taken it.

"I'll have to go inside and examine it," said Kandus' voice, "for of course I cannot see it now that it has become invisible. I'll not be gone long."

"That is very decent of you, Ptor Fak," I said, "that medallion must be almost invaluable."

"One of my remote ancestors was a jeddak," explained Ptor Fak; "that medallion belonged to him, and it has been in the family for thousands of years."

"You must be quite certain of my swordsmanship," I said.

"I am," he replied; "but even had I been less certain, I should have done the same."

"That is friendship," I said, "and I appreciate it."

"It is priceless," said a voice at my side, and I knew that Kandus had returned. "I will go at once and see what can be done about the duel."

"Don't forget what I asked you to tell Rojas," I reminded him.

8

After Kandus left us, time dragged heavily. The afternoon wore on and it became so late that I was positive that he had failed in his mission. I was sitting dejectedly thinking of the fate that was so soon to overtake Llana of Gathol. I knew that she would destroy herself, and I was helpless to avert the tragedy. And, while I was thus sunk in the depths of despair, a hand was placed on mine. A soft hand; and a voice said, "Why didn't you tell me?"

"You didn't give me a chance," I said; "you just ran out on me without giving me a chance to explain."

"I am sorry," said the voice, "and I am sorry for the harm I have done Llana of Gathol; and now I have condemned you to death."

"What do you mean?" I asked.

"Ptantus has commanded Motus to fight you and kill you."

I threw my arms around Rojas and kissed her. I couldn't help it, I was so happy. "Good!" I exclaimed. "Though neither of us realized it at the time, you have done me a great favor."

"What do you mean?" she demanded.

"You have given me the chance to meet Motus in a fair fight; and now I know that Llana of Gathol will be safe—as far as Motus is concerned."

"Motus will kill you," insisted Rojas.

"Will you be there to see the duel?" I asked.

"I do not wish to see you killed," she said, and clung to me tightly.

"You haven't a thing to worry about, I shall not be killed; and Motus will never have Llana of Gathol or any other woman."

"You can tell his friends to start digging his grave immediately," said Ptor Fak.

"You are that sure?" said Rojas.

"We have the princess," said Ptor Fak, which is the same as saying in America "It is in the bag." The expression derives from the Barsoomian chess game, jetan, in which the taking of a princess decides the winner and ends the game.

"I hope you are right," said Rojas. "At least you have encouraged me to believe, and it is not so difficult to believe anything of Dotar Sojat."

"Do you know when I am to fight Motus?" I asked.

"This evening," replied Rojas, "before the whole Court in the throne room of the palace."

"And after I have killed him?" I asked.

"That is to be feared, too," said Rojas, "for Ptantus will be furious. He will not only have lost a fighting man but all the money he has wagered on the duel. But it will soon be time," she added, "and I must go now." I saw her open my pocket pouch and drop something into it, and then she was gone.

I knew from the surreptitious manner in which she had done it that she did not wish anyone to know what she had put in my pocket pouch, or in fact that she had put anything into it; and so I did not investigate immediately, fearing that someone may have been watching and had their suspicions aroused. The constant strain of feeling that unseen eyes may be upon you, and that unseen ears may be listening to your every word was commencing to tell upon me; and I was becoming as nervous as a cat with seven kittens.

After a long silence Ptor Fak said, "What are you going to do with her?"

I knew what he meant; because the same question had been worrying me. "If we succeed in getting out of this," I said, "I am going to take her back to Helium with me and let Dejah Thoris convince her that there are a great many more charming men that I there." I had had other women fall in love with me and this would not be the first time that Dejah Thoris had unscrambled things for me. For she knew that no matter how many women loved me, she was the only woman whom I loved.

"You are a brave man," said Ptor Fak.

"You say that because you do not know Dejah Thoris," I replied; "it is not that I am a brave man, it is that she is a wise woman."

That started me off again thinking about her, although I must confess that she is seldom absent from my thoughts. I could picture her now in our marble palace in Helium, surrounded by the brilliant men and women who crowd her salons. I could feel her hand in mine as we trod the stately Barsoomian dances she loves so well. I could see her as though she were standing before me this minute, and I could see Thuvia of Ptarth, and Carthoris, and Tara of Helium, and Gahan of Gathol. That magnificent coterie of handsome men and beautiful women bound together by ties of love and marriage. What memories they evoked!

A soft hand caressed my cheek and a voice, tense with nervousness said, "Live! Live for me! I shall return at midnight and you must be here;" then she was gone.

For some reason or other which I cannot explain, her words quieted my nerves. They gave me confidence that at midnight I should be free. Her presence reminded me that she had dropped something into my pocket pouch and I opened it casually and put my hand into it. My fingers came in contact with a number of spheres, about the size of marbles, and I knew that the secret of invisibility was mine. I moved close to Ptor Fak; and once again with the remaining bit of wire I picked the lock of his shackle, and then I handed him one of the spheres that Rojas had given me.

I leaned very close to his ear. "Take this," I whispered; "in an hour you will be invisible. Go to the far end of the courtyard and wait. When I return I too shall be invisible and when I whistle thus, answer me." I whistled a few of the opening notes of the national anthem of Helium, a signal that Dejah Thoris and I had often used.

"I understand," said Ptor Fak.

"What do you understand?" demanded a voice.

Doggonit! there was that invisibility nemesis again and now all our plans might be knocked into a cocked hat. How much had the fellow heard? What had he seen? I trembled inwardly, fearing the answer. Then I felt hands at my ankle and saw my shackle fall open.

"Well," repeated the voice peremptorily, "what was it that you understood?"

"I was just telling Ptor Fak," I said, "how I was going to kill Motus, and he said he understood perfectly."

"So you think you are going to kill Motus, do you?" demanded the voice. "Well, you are going to be very much surprised for a few minutes, and after that you will be dead. Come along with me; the duel is about to take place."

I breathed a sigh of relief. The fellow had evidently seen or heard nothing of any importance.

"I'll see you later, Ptor Fak," I said.

"Good-by and good luck," he replied. And then, accompanied by the warrior, I entered a city street on my way to the throne room of Ptantus, jeddak of Invak.

9

"So you think you're pretty good with the sword," said the warrior walking at my side and who was now visible to me.

"Yes," I replied.

"Well, you're going to get a lesson in swordsmanship tonight. Of course it won't do you much good because after it is all over you will be dead."

"You are very encouraging," I said, "but if you are fond of Motus, I suggest that you save your encouragement for him. He is going to need it."

"I am not fond of Motus," said the warrior; "no one is fond of Motus. He is a calot and I apologize to calots for the comparison. I hope that you kill him but of course you won't. He always kills his man, but he is tricky. Watch out for that."

"You mean he doesn't fight fair?" I asked.

"No one ever taught him the word," said the warrior.

"Well, thank you for warning me," I said; "I hope you stay to see the fight, maybe you will be surprised."

"I shall certainly stay to see it," he said. "I wouldn't miss it for the world. But I am not going to be surprised; I know just what will happen. He will play with you for about five minutes and then he'll run you through; and that won't please Ptantus for he likes a long drawn out duel."

"Oh, he does does he?" I said. "Well, he shall have it." That fitted in perfectly with my plans. I had swallowed one of the invisibility spheres just before the warrior unshackled me, and I knew that it would take about an hour for it to effect perfect invisibility. It might be difficult to drag the duel out for an hour, but I hoped to gain a little time by stalling up to the moment that we crossed swords. And I accomplished it now by walking slowly to kill as much time as possible, and twice I stopped to tighten the fastenings of my sandals.

"What's the matter?" demanded the warrior. "Why do you walk so slow? Are you afraid?"

"Terrified," I replied. "Everyone has told me how easily Motus is going to kill me. Do you think that a man wants to run to his death?"

"Well, I don't blame you much," said the warrior, "and I won't hurry you."

"A lot of you Invaks are pretty good fellows," I remarked.

"Of course we are," he said. "What made you think anything different?"

"Pnoxus, Motus, and Ptantus," I replied.

The warrior grinned. "I guess you are a pretty shrewd fellow," he said, "to have sized them up this quickly."

"Everybody seems to hate them," I said; "why don't you get rid of them? I'll start you off by getting rid of Motus tonight."

"You may be a good swordsman," said the warrior, "but you are bragging too much; I never knew a braggart yet who could 'take the princess.'"

"I am not bragging," I said; "I only state facts." As a matter of fact, I often realize that in speaking of my swordsmanship, it may sound to others as though I were bragging but really I do not feel that I am bragging. I know that I am the greatest swordsman of two worlds. It would be foolish for me to simper, and suck my finger, and say that I was not. I am, and everyone who has seen me fight knows that I am. Is it braggadocio to state a simple fact? It has saved a number of lives, for it has kept no end of brash young men from challenging me. Fighting has been, you might say, my life's work. There is not a lethal weapon in the use of which I do not excel, but the sword is my favorite. I love a good blade and I love a good fight and I hoped that tonight I should have them both. I hoped that Motus was all that they thought him. The thought might have obtruded on the consciousness of some men that perhaps he was, but no such idea ever entered my head. They say that overconfidence often leads to defeat, but I do not think that I am ever overconfident. I am merely wholly confident, and I maintain that there is all the difference in the world there.

At last we came to the throne room. It was not the same room in which I had first seen Ptantus; it was a much larger room, a more ornate room; and at one side of it was a raised dias on which were two thrones. They were empty now, for the jeddak and the jeddara had not yet appeared. The floor of the room was crowded with nobles and their women. Along three sides of the room were several tiers of benches, temporary affairs, which had evidently been brought in for the occasion. They were covered with gay cloths and cushions; but they were still empty, for, of course, no one could sit until the jeddak came and was seated.

As I was brought into the room, a number of people called attention to me and soon many eyes were upon me.

In my well-worn fighting harness, I looked rather drab in the midst of this brilliant company with their carved leather harness studded with jewels. The Invaks, like most of the red nations of Barsoom, are a handsome people and those in the throne room of this tiny nation, hidden away in the Forest of Lost Men, made a brave appearance beneath the strange and beautiful lights which gave them visibility.

I heard many comments concerning me. One woman said, "He does not look like a Barsoomian at all."

"He is very handsome," said a sweet voice, which I immediately recognized; and for the second time I looked Rojas in the face. As our eyes met I could see her tremble. She was a beautiful girl, by far the most beautiful of all the women in the room, I am sure.

"Let's talk with him," she said to a woman and two men standing with her.

"That would be interesting," said the woman, and the four of them walked toward me.

Rojas looked me square in the eye. "What is your name?" she asked, without a flicker of recognition.

"Dotar Sojat," I replied.

"The Sultan of Swat," said one of the men, "whatever a sultan is and wherever Swat may be." I could scarcely repress a smile.

"Where is Swat?" inquired the woman.

"In India," I replied.

"I think the fellow is trying to make fools of us," snapped one of the men. "He is just making up those names. There are no such places on Barsoom."

"I didn't say they were on Barsoom," I retorted. "They are forty-three million miles from Barsoom."

"If they're not on Barsoom, where are they?" demanded the man.

"On Jasoom," I replied.

"Come," said the man, "I have had enough of this slave's insolence."

"I find him very interesting," said the woman.

"So do I," said Rojas.

"Well, enjoy it while you may," said the man, "for in a few minutes he will be dead."

"Have you laid a wager on that?" I asked.

"I couldn't find anyone to bet against Motus," he growled. "Kandus was the only fool to do that and the jeddak covered his entire wager."

"That is too bad," I said; "someone is losing an opportunity to make some money."

"Do you think you will win?" asked Rojas, trying to conceal the eagerness in her voice.

"Of course I shall win," I replied. "I always do. You look like a very intelligent girl," I said, "if I may speak to you alone I will tell you a little secret."

She saw that I had something that I wished to say to her in private, but I will admit that I had put her in rather an embarrassing position. However, the other woman helped me out."

"Go ahead, Rojas," she urged. "I think it would be fun to hear what he has to say."

Thus encouraged Rojas took me to one side. "What is it?" she asked.

"Llana of Gathol," I said. "How are we to get her?"

She caught her breath. "I never thought of that," she said.

"Could you get one of those invisibility spheres to her right away?" I asked.

"For you, yes," she said. "For you I would do anything."

"Good; and tell her to come out into the courtyard by the quarters of the slave women. A little after midnight she will hear me whistle. She will recognize the air. She must answer and then wait for me. Will you do that for me, Rojas?"

"Yes, but what excuse am I to make for leaving my friends?"

"Tell them you are going to get some money to wager on me," I said.

Rojas smiled. "That is a splendid idea," she said. And a moment later she had made her explanations to her friends and I saw her leave the throne room.

10

The crowd was growing restless waiting for the jeddak, but I was more than pleased by this delay as it would shorten the time that I should have to wait before I could achieve invisibility.

It seemed now that everything had been nicely arranged; and when I saw Rojas return to the throne room and she gave me a quick fleeting smile, I was convinced that almost the last of my worries were over. There was really only one doubt remaining in my mind, and that was as to what might happen to me after I had killed Motus. I had no doubt but that Ptantus would be furious; and being a tyrant with the reactions of a tyrant, he might order my immediate death. Anticipating this, however, I had decided to make a run for the nearest courtyard; and if sufficient time had elapsed since I had taken the invisibility sphere, I would only have to step out into the open to elude them. And, once in one of the courtyards, and invisible, I knew that I could escape.

Suddenly trumpets blared and the people fell back to each side of the throne room. Then, preceded by the trumpeters, Ptantus and his jeddara entered the throne room accompanied by a band of gorgeously trapped courtiers.

I glanced at the great clock on the wall. It was exactly the 8th zode which is the equivalent of 10:48 P.M. Earth time. By midnight Llana of Gathol would have achieved invisibility—if Rojas had given her the sphere. That was the question. Yet I felt that Rojas had not failed me. I firmly believed that she had done her part.

The royal pair made their way slowly across the room to the dais and seated themselves upon their thrones, whereat the nobles and their women found their places on the benches.

From somewhere Motus had appeared; and he, and a noble who accompanied him, and I, and my warrior guard, were alone upon the floor. A fifth man then appeared who I later discovered was what you might call a referee, or umpire. He summoned me forward, and the five of us advanced and stopped before the throne.

"I bring you the noble Motus," he said addressing Ptantus, "and Dotar Sojat, the Sultan of Swat, who are to duel to the death with long-swords."

The jeddak nodded. "Let them fight," he said, "and see that you fight fair," he added, glaring directly at me.

"And, I suppose that Motus does not have to fight fair," I said; "but that is immaterial to me. I shall kill him however he fights."

The referee was almost beside himself with embarrassment. "Silence, slave!" he whispered. He carried an extra sword which he handed to me and then motioned us to cross swords.

Instead of adhering to this honorable custom, Motus lunged for my heart.

"That was unwise, Motus," I said, as I parried the thrust; "I am going to make you suffer a little more for that."

"Silence, slave," demanded the referee.

"Silence yourself, calot," I replied, "and get out of my way. I am not supposed to be fighting two men," I pricked Motus on the right breast and brought blood, "but I shall be glad too if you will draw."

Motus came at me again, but he was wary and he was a good swordsman.

"Your face is all black and swollen, Motus," I said; "it looks as if someone had hit you, for that is what a son-of-a-calot is apt to get when he kicks a blind man."

"Silence," screamed the referee.

I fought on the defensive at first with one eye on the great clock. It had been over half an hour since I had taken the invisibility sphere, and I planned on letting Motus live another half hour so as to be quite sure that I had gained potential invisibility before I finished him off.

By fighting on the defensive, I compelled Motus to do all the work; and by repeatedly side-stepping his most vicious lunges, letting them slip off my blade so that he had to leap quickly back, I subjected him to considerable nervous as well as physical strain, so that presently the sweat was streaming down his body. And, now I commenced to touch him here and there; and blood mixed with the sweat until he was a sorry looking spectacle, although nowhere had he received a severe wound.

The crowd was all on Motus's side; that is, all who were vocal. I knew of two at least who hoped that I would win, and I guess that there were many others who disliked Motus but who dared not cheer on an alien and a slave.

"You are tiring, Motus," I said to him; "hadn't you better finish me off now before you become wholly exhausted?"

"I'll finish you off all right, slave," he came back, "if you'll stand still and fight."

"It is not time to kill you yet, Motus," I said, glancing up at the clock, "when the hand points to eleven xats past the 8th zode, I shall kill you."

"Silence," screeched the referee.

"What is the slave saying?" demanded Ptantus in stentorian tones.

"I said," I shouted back at him, "that I should kill Motus at exactly 8 zodes, 11 xats. Watch the clock, Ptantus, for at that instant you are going to lose your wager, and Motus his life."

"Silence," commanded the jeddak.

"Now, Motus," I whispered, "I am going to show you how easily I can kill you when the time comes," and with that I disarmed him and sent his sword clattering across the floor.

A mighty gasp arose from the audience, for now under the rules of a duel of this nature, I was at liberty to run Motus through the heart; but instead I rested my point upon the floor and turned to the referee.

"Go and fetch Motus's sword," I said, "and return it to him."

Motus was trembling a little. I could see his knees shake though almost imperceptibly. I knew then what I had suspected before—Motus was yellow.

While the referee was retrieving Motus' sword, a little ripple of applause ran through the stands. But Ptantus only sat and scowled more fiercely; I fear that Ptantus did not like me.

When Motus' sword was returned to him, he came for me furiously; and I knew perfectly well what was in his mind; he was going to finish me off immediately. I disarmed him again; and again I lowered my point, while the referee without waiting to be told ran after the blade.

Now Motus was more wary. I could see that he was trying to work me around to some position in which he wished to have me. I noticed presently that the referee was not within my range of vision, and a quick glance told me he was standing directly behind me; it was not intuition that told me why, for I had seen that trick played before by crooked swordsmen with an accomplice. I heard a few groans from the stands; and then I knew that I was right, for no honorable person could witness such a thing without voicing his disapproval.

When Motus next lunged, hoping to force me back, the referee would "accidentally" be close behind me; I would bump into him, and Motus would have me at his mercy. It is a despicable trick; and Ptantus must have seen it coming, but he made no move to prevent it.

I watched Motus' eyes and they telegraphed his intention to me an instant before he lunged, throwing all his weight behind it. I had slightly crouched in anticipation of this and my earthly muscles carried me to one side, and Motus's sword drove to the hilt through the body of the referee.

For a moment pandemonium reigned in the throne room. The entire audience stood up in the stands and there were cheers and groans, and something told me that the cheers were for me and the groans for Motus and the referee.

Motus was a terribly unstrung and rattled man as he jerked his blade from the body of the dead man, but now I gave him no respite. I went after him in earnest, though not yet for the kill. I cut a deep gash across his swollen jaw. "You will not make a good looking corpse now, Motus," I said, "and before I am through with you, you are going to look a great deal worse."

"Calot!" he snapped, and then he rushed me, cutting and thrusting violently. I parried every cut and thrust and wove a net of steel around him, and every time he missed I brought blood from some new spot on his body.

"You have three xats to live, Motus," I said; "you had better make the best of them."

He rushed at me like a madman; but I sidestepped him and as he turned I took off one of his ears as neatly as a surgeon could have done it—I thought he was going to faint, for his knees seemed to give beneath him and he staggered about for a moment.

I waited for for him to recover control of himself, and then I went to work on him again. I tried to carve my initials on his breast, but by this time there was not a whole place large enough; from the waist up he looked like a plate of raw hamburger.

The floor was covered with his blood by now; and as he rushed me again furiously, he slipped and fell. He lay there for a moment glaring at me, for I am sure he expected that I would finish him off then; but instead I said, "You have a xat and a half to live yet, Motus."

He staggered to his feet and tried to throw himself upon me, screaming imprecations as he came. I think that by this time Motus had gone quite mad from pain and terror. I felt no sympathy for him—he was a rat; and now he was fighting like a cornered rat.

"The floor is too slippery here," I said to him; "lets go over by the jeddak's throne—I am sure that he would like to see the finish."

I maneuvered him around into position and backed him across the floor until we stood directly in front of Ptantus.

It is seldom that I have ever punished a man as I punished Motus; but I felt that he deserved it, and I was the plaintiff, prosecuting attorney, jury, and judge; I was also the executioner.

Motus was gibbering now and making futile passes at me with his blade. Ptantus was glaring at me, and the audience was tense with breathless expectancy. I saw many an eye glance quickly at the clock.

"One more tal, Motus," I said. A tal is about eight tenths of an earthly second.

At that Motus turned suddenly and ran screaming toward the great doorway that led from the throne room; and again the audience rose to its feet, and there were groans and cries of "Coward!"

The fight was to have been to the death and Ptantus had wagered that I would not kill Motus. If I did not kill him, I feared that Ptantus would then claim the money; so I risked everything on an art I had often practiced for my own amusement. I carried my sword hand far behind my right shoulder and then brought it forward with all my strength, releasing the blade point first. It flew like a sped arrow and drove through Motus' body below the left shoulder blade at exactly 11 xats past the 8th zode.

11

I turned and bowed to Ptantus, now having no sword with which to salute him. He should have acknowledged this customary courtesy but he did nothing of the sort, he merely glared at me and stood up. The jeddara arose too; and, with the trumpeters before them and the courtiers behind, the two stalked out of the throne room, making a wide detour to avoid the blood and the two corpses.

After they had left, the warrior who had brought me from the courtyard came and touched me on the arm. "Come," he said. "All you get out of this is to be chained to your tree again."

"I got a great deal more than that out of it," I replied, as I accompanied him across the throne room; "I had the satisfaction of avenging a cowardly kick."

As we crossed towards the doorway, someone started cheering and then practically the entire audience took it up. "That is an unusual demonstration," said the warrior, "but you deserve it. No one on Barsoom ever saw such swordplay as you showed us tonight—and I thought you were boasting!" He laughed.

I knew that it would be necessary for us to cross a couple of courtyards before we reached the one in which I had been confined; and I realized that if I suddenly disappeared before the warrior's eyes, he would know that I had obtained invisibility spheres; and while of course he couldn't have found me, it would certainly have started an investigation and would have upset our plans for escape. If they knew that I was at large and invisible, one of the first things that they would most naturally have done would have been to place a guard over my flier.

If, however, they merely thought that I had escaped, and was not invisible, they would feel that they need only search for me to find me very quickly. Of course, they might still place a guard over the flier; but such a guard would not be so on the alert, and we still might board the ship and get away before they were aware of our presence.

As we approached the first courtyard, I suddenly broke away from my guard and ran ahead with all my earthly speed. The warrior shouted for me to halt, and broke into a run. As I reached the entrance to the courtyard I pretended to dodge around the corner, which would of course have hidden me from him.

I must confess that in that short sprint my heart had been in my mouth, for of course I could not know whether or not I should become invisible.

However, the moment that I left the lighted corridor I absolutely disappeared; I could not see any part of my body—it was the strangest sensation that I have ever experienced.

I had made my plans, and now I ran to the far end of the courtyard and leaped lightly to the roof of the city.

I could hear the warrior guard rushing about calling to me; my disappearance must certainly have mystified him, for having no idea that I could become invisible, there was really no way in which he could account for it except on the theory that I had run into the entrance to another street. However, he was probably confident that I did not have time to do this.

Well, I did not bother much about him or what he was thinking; instead I took off across the roof in search of the courtyard where Ptor Fak was awaiting me and where I expected to meet Rojas at midnight; and it was pretty close to what we call midnight then, the Barsoomian midnight occurring twenty-five xats after the eighth zode.

A Martian day is divided into ten zodes, there being four tals to a xat, or two hundred to a zode. The dials of their clocks are marked with four concentric circles; between the inner circle and the next outer one the Zodes are marked from one to ten; in the next circle, the xats are marked from one to fifty between each two zodes; and in the outer circle two hundred tals are marked between the radii which pass through the zode numbers and extend to the outer periphery of the dial. Their clock has three different colored and different length hands, one indicating the zode, the second one the xat, and the longest one the tal.

(Editor's note: I have before me the diagram of the dial of a Martian clock drawn for me by John Carter many years ago.)

I had no difficulty in finding the courtyard in which I had been confined; and when I reached it I whistled, and Ptor Fak answered. I dropped down into it and whistled again, and when Ptor Fak answered I groped around until I bumped into him.

"How well you look," he said, and we both laughed. "It took you much longer to dispose of Motus than I had anticipated," he continued.

"I had to drag it out so that I would be sure to be invisible when I had returned here," I explained.

"And now what?" asked Ptor Fak.

I found his head and placed my lips close to one of his ears. "After Rojas comes," I whispered, "we'll cross the roof to the quarters of the slave women and get Llana of Gathol. In the meantime, you climb this tree which overhangs the roof and wait for us up there."

"Whistle when you come up," he said, and left me.

Invisibility I discovered was most disconcerting; I could see no part of my body; I was only a voice without visible substance—a voice standing in an apparently deserted courtyard which might be filled with enemies, as far as I knew. I couldn't even have heard them had there been any there, for the Invaks have taken the precaution of covering all the metal parts of their accouterments so that there is not the usual clank of metal upon metal when they move about.

Knowing as I did that a search for me must have been instituted, I felt positive that there must be Invak warriors in the courtyard, notwithstanding the fact that I neither heard nor saw anyone.

As I waited for Rojas, I took the precaution of not moving about lest I inadvertently bump into someone who might require me to identify myself; but I could not prevent someone from bumping into me, and that is exactly what happened. Hands were laid upon me and a gruff voice demanded, "Who are you?"

Here was a pretty kettle of fish. What was I to do? I doubted that I could pass myself off as an Invak—I knew too little about them to do that successfully; so, I did the next best thing that occurred to me.

"I am the ghost of Motus," I said, in a sepulchral voice. "I am searching for the man who killed me, but he is not here."

The hands relinquished their hold upon me; I could almost feel the fellow shrink away from me, and then another voice said, "Ghost of Motus nothing—I recognize that voice—it is the voice of the slave who killed Motus. Seize him!"

I jumped to one side but I jumped into the arms of another voice, and it seized me. "I have him!" cried the voice. "How did you achieve the secrets of invisibility, slave?"

With my left hand I groped for the hilt of the fellow's sword; and when I found it, I said, "You have made a mistake," and drove his sword through the heart of the voice.

There was a single piercing scream, and I was free. Holding my sword point breast high, I turned and ran for the tree by which Ptor Fak had mounted to the roof. One of my shoulders brushed a body, but I reached the tree in safety.

As I climbed carefully to a lower branch so as not to reveal my presence by the shaking of the foliage, I heard a low whistle. It was Rojas.

"Who whistled?" demaded a voice somewhere in the courtyard. There was no reply.

Rojas could not have come at a worse time; I did not answer her; I did not know what to do, but Ptor Fak evidently thought that he did, for he answered the whistle. He must have thought that it was I who was signalling to him.

"They're on the roof!" cried a voice. "Quick! up that tree!"

Now the only tree that overhung the roof was the one that I was in, and if I remained there I was sure to be discovered. There was only one thing for me to do and that was to go up on the roof myself, and I did so as quickly as I could.

I hadn't taken half a dozen steps after I arrived, before I bumped into someone. "Zodanga?" I whispered. I didn't wish to speak Ptor Fak's name, but I knew that he would understand if I spoke the name of the country from which he came.

"Yes," he replied.

"Find the flier and stay near it until I come." He pressed my arm to show that he understood, and was gone.

I could see the tree up which I had come shaking violently; so I knew that a number of warriors were climbing up in pursuit of me, though how in the world they expected to find me, I don't know.

It was a most amazing situation; there must have been at least a dozen men on the roof and possibly still others down in the courtyard where I knew Rojas to be, yet both the roof and the courtyard were apparently deserted—neither the eye nor the ear could perceive any living thing; only when someone spoke was the illusion dispelled, and presently I heard a voice a short distance away. "He has probably gone this way —the city wall lies nearest in this direction. Spread out and comb the roof right to the city wall."

"It's a waste of time," said another voice. "If someone has given him the secret of invisibility, we can never find him."

"I do not think it was he, anyway," said a third voice; "there is no way in which he could have become invisible—it was unquestionably the ghost of Motus that spoke."

By this time the voices were dwindling in the distance, and I felt that it was safe to assume that all the warriors had gone in search of me; so I walked to the edge of the roof and jumped down into the courtyard. I stood there a moment concentrating all my mental powers in an endeavor to sense the presence of others near me, as Kandus had said that he was able to do, but I got no reaction. This might mean either that I failed to sense the presence of others or that there was no one there—at least near me; so I took the chance and whistled again. An answer came from the other side of the courtyard; I waited. Presently I heard a low whistle much nearer, and I replied—a moment later Rojas' hand touched mine.

I did not speak again for fear of attracting other pursuers, but I led her to the tree and helped her to clamber to the roof.

"Where is my flier?" I whispered.

She took me by the arm and led me in a direction at right angles to that which my pursuers had taken. The outlook appeared brighter immediately.

Rojas and I walked hand in hand so as not to lose one another. Presently I saw my flier standing there in the light of the farther moon, and it certainly looked good to me.

"The quarters of the slave women are near by, are they not?" I asked in a whisper.

"Right there," she said, and I suppose she pointed; then she led me to the edge of the roof overlooking a courtyard.

12

Rojas and I stood hand in hand at the edge of the roof looking down into a seemingly deserted courtyard. "You gave Llana of Gathol the invisibility sphere?" I asked.

"Yes," replied Rojas, "and she must be invisible by this time." She pressed my hand. "You fought magnificently," she whispered. "Everyone knew that you could have killed Motus whenever you wished; but only I guessed why you did not kill him sooner. Ptantus is furious; he has ordered that you be destroyed immediately."

"Rojas," I said, "don't you think that you should reconsider your decision to come with me? All of your friends and relatives are here in Invak, and you might be lonesome and unhappy among my people."

"Wherever you are, I shall be happy," she said. "If you do not take me with you I shall kill myself."

So that was that. I had involved myself in a triangle which bid fair to prove exceedingly embarrassing and perhaps tragic. I felt sorry for Rojas, and I was annoyed and humiliated by the part that I was forced to play. However, there had been no other way; it had been a question of Rojas' happiness or of Llana's life, and the lives of Ptor Fak and myself. I knew that I had chosen wisely, but I was still most unhappy.

Motivated by the habits of a lifetime, I strained my eyes in search of Llana of Gathol, who perhaps was down there somewhere in the courtyard; and then, realizing the futility of looking for her, I whistled. There was an immediate response from below and I sprang down from the roof. It did not take us long to locate one another; and as we were not challenged, I assumed that we were fortunate enough to be alone.

Llana touched my hand. "I thought that you would never come," she said. "Rojas told me about the duel that you were to fight; and while I had no doubts about your swordsmanship, I realized that there is always the danger of an accident or trickery. But at last you are here; how strange it is not to be able to see you. I was really quite frightened when I stepped out here into the courtyard and discovered that I could not even see myself."

"It is the miracle of invisibility that will save us," I said, "And only a miracle could have saved us. Now I must get you to the roof."

There was no overhanging tree in this courtyard, and the roof was fifteen feet above the ground. "You are about to have an experience, Llana," I said.

"What do you mean?" she asked.

"I am going to toss you up onto the roof," I told her, "and I hope you land on your feet."

"I am ready," she said.

I could see the roof all right, but I couldn't see Llana; all I could do was pray that my aim would be true. "Keep your whole body perfectly rigid," I said, "until I release you; then draw your feet up beneath you and relax. You may get a bad fall, but I don't think that it can hurt you much; the roof is heavily padded with vines."

"Let's get it over," said Llana.

I grasped one of her legs at the knee with my right hand and cradled her body on my left forearm; then I swung her back and forth a couple of times, and tossed her high into the air.

Llana of Gathol may have been invisible, but she was also definitely corporeal. I heard her land on the roof with anything but an invisible thud, and I breathed a sigh of relief. To spring lightly after her was nothing for my earthly muscles, and soon a low whistle brought the three of us together. I cautioned the girls to silence, and we walked hand in hand in the direction of the flier.

This was the moment that aroused my greatest apprehension, as I realized that the flier might be surrounded by invisible warriors; and, as far as I knew, the only sword among us was the one I had taken from the warrior I had killed in the courtyard; but perhaps Rojas had one.

"Have you a sword, Rojas?" I whispered.

"Yes," she said; "I brought one."

"Can you use it?" I asked.

"I never have used one," she replied.

"Then give it to Llana of Gathol; she can use if it necessary, and very effectively too."

We approached to within about a hundred feet of the flier and stopped. This was the crucial moment; I was almost afraid to whistle, but I did. There was an immediate answer from the vicinity of the flier. I listened a moment for voices that might betray the presence of the enemy, but there were none.

We advanced quickly then, and I helped the girls over the rail. "Where are you, Ptor Fak?" I asked. "Are you alone?"

"On deck," he said, "and I don't think there is anyone around."

"All the warriors of Invak could be here now," I said, as I reached the controls and started the motor.

A moment later the little ship rose gracefully into the air, and almost immediately from below us, we heard shouts and imprecations. The Invaks had seen the ship, but too late to prevent our escape. We were safe. We had accomplished what a few hours before would have seemed impossible, for then Ptor Fak and I were chained to trees and Llana of Gathol was a captive in another part of the city.

"We owe Rojas a great debt of gratitude," I said.

"A debt," she replied, "which it will be very easy, and I hope pleasant, for you to repay."

I winced at that; I saw a bad time ahead for me. I would rather face a dozen men with my sword than one infuriated or heartbroken woman. Before we reached Helium, I would have to tell her; but I decided to wait until we had regained visibility.

Perhaps it would have been easier to tell her while we were both invisible, but it seemed a cowardly way to me.

"You are going on to Helium, John Carter?" asked Llana.

"Yes," I said.

"What will they think of a flier coming in by itself with no one on board?" she asked.

"We will have to wait until we become visible before we approach the city," I replied. "We must not take any more of the invisibility spheres."

"Who is John Carter?" asked Rojas. "Is there another here of whom I did not know?"

"I am John Carter," I replied. "Dotar Sojat is merely a name that I assumed temporarily."

"Then you are not the Sultan of Swat?" demanded Rojas.

"No," I replied, "I am not."

"You have deceived me."

"I am sorry, Rojas," I said; "I was not trying to deceive you—about my name; as a matter of fact I never told you I was the Sultan of Swat; I told some warrior who questioned me." If she were angry about my deceiving her concerning my name and status, how was she going to take the fact that I did not love her, and that I already had a mate! I was as unhappy as a live eel in a frying pan; then of a sudden I decided to take the bull by the horns and get the whole thing over with. "Rojas," I began, "though I did not deceive you about my name, I did deceive you in a much more important matter."

"What is that?" she asked.

"I used your—ah—friendship to gain freedom for Llana of Gathol. I pretended to love you when I did not; I already have a mate."

I waited for the explosion, but no explosion came; instead there was a faint, tinkling, little laugh. I continued to wait; no one spoke; the silence became oppressive. Momentarily I expected a dagger to be slipped into me; or that Rojas would leap overboard; but neither of these things occurred, and I sat there at the controls wondering about that laugh. Perhaps the shock of my avowal had unbalanced Rojas' mind. I wished that I could see her, and at the same time I was glad that I could not—and I was certainly glad that no one could see me, for I felt like a fool.

I couldn't think of anything to say, and I thought the silence was going to last forever, but finally Llana of Gathol broke it. "How long will we remain invisible?" she asked.

"A little more than ten zodes from the time you took the sphere," said Rojas. "I shall become visible first, and then probably either John Carter or Ptor Fak, as I imagine that they took the spheres about the same time; you will be the last to regain visibility." Her voice was perfectly normal; there was no trace of nervousness nor bitterness in it. I couldn't make the girl out.

Perhaps she was the type that would bide its time until it could wreak some terrible revenge. I'll tell you that I had plenty to think about on that trip to Helium.

13

Shortly after dawn, I saw a most amazing phenomenon—I saw just a suggestion of the outline of a shadowy form beside me; it took shape slowly: Rojas was materializing! The effects of the invisibility compound were disappearing, and as they disappeared Rojas appeared. There she sat gazing out across the Martian landscape, the shadow of a happy smile upon her lips; somehow she reminded me of a cat which had just swallowed a canary.

"Kaor!" I said, which is the Barsoomian equivalent of Good Morning, Hello, or How do you do?—in other words, it is a Barsoomian greeting.

Rojas looked in my direction but of course she could not see me.

"Kaor," she replied, smiling. "You must be very tired, John Carter; you have had no sleep all night."

"When Llana of Gathol awakens, I shall sleep," I replied; "she can handle the controls quite as well as I."

"I have never been beyond the forests of Invak before," said Rojas. "What a drab, lonely world this is."

"You will find the twin cities of Helium very beautiful," I said. "I hope that you will like it there, Rojas."

"I am sure that I shall," she said; "I am looking forward to being in Helium with you, John Carter."

I wondered what she meant by that. The girl was an enigma; and I gave up trying to find a solution for her, and when Llana of Gathol spoke a moment later, and I knew that she was awake, I asked her to take the controls.

"We will cruise around outside of Helium," I said, "until we have all regained visibility," and then I lay down and fell asleep.

It was late that night before we had all regained visibility, and the next morning I approached Helium. A patrol boat came up to meet us, and recognizing my flier, it came alongside. The officer in command, and, in fact, the whole crew were overjoyed to see both Llana of Gathol and myself, alive and safe. The patrol boat escorted us to the hangar on the roof of my palace, where we received a tremendous welcome, as we had both been given up for dead long since.

Ptor Fak, Llana, and Rojas were behind me when I took Dejah Thoris in my arms; then I turned and presented Rojas and Ptor Fak to her.

"Had it not been for Rojas," I told Dejah Thoris, "none of us would have been here," and then I told her very briefly of our capture and incarceration in Invak.

I watched Rojas very closely as Dejah Thoris took both her hands in hers and kissed her on the forehead; and then, to my surprise, Rojas threw her arms about her and kissed her squarely on the mouth; the girl was absolutely bewildering.

After we had all breakfasted together Dejah Thoris asked me what my plans were now. "I shall see Tardos Mors immediately," I replied, "and after I have arranged for the dispatch of a fleet for Gathol, I shall fly there myself, alone, to reconnoiter."

"Why alone?" demanded Dejah Thoris; "But why should I ask? It has always been your way to do things alone."

I saw Tardos Mors and made the necessary arrangements for the dispatch of a fleet to Gathol; and then I returned to my palace to bid Dejah Thoris good-bye; and as I passed through the garden, I saw Rojas sitting there alone.

"Come here a moment, John Carter," she said; "I have something to say to you."

Here it comes, I thought; well, it would have to be gotten over sooner or later, and it would be a relief to get it over at once.

"You deceived me, John Carter," she said.

"I know I did," I replied.

"I am so glad that you did," she said, "for I deceived you. I admired you, John Carter, tremendously; but I never loved you. I knew that you had come to Invak in a flier; and I knew that if you could be helped to escape in it, you might be persuaded to take me with you. I hate Invak; I was most unhappy there; I would have sold my very soul to have escaped, and so I tried to make you love me so that you would take me away. I thought I had succeeded, and I was very much ashamed of myself. You can never know how relieved I was when I found that I had failed, for I admired you too much to wish to bring unhappiness to you."

"But why did you pretend to be so jealous of Llana of Gathol?" I asked.

"To make my love seem more realistic," she said.

"You have lifted a great weight from my conscience, Rojas.

I hope that you will like it here and that you will be very happy."

"I shall love it," she said, "for I already love Dejah Thoris, and she has asked me to stay here with her."

"Now I know that you will be happy here," I told her.

"I am sure of it, John Carter—I have seen some very handsome men already, and they can't all have mates."

The flight to Gathol was uneventful. I had taken an invisibility sphere some time before leaving Helium, and before I reached Gathol I had completely disappeared.

As I approached the city, I could see Hin Abtol's army drawn up around it; there were many more than there had been when I escaped in the Dusar; and on the line from which I had stolen the ship were at least a hundred more fliers, many of them large fighting ships, with some transports.

Presently several patrol boats rose to meet me. I was flying no colors, and when they hailed me I made no response. A couple of them ranged alongside me, and I could hear the exclamations of astonishment when they discovered that there was no one aboard the ship and no pilot at the controls.

I think they were rather frightened, for no one attempted to board me; and they let me fly on without interfering.

I dropped down to the Panar line, and set my flier down beside the last ship in it. One of the patrol ships landed also, and was soon surrounded by a crowd of officers and warriors, who approached my ship with every sign of curiosity written on their faces.

"This ship is piloted by Death," I said in a loud voice; "it is death to approach too close or to try to board it."

The men stopped then, and most of them fell back. I dropped to the ground and wandered about at will, my purpose being to gather what information I could from conversations among the officers. These men, however, were so interested in my ship that I gained no information from them; and so I wandered away and walked down the line to the flagship, which I boarded, passing the sentry at the foot of the ladder and the watch on deck. It seemed strange to walk there among the enemy, unseen; all that I had to do was to avoid contact with any of them, and I was safe from detection.

I went to the cabin of the commander of the fleet. He was sitting there with several high ranking officers, to whom he was giving instructions.

"As soon as Hin Abtol arrives from Pankor," he was saying, "we are to take up several thousand men equipped with equilibrimotors and drop them directly into the city; and then, with Gathol as a base, we shall move on Helium with fully a million men."

"When will Hin Abtol arrive?" asked one of the officers.

"Tonight or tomorrow morning," replied the commander. "He is coming with a large fleet."

Well, at last I had learned something; and my plans were formulated instantly. I left the flagship and returned to my flier, which was being examined by a considerable number of officers and men, but from a safe distance.

I had difficulty in finding an opening through which I could pass without touching any of them; but at last I succeeded, and I was soon at the controls of my flier.

As it rose from the ground apparently without human guidance, exclamations of awe and astonishment followed it. "It is Death," I heard a man cry; "Death is at the controls."

I circled low above them. "Yes, it is Death at the controls," I called down to them; "Death, who has come to take all who attack Gathol;" then I zoomed swiftly aloft and turned the nose of my ship toward Pankor.

I only went far enough from Gathol to be out of sight of Hin Abtol's forces; and then I flew in wide circles at considerable altitudes, waiting for Hin Abtol's fleet.

At long last I saw it in the distance. With it was the man who, with the enormous number of his conscripts, would surely take Gathol and sack it, were he not stopped.

I spotted Hin Abtol's flagship immediately and dropped down alongside it. My little flier evoked no alarm, as it would have been helpless in the midst of this great fleet; but when those aboard the flagship saw that the flier was maneuvering without human control, their curiosity knew no bounds, and they crowded to the rail to have a better look.

I circled the ship, drawing nearer and nearer. I could see Hin Abtol on the bridge with a number of officers, and I saw that they were as much intrigued as were the warriors on deck.

Hin Abtol was leaning far out over the rail to have a better look at me; I moved in closer; the side of the flier touched the bridge lightly.

Hin Abtol was peering down at the deck and into the little control room. "'There is no one aboard this ship," he said; "some one had discovered the means of flying it by remote control."

I had set the wheel to hold the flier tightly against the bridge; then I sprang across the deck, seized Hin Abtol by his harness, and dragged him over the rail onto the deck of the flier. An instant later still holding Hin Abtol, I was at the controls; the flier nosed down and dove beneath the flagship at full speed. I heard shouts of astonishment mingled with cries of rage and fear.

A number of small craft took after me; but I knew that they could not overtake me, and that they would not dare fire on me for fear of killing Hin Abtol.

Hin Abtol lay trembling at my side, almost paralyzed with terror. "What are you?" he finally managed to stammer. "What are you going to do with me?"

I did not reply; I thought that that would terrify him the more; and I know that it did, for after a while he implored me to speak.

We flew back, high over Gathol, which was now safe from attack. Early the next morning I saw a great fleet coming out of the southeast—it was the fleet from Helium that Tardos Mors was bringing to relieve Gathol.

As I was approaching it, the effects of the invisibility sphere diminished rapidly; and I materialized before the astounded gaze of Hin Abtol.

"Who are you? What are you?" he demanded.

"I am the man whose flier you stole at Horz," I replied. "I am the man who took it from beneath your nose in Pankor, and with it Llana of Gathol—I am John Carter, Prince of Helium; have you ever heard of me?"

Nearing the fleet, I broke out my colors—the colors of the Prince of Helium; and a great cheer rose from the deck of every ship that could distinguish them.

The rest is history now—how Helium's great fleet destroyed Hin Abtol's fleet, and the army of Helium routed the forces which had for so long invested Gathol.

When the brief war was over, we set free nearly a million of the frozen men of Panar; and I returned to Helium and Dejah Thoris, from whom I hope never to be separated again.

I had brought with me Jad-han and Pan Dan Chee, whom we had found among the prisoners of the Panars; and though I was not present at the meeting between Pan Dan Chee and Llana of Gathol, Dejah Thoris has assured me that the dangers and vicissitudes he had suffered for love of the fair Gatholian had not been in vain.

ABOUT EDGAR RICE BURROUGHS

Edgar Rice Burroughs is one of the world's most popular authors. With no previous experience as an author, he wrote and sold his first novel—*A Princess of Mars*—in 1912. In the ensuing thirty-eight years until his death in 1950, Burroughs wrote 91 books and a host of short stories and articles. Although best known as the creator of the classic *Tarzan of the Apes* and *John Carter of Mars,* his restless imagination knew few bounds. Burroughs' prolific pen ranged from the American West to primitive Africa and on to romantic adventure on the moon, the planets, and even beyond the farthest star.

No one knows how many copies of ERB books have been published throughout the world. It is conservative to say, however, that of the translations into 32 known languages, including Braille, the number must run into the hundreds of millions. When one considers the additional world-wide following of the Tarzan newspaper feature, radio programs, comic magazines, motion pictures and television, Burroughs must have been known and loved by literally a thousand million or more.